"Are you hurt?" Zeke knelt close beside Myra.

"Only my pride." She stood, wiping wet snow from her jeans. "Cayenne's never thrown me before."

"If you're sure you're okay to ride, come on." Zeke boosted her up onto Ember's back. "We'll ride double."

"I can sit behind you," Myra said, attempting to swing down again.

"Stay. We've gotta make tracks home and I want to know you're not so woozy you'll fall off." He landed in the saddle behind her.

Myra tried to keep from leaning against Zeke, but snuggled between his solid thighs and cradled by his arms, she relaxed against her will.

"It's really dark now," Zeke said, his breath rustling Myra's hair. "Do you think your horse will head straight to the ranch?"

"I hope so." Myra turned slightly to look at him. Part of her liked the comfort afforded by Zeke Maxwell's strong arms. Another part of her whispered, *But he's the enemy*.

Dear Reader,

The theme idea for the Snowy Owl Ranchers books started when I read a great article in *National Wildlife* magazine about a study done on snowy owls in the lower forty-eight. Snowy owls used to nest only in the cold lands of the far north. The study shows these gorgeous birds are having to travel farther afield for food and nesting.

Book characters generally come to me in the night. Odd as it may sound to people who don't write down stories that pop into their minds, the town of Snowy Owl Crossing is fictional, as are all of the people who populate *His Ranch or Hers*, the first of three connected books for the Harlequin American Romance line.

I hope readers come to love the owls as I have and also develop a fondness for folks like Zeke Maxwell, Myra Odell, and their friends and family who live and work in my fictional Montana ranching community.

As always I love hearing from readers via mail at 7739 E. Broadway Blvd #101 Tucson, AZ 85710-3941, or email: rdfox@cox.net.

Sincerely,

Roz Denny Fox

HIS RANCH
OR HERS

———

Roz Denny Fox

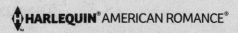

HARLEQUIN® AMERICAN ROMANCE®

ISBN-13: 978-0-373-75606-3

His Ranch or Hers

Copyright © 2016 by Rosaline Fox

Recycling programs for this product may not exist in your area.

The publisher acknowledges the copyright holder of the additional work:

My Funny Valentine
Copyright © 1991 by Debbie Macomber

Printed in U.S.A.

CONTENTS

Roz Denny Fox's first book was published by Harlequin in 1990. She writes for several Harlequin lines and her books are published worldwide and in a number of languages. Roz's warm home-and-family-focused love stories have been nominated for various industry awards, including the Romance Writers of America's RITA® Award, the Holt Medallion, the Golden Quill and others. Roz has been a member of the Romance Writers of America since 1987 and is currently a member of Tucson's Saguaro Romance Writers, where she has received the Barbara Award for outstanding chapter service. In 2013 Roz received her fifty-book pin from Harlequin. Readers can email her through Facebook or at rdfox@cox.net, or visit her website at korynna.com/rozfox.

Books by Roz Denny Fox

Harlequin American Romance

The Maverick Returns
Duke: Deputy Cowboy
Texas Dad
Texas Mom

Harlequin Heartwarming

Annie's Neighborhood
An Unlikely Rancher
Molly's Garden

Visit the Author Profile page
at Harlequin.com for more titles.

HIS RANCH OR HERS

Roz Denny Fox

I want to thank the hardworking editors at Harlequin who have so kindly shared my vision for the Snowy Owl books and others. Always to Paula Eykelhof and Kathleen Scheibling. Also to Dana Hopkins, and to Victoria Curran for whom I have written stories for the Harlequin Heartwarming line. Harlequin books across all lines are my favorite books to read.

Chapter One

Myra Odell parked the tractor in the implement barn and went out to the fenced acres of grass. Recent rains had greened the pasture nicely. Good. Maybe tomorrow she'd bring the new crop of young animals down to ready them for market. Her neighbor Hank Watson had offered to truck them to the stockyard before winter storms hit northeastern Montana. With August close to the end, she'd still hoped for a few more weeks of decent weather. But all morning the sky had looked ominous. She'd gotten fairly good at predicting weather disruptions. She'd grown up in this country, and for most of her twenty-eight years she'd spent summers here on Flying Owl Ranch with her dad's parents. Three summers ago she'd come to help out Gramps, who's health had declined after her grandmother passed away the previous year.

Rather than return to teaching high school math in Great Falls that year, she'd stayed to run the ranch she loved. Her mom fussed about it, but truth be told Myra liked cattle ranching way more than teaching. Although after losing Gramps, the loneliness took some getting used to. Thankfully, she'd made friends with neighbors and some in the nearby town of Snowy Owl Crossing. And Gramps said she was a born rancher. Which was good because Myra saw herself spending the rest of her life right here.

Stepping down from the last rung of the split-rail fence, Myra checked her watch. She could feed the two saddle horses she kept for herding cattle before driving into town to grab staples in case the *Farmer's Almanac* was right about them getting an early snow. She might drop in to see a couple of her girlfriends, especially Jewell Hyatt, to ask if she had any news from the state. Their committee had put in a request to designate some local land as a snowy-owl habitat.

A waterfowl preserve was already adjacent to a nearby lake, but snowy owls nested in tall fir trees too often being logged off. The birds weren't yet endangered, but everyone in the area who loved watching them raise their young knew the owl population was shrinking. Quite a bit just since Myra had made her home here.

The horses whinnied a welcome. Both stuck their heads over their stall doors to see if she'd brought apples or a carrot in addition to their daily rations. Today she had neither, but they made do with muzzle rubs.

She left the barn and was heading toward Gramps's aging Ford pickup when her cell phone rang. Myra dug her phone out of her jacket pocket and was surprised to see her dad's number on the screen. She rarely heard directly from him as he tended to let her mom or her younger brother, Eric, touch base for the whole family. Her folks owned a much larger cattle ranch off the highway that ran between Miles City and Billings. Because it was rarer still that any of the busy Odells took time to phone during a weekday, worry knotted in Myra's stomach as she swiped the bar to answer.

"Hello, Dad? Is everything all right at Rolling Acres?" Myra heard the tremor in her voice and took a deep breath to dispel her concerns.

"Everything is fine. I have good news. Lieutenant Maxwell is here."

"You mean the guy who saved Eric's life in Afghanistan? I didn't know he was out of the hospital."

"Zeke, that's right. He's out of the VA hospital after an extensive stay after he saved Eric's life."

"Doesn't he live on the East Coast?"

"Yup, he was renting an apartment in Boston, where he grew up. Seems his folks have retired to some island."

"Eric told me they'd kept in contact. I recall him saying the lieutenant had to have his left shoulder and elbow rebuilt. It sounded serious. I think Eric felt some guilt because the guy got hurt saving him and the others."

"I don't know that he felt guilty. Certainly grateful. Your mother and I can't thank him enough, either."

"For sure. So what's he doing in Montana?"

"That's really what I called to tell you. Zeke's

friends and family have all left Boston for other opportunities. Eric thought he needed cheering up."

"So you invited him to visit. That's thoughtful of you guys."

Myra's father cleared his throat. "Actually, kiddo, your mom and I had this brilliant idea to gift him the Flying Owl. With Dad gone and you needing to get back to the job you went to college for, we dug out the deed. As co-owner on Dad's trust, it was simple to have Don Jarvis draw up a new deed. I sent it off to Lieutenant Maxwell last month. At first we didn't hear back and so weren't sure he'd accept. Then yesterday he showed up to ask if it was legitimate. I assured him it is. Expensive as land is, nothing on earth can ever equal the worth of him saving Eric's life."

Myra's ears started to buzz. She wasn't sure she'd processed everything she thought she'd heard her dad say. Turning around, she sat heavily on the old truck's running board. A sick feeling gripped her stomach and washed over her. "I...I love the Flying Owl. Wh... why didn't you call and discuss this with me?"

"Now, honey, your mother and I know you felt obligated to stick around and help your gramps. We appreciate all you did to make his last years easier. He was a lost soul after Mom died, and I was tied down here. Like your mother keeps telling me, you've dedicated enough time in that out-of-the-way place. This way, you have a week or so before a new school year starts to look for teaching jobs. You deserve to get back to living and working in a city where you'll meet young men and women your own age."

Myra couldn't force the plethora of objections past her constricted throat.

"Honey, did I lose you?"

"Uh, no," she managed to rasp. She swallowed a bunch of times and swabbed at tears trickling from her eyes. She heard doors slamming in the background on her dad's end, followed by loud male laughter. "Dad, you don't understand—"

He cut her off. "Listen, hon, Eric and Zeke are back from riding ATVs around the ranch. Zeke's joining us for supper, and he'll spend the night. Tomorrow he'll drive to the Flying Owl. That gives you this afternoon and evening to pack your stuff and take any mementos from the ranch you want. I figure he'll arrive by noon. Maybe you'd be so kind as to give him a quick tour of the ranch. Afterward, come stay with us until you get a job offer. We haven't seen enough of you," he said, his tone gruff with emotion.

Myra remained at a loss for words. She loved her family. She didn't doubt they loved her. Possibly she was partly to blame for this awful turn of events. After all, she'd never told them how much living here and running the ranch meant to her. "Sure. Bye, Dad," she managed to whisper past a growing lump in her throat. She quickly disconnected and buried her face in her hands.

Numb, but not one to wallow in self-pity, she decided to get on with her earlier plan of going to town.

If this wasn't all a bad dream, she had friends to no-
tify of the sudden, colossal change in her life.

As she drove the two-lane road toward Snowy Owl
Crossing, gray clouds obscured the jagged tops of
the mountain range she loved. With its rock-strewn
mountains, patches of evergreen trees and gentle hills
flattening into rich farm and ranch lands, this area
had everything. She hurt to think of leaving it.

The town had a single major street lined with businesses. At one end sat a combination grocery store–
post office, at the other, a very busy feed store. Myra
remembered a time Main Street wasn't paved, when
she'd spent summers here as a young girl tagging
after Gram and Gramps. Little else had changed about
the weathered wood stores, except for a new generation of proprietors.

She parked near the coffee shop owned by the
mother of one of her good friends, Lila Jenkins. Only
a year older than Myra, Lila was already a widow
with a nine-year-old son. Following her husband's
death, Lila had begun working part-time for her mom.
She also owned a bed-and-breakfast that catered to
fishermen, but she was struggling to keep it afloat.

Still discombobulated by her dad's call, Myra
hoped a strong cup of coffee would help snap her
out of the pain gripping her.

As she entered the cheery, warm café, it surprised
her to see a couple of her other friends seated at a
back table. Jewell Hyatt, born and raised in Snowy
Owl Crossing, now served as the area's main veteri-

narian. Shelley Price was a few years older than the other women in the Artsy Ladies group. Her husband was a park ranger and she taught ceramics out of her home. Shelley made beautiful items for the November bazaar they all participated in to raise money for the snowy owls.

Lila emerged from the kitchen, saw Myra and smiled. But Myra's heart sank. Saying goodbye, telling her friends she wouldn't be able to finish her projects for the bazaar this year would be harder than she'd imagined.

Spotting her, Jewell stood and beckoned her to their table. "Gosh, Myra. Sit down. What's wrong? You look… I don't know, sad-eyed. Not exactly sick, but not well."

Myra pulled out a chair just as Lila reached them. "Can I get you something? I made chocolate pie today. I know it's your favorite."

"Just coffee. But hurry back," she said, sinking down on the chair across from Jewell. "I've got news. Bad news." She shed her jacket as Lila dashed behind the counter to pour coffee for herself and Myra. As soon as her friend returned, Myra blurted out everything she'd learned from her dad's call.

For an elongated moment her three friends looked stunned. Then Lila leaned over and hugged her. "Is there nothing you can do to change your father's mind?"

Myra blinked away a sudden rush of tears. Not trusting herself to speak, she shook her head.

Jewell reached across the table and squeezed her friend's arm. "Let's think a minute. You say your dad jointly owned the ranch with your grandfather. So as awful as it seems, I guess he has a right to give the property away. Too bad you can't just run this new guy off."

Lila glanced at the others. "Dare she even try running off a former Green Beret? They're tough. Plus, he saved her brother. That makes the guy a hero, right?"

Myra paused before drinking from her steaming mug. "How would I even run him off?"

Jewell clasped her own cup. "Maybe you won't have to run him off. Didn't you say he's from Boston? Managing a cattle ranch isn't like doing a bunch of sit-ups. Even if he led a squad or a platoon or whatever they call it, I don't think that compares to keeping a herd of cattle alive during a Montana winter. What's to say he'll stick it out?"

Shelley, who'd been quietly sipping her tea, smiled. "That's brilliant, Jewell. Myra, why not volunteer to stay on and help this dude like you did your grandpa? Only, you let him do all the dirty, messy chores. Get my drift?"

Myra brightened then frowned. "The folks want me to stay with them while I apply for teaching jobs. They'd probably veto any notion of me sharing a house with a stranger. Even if he did save Eric's life."

Lila leaned forward to stare at Myra. "You're an

adult woman. I work part-time for my mother, but she has no say over my private life."

The others all nodded and Myra blew out a noisy breath. "You make good points. But my parents paid for my education. I never talk to Mom that she doesn't work in how I'm wasting my time tucked away here. She likes living nearer Billings where she has access to big stores and such. City amenities we don't have."

"But that's not you," Jewell stressed. "It's your life. And you know we'll all be disappointed if you leave."

"Not as disappointed as me," Myra admitted, thinking it over. "I usually hire help with haying and branding and such. High school kids from neighboring towns or the reservation. The Flying Owl doesn't have a bunkhouse, so Gramps never kept full-time hired hands. I suppose if I didn't take anyone on this winter, this Lieutenant Maxwell would have to do all the worst chores himself."

"That's right," Jewell said with a smile.

"But I don't know much about him. Eric spent a year under his command. They kept in touch after they both left the service. I can phone my brother and ask if it's safe for me to live under the same roof at least long enough to see he doesn't ruin Gramps's ranch." She perked up the more she talked.

"Now you're sounding like the Myra we all love," Jewell said, grinning. She lifted her coffee mug and all the women did the same, touching their rims in solidarity.

Myra set money on the table for her coffee. "I need

to get to Hadley's store before it closes to stock up on a few things. Zeke Maxwell is due in sometime tomorrow morning. I'll see how our meeting goes. Then I'll phone one of you."

"Zeke? Is that short for something?"

Myra shook her head as she shrugged into her jacket. "Dunno. Eric's mentioned he has a twin brother, who travels the world hunting gems. And I think their parents retired to the Caribbean. I know he bunged up a shoulder and elbow saving Eric and other men while under enemy fire. And for that my dad gave him the Flying Owl." She made a face.

Shelley patted Myra's hand. "Tonight I'll burn a candle with the hope he sees right away that he doesn't fit in. The hard work and isolation in Snowy Owl Crossing might well be too much for him."

"Thanks, everyone. I'd best get moving. I probably still should gather the family albums and put them in a box. And drag out my suitcases. I can't make this visit goodbye. However things shake out, I'll come see you all again." She left then before the tears that sprang to her eyes could fall.

THICK CLOUDS THAT had blanketed the mountaintops for most of the previous day had blown in overnight. By 10:00 a.m. stinging snow had dusted and showed little sign of letting up.

If it continued for long, Myra knew she'd need to haul hay out to the herd. But she wanted to wait for the new owner to put in an appearance. Boy, that title almost gagged her. She had phoned Eric last night. When she'd asked if his former lieutenant suffered from any post-traumatic stress problems, he'd laughed and said Zeke was a solidly good guy through and through. Her brother asked why she wanted to know, but she hadn't told him. Really, she hadn't made up her mind. She'd yet to search online for teaching jobs. She felt qualified to hire on as a ranch hand, too. But with the flat economy, not a lot of ranches were advertising. At least none in the immediate area. She had checked on that.

While she could delay ferrying hay out to the main herd, she didn't want to put off bringing the young steers down from the summer lease in the foothills. Too bad the grass that yesterday had been so green and lush was now white with snow. If need be, she could clear a few patches with her snowblower.

Donning boots, a ski hat with earflaps and a Sherpa-lined leather jacket, Myra tramped to the barn. At the sound of an engine, she glanced toward the private lane. Not recognizing the big black Chevy pickup sporting off-road tires, she assumed her nemesis had arrived.

The man who emerged from the pickup—newer than Gramps's old Ford by at least a decade—looked to top six feet by a couple of inches or so. Bareheaded in a snowstorm, his dark hair was cut military short. He did wear boots and a far-from-new bomber jacket with some insignia patches sewn on the left side. The US flag stood out. It was hard not to notice that his shoulders were broad, but as he strode toward her she detected no sign of an injury to his left side. He walked straight as a telephone pole, a thirtyish guy in perfect shape. So if the VA had put him back together, they'd done a bang-up job.

He stopped a foot or so from her. "Hi. I'm Zeke Maxwell. You must be Myra, Eric's sister."

She lost track of a few seconds as she gazed up into warm dark brown eyes fringed by to-die-for long, thick eyelashes. Caught assessing him, Myra fumbled worn gloves out of her jacket pocket. That gave her a moment before answering as she bent to retrieve one from the snow-covered ground. "Is Zeke a nickname?" she asked, blurting out the question Jewell had asked yesterday.

The man wrinkled his nose. "Ezekiel. A family name that got passed down through generations. As twin A in a set, I drew the short straw. I still haven't forgiven my mother, so you don't want to call me that." He pivoted in a slow circle, dusting snow off his head as he took in the house, barn, sheds and corral before circling back to examine Myra from head to toe. "Why are we standing out here in the weather? I could use a cup of coffee and a fire to warm up."

"The house is unlocked. Coffee's in a thermos by the pot. I'm heading out to drive the cows and yearlings down from the foothills into that enclosure." She stabbed a finger, which he followed without moving his head.

His right shoulder rose slightly then fell. "Give

me a minute to grab a hat and gloves from my truck and I'll join you."

"Being from Boston and all, do you even ride? Do you need me to saddle your horse?" she drawled.

"Unless you give me a nag, I won't hold you back." He spun on a heel and stalked back to his pickup.

Myra tugged on her gloves, flipped up her jacket collar and stomped into the barn. She should probably apologize, but really, if he thought one ran a ranch sitting by a fire drinking coffee, the Flying Owl would be in shambles before spring thaw.

Marching to the back of the barn, she led Cayenne, a sorrel mare, out of her stall and had the saddle on and cinched as Zeke appeared in a Boston Red Sox ball cap. *His ears were gonna freeze, but he'd learn.* "You get the black gelding," she told him. "His name is Ember. Saddle's on the rack. Bridles are on the wall peg." She took one down and settled it over the sorrel's head.

He flashed her a glance, as if he had something to say, but then yanked up the saddle, smoothed the blanket over the gelding's back and settled the saddle as easily as if it were an everyday occurrence. Same with the bridle.

In silence they left the barn. Zeke mounted while Myra closed the barn door, then she, too, swung into the saddle.

Zeke let her lead. As they moved from a trot into a canter, he pulled alongside. "Feels like we're in the middle of a snow globe. Is snow usual this time of

year? Will it last? At supper Eric said the weather-
man predicted mountain snow. Your dad scoffed."

"The almanac shows it could last a few days. It's
early. As a rule, the first snowfall is late September
or early October. If this is a harbinger of what's to
come, it could wreck winter-wheat crops."

"Do you raise and sell wheat, too?"

"Ranchers raise, cut and bale wheat, grass and alfalfa for cattle feed. Lose a crop and you either have
to buy grain at outrageous costs or sell stock you can't
afford to feed at a loss." It was plain he didn't know
diddly-squat about ranching. Maybe Jewell was right,
maybe he'd opt out. She wasn't a fan of feeding the
greater herd by hand this early in the season. But if
it made him leave, she'd say, let it snow.

They reached the foothills where her stock huddled
in a cut between the hills that blocked the windblown
snow. Myra rode past them, uncoiled her rope, swung
it around and yelled "Hi yi yi" several times. Startled,
the animals bolted away from the noise.

"What do you want me to do?" Zeke called.

"Watch for stragglers. Make noise to bring 'em
back into the fold. I see some have my neighbor's
brand. We'll take them in. He can collect them when
it's convenient. Hank Watson runs the Bar W. He's
kindly volunteered to truck my yearlings—uh, your
yearlings—to market shortly. If you see the slant R
brand, that's Dave Ralston, your other neighbor. He's
a good guy to know. He rents out his baler. A ranch
this size can't afford to buy one."

Zeke bobbed his head.

Myra noticed he rode well, and he brought in a number of strays as they rode down the hillside and made their way to the large enclosure. Subconsciously she'd hoped he'd screw up.

As the ranch came into sight through falling snow-flakes, Myra raced ahead, hopped off Cayenne and opened the gate.

Without asking, Zeke hung back and drove the cattle through.

"Phew," he said, swinging down to help Myra shut the gate. "I see they're pawing up the snow to get to grass. Good they know to do that."

"Yep. The snow is slacking some, but we still have to take hay out to the main herd. We'll go put our horses up, hook the big tractor to the flatbed and load up twenty or so bales."

"Okay."

Myra couldn't help but notice he sounded unsure. Maybe she should let him stop for coffee. On the other hand, if she kept the pressure on, by nightfall he could give up.

"Just unsaddle Ember. I'll brush both horses down and feed them later. We need to get the hay distributed while it's light."

Again Zeke followed orders.

Myra fetched the tractor and hooked up the flat-bed. Backing the trailer into the barn, she climbed a ladder to the hayloft and began tossing down large bales.

"Do you need assistance?" Zeke asked, squinting up at her.

"You could straighten them on the trailer. If I don't have to do it at the end of pitching off twenty bales, it'll save us time."

He stepped up on the trailer and that was the first time Myra noticed he greatly favored his left arm. She heard him grunt as he hefted the heavy bales one-handed. For someone her size—and at five-seven she wasn't petite—moving bales took knowing how to leverage the weight. Obviously it was the same for a man with an injured arm. She debated telling him to leave the stacking for her, after all. But she didn't want to insult him. When she left, the work would all fall on him unless he hired help. Maybe he had a disability pension that would help cover costs. She and Gramps hadn't had extra money to work with.

"I'll drive the tractor this time because I know the route," she said once they were ready. "You can sit on the bales. See, I've fitted one like a chair so you won't bounce off." She'd thought Zeke might laugh, but he had begun to look weary. And a dense fog had settled down, covering the mountains.

"Feels like we've landed on an alien planet," Zeke hollered after she fired up the tractor and drove into the whirling mist.

So he did have a sense of humor. Myra tossed him a smile over her shoulder.

It took about half an hour to reach the pasture where the Angus heifers milled about on either side of a coulee. A bull stood in the brush beyond the fence. Stopping, Myra took her cutters out of the toolbox welded onto the tractor. Crawling back across hay bales, she cut one open, stood and spread hay into the draw. Big, snorting, drooling cows immediately jockeyed for access to the new hay and began to eat.

Taking his cue, Zeke snipped open the next bale and manhandled it farther along the natural trough. "Listen, this will go quicker if you drive the tractor and I do the bales."

Taking pity on him, because Myra saw it wasn't easy for him to do the lion's share while favoring one arm, she said, "We can take turns. I'll drive the length of this coulee. There's another like it a few hundred yards over nearer the stream. We'll catch it on the return trip. Oh, wait. Can you drive a tractor?"

"I learned to drive anything with a gas pedal and a steering wheel in the army, and we had to improvise if either of those pieces got shot out."

She hid a grimace but nodded. It'd been over a year since her grandfather had been able to help her with any of the heavy chores. Working in tandem with Zeke cut the time by more than half what she'd thought it would take to attend to the herd.

"How many cattle did we just feed?" he asked as she broke apart the last bale.

"A hundred fifty, plus or minus any that wandered off or were taken down by coyotes. There are close to a hundred moms with yearlings that we put in the grassy pen by the barn. Those youngsters will be sold before true winter sets in. You calve in the spring, sell in the fall."

Zeke looked around at the snow falling in earnest. "This isn't winter?"

She rolled her eyes. "Far from it. For a Montana winter you're talking snow too deep to trek through. Once the calves are shipped, you'll bring the main herd down to pastures around the barn. Even then it can snow so hard you'll have to take grain out on a sled. Every day you'll break the ice on the water troughs."

He hunched over the steering wheel and followed their earlier tracks back to the barn. Parking, he let the motor idle. "What next?"

"I'll store the tractor and see to the horses. Then I'll go in and start supper. Why don't you go on to the house and get settled. I cleared out Gramps's bedroom and put fresh sheets on the bed and towels in the bathroom. It's the room to the right of the living room. My bedroom is at the back of the house. I could pack up and head out tonight, but with this storm I'd rather wait until morning."

Zeke studied her as he took his ball cap off. "I thought maybe you'd spend a few days showing me the ropes. But we can discuss that later. Tell you what, I'll take KP duty tonight while you finish up out here. Then we can talk, and maybe you'll go over the ranch accounts. Your dad said you kept the books and your mom jumped in to tell me you're a high school math teacher."

"I was. I won't turn down your offer to cook. It's my least favorite chore. The kitchen is old and small, but at least everything is functional and stocked."

"Your father mentioned the house might need some work. He said not much has been changed since he was born and raised here."

"I like it as is. The roof doesn't leak and the fireplace works. So do the showers."

"Uh-huh. It's snowing harder. How much time do you need, so I know when to have supper on the table?"

"An hour should do it."

He tipped his cap and made tracks for his pickup.

Myra climbed onto the tractor, ratcheted up the engine and backed the trailer into its spot in the shed. She watched Zeke take two duffel bags from under his pickup's canopy and hike on to the house.

Sighing, she went in to take care of the horses, dialing her brother on the way to inform him that due to the snow she wasn't leaving the ranch just yet. She contacted Eric instead of her parents because she still resented how they had given away a ranch they should have known she loved.

His ears stung from the cold as he walked into a warm house he now owned. It all still felt surreal to Zeke. Particularly since he hadn't realized the house would be occupied by Eric's sister. He'd spent half a day with her, but as yet couldn't pigeonhole her. Figuring her out became more difficult once he entered this home. At his first glance around the living room, on nearly every flat surface in the living room sat dollhouses. *A grown woman had dollhouses?* They were all so elaborate. On closer inspection he saw not all of them were complete. Several had walls but no roofs. A few were unpainted. Taking care not to knock into any of them with his duffels, he located the bedroom Myra had mentioned. He flipped on a light switch that lit two bedside lamps. The big bed, covered with a thick quilt, looked inviting. Thankfully, the decor was neutral. No frills. Having noted ruffled curtains on some of the dollhouse windows, he hadn't known what to expect.

Since he'd promised to cook, he dropped the bags and found the kitchen. *Vintage* didn't begin to describe the space. Outdated but spotless. He didn't see a microwave, and the stove and fridge were surely older than his thirty-one years. He opened cupboards and took stock, then peered inside the fridge. A clicking sound, like dog toenails striking the linoleum, had Zeke straightening and looking around. The noise was coming from the corner where the back door was, behind a dinette set with four chairs. A pen fashioned by baby gates held a quilt, plastic toys, metal dishes of water, lettuce and some kind of pellets. Therein roamed a pig. A pig. Small and white with gray spots. A door with a doggie flap opened onto what looked like a screened porch.

He was still shaking his head in disbelief when his cell phone rang. Plucking it from his pocket he saw his twin's number. "Seth, buddy, where are you this month?"

"I'm back in Afghanistan. My gem contact phoned to say his men found an area of pure lapis. I flew in yesterday to have a look. He was right, and it's rare to find lapis without occlusions, so we're dickering on price. I got your text saying you were going to Montana. The family of one of the guys you saved gave you a ranch? Is that true, or did you injure your head as well as your shoulder?"

"It's true. In fact, I'm there now. I spent my first afternoon hauling hay to cattle in a snowstorm."

"You're kidding! What do you know about ranching, dude?"

"Nothing. But Eric Odell's sister—his folks are the ones who gave me the ranch—she's been running the ranch. Their grandfather owned it before he died. She's a teacher, and Eric's parents told me she wants to get back to her career. But I had to admit, trekking after her today I saw how much I don't know. I had hoped she might stay awhile to give me pointers."

"But?"

"But…then I came in the house. She's got dollhouses everywhere. Like, is it a fetish? And, Seth, I discovered she keeps a pig as a house pet. Now I wonder if she's been tucked away in this remote spot to hide the fact she's eccentric, to put it mildly."

His brother laughed loudly. "If you have the deed, kick her out. Hire an old cowboy to teach you what you need to know. Seems to me you've stepped into a sweetheart deal. I'm envious that you get to live in wide-open spaces. Sometimes I'm so tired of eating and sleeping in hotels."

"Take a break and come visit me. We can learn how to run a ranch together."

"Maybe. Not for a while. I have this lapis I want, then I'm off to Tanzania. Tanzanite is getting scarce. I've got a friend who has staked a claim that he's sure will yield a vein. I haven't actually done any digging in months. It'll be fun."

"Yeah, yeah. I've heard this song and dance from you for years. You don't want to set down roots. You've got the wanderlust, bro."

"Hmm. We'll see. It gets to be a hard-knock life. Email me pictures of your ranch. It'll remind me what it's like to have a home."

"Sure. I'll take some after this snowstorm passes. You take care. Especially in the Hindu Kush. Our forces have drawn down. It's less safe than when you visited me there."

"So I hear. We'll keep in touch. Good luck with Pet-Pig Woman."

Zeke grimaced, gave the round little pig a last glance then started fixing supper. Midway through preparations, he heard the front door open and close, and then footsteps going toward the back of the house. Then he heard water running and figured Myra had opted to take a shower. It was probably something he should have done, he thought as he found dishes and set the table. Were they really going to eat next to a penned pig? *Apparently so.*

It wasn't long before Myra appeared in the doorway. She wore slippers, clean jeans and a checked flannel shirt, and her shoulder-length, tawny-gold hair fell in damp waves around a face scrubbed clean of makeup. Zeke hadn't paid such close attention before. Framed in the doorway, she seemed younger and prettier than he recalled while she'd dragged him through a snowstorm.

"Wow, something smells good. Can I help? Oh, I see you've even set the table. Sorry I was so long. I took time to oil the tack. Saddles and bridles are expensive. Oiled, they hold up better in the weather."

Zeke shook himself loose from eyeing her. "Your timing is great. Go on and choose where you normally sit. I'll bring everything to the table."

Myra crossed the room and pulled out a chair. Like magic, steaming dishes began to fill up the table. Her mouth dropped open. "You made scalloped potatoes and green beans with almonds?" She blinked up at Zeke as he set a basket of homemade biscuits in front of her, followed by a slice of sirloin steak he pulled out from under the broiler.

"Dig in while everything's hot," he said. "Oh, wait." He snapped his fingers and turned to rummage in the fridge. "I saw butter somewhere."

"In the top compartment on the fridge door."

He carried the butter dish to the table even as Myra broke open a hot biscuit. "These are as flaky as my gram used to make. Mine are like lead weights. Everything looks scrumptious. Where did you learn to cook like this?"

"Before I joined the military, I worked in restaurants. I also pulled my share of KP duty prior to getting into a Green Beret unit."

"I'll do dishes tonight, but I draft you to fix breakfast." Her mouth was full when he shot a deliberate glance toward her pet pig.

"I've never had bacon or ham on the hoof, but I guess I can make do." He smiled crookedly as he cut a slice of steak.

Her fierce glare made plain that Myra wasn't amused.

Chapter Two

"Orion is a hundred percent pet." Myra's tone was challenging. "Our local vet found him when she responded to a tip about a family who skipped town in the middle of the night leaving a goat, a donkey and a young indoor pig to fend for themselves. Some call him a potbellied pig, but he's really a micromini. Jewell knew I didn't have a dog or cat, so she talked me into adopting him."

"Jewell?" Zeke looked blank.

"Our vet. You'll meet her. She takes care of animals large and small, plus she heads the committee trying to obtain a habitat for our snowy owls."

"I see. In the developing world, I got used to seeing animals in people's homes that you never see in the US. Really, the quilt and squeaky toys in his pen tipped me off that you weren't raising him for food."

"Teacup pigs and microminis are intelligent, curious, funny, affectionate, clean animals. Orion was good company for Gramps, and now me." She paused, her fork in the air. "I expect Mom will pitch a fit when I show up at their house with him." Myra's agitation showed in the short, stabbing cuts she made to her steak.

"Uh, hey, I forgot to pour coffee." Zeke rose, went to the counter and picked up the pot. "Do you take cream or sugar?"

"No."

"Look, I was teasing about the pig. I didn't mean to upset you." Zeke poured their coffee and returned the pot to the burner.

She dropped her utensils and picked up her cup. But when their eyes met over the rim, Myra hurriedly averted her gaze. "Nothing to do with the Flying Owl is a joke."

He gestured with his cup. "I…ah…don't know a lot about cattle ranching."

"No kidding."

Leaning back, Zeke studied her, his expression pensive. "It strikes me you weren't prepared to have me show up today to take over."

Her eyes flashed. "Take over? Listen, you fixed a great meal. I want to enjoy it."

"No problem." He took a second helping. "I'm just getting way different vibes from you than I got from your family. Your mom went on and on about how anxious you are to get back to teaching in the city."

Myra took more green beans, knowing she was being uncharacteristically surly. "My parents think I should be anxious. Especially Mom." She couldn't seem to stop resenting Zeke. But soon the only noise in the kitchen was the ticktock of the old wall clock and Orion rooting in his dish.

Zeke drained his cup and got up for more coffee. Retaking his seat, he said, "Is it safe to ask you about the ranch finances? I don't want to cast aspersions on your dad, because he and your mother treated me really well. But did he give me an albatross? I can see the house needs work, but my brother said the land must be worth a lot."

Myra's heart gave a kick. She hunched forward. Had he given her an opening to lay it on thick and convince him the ranch was a dud? *She couldn't lie. It wasn't in her.* She took her time before looking him in the eye. "To my dad, who left here at twenty-five when he got married and began to build his own spread on a ranch that belonged to my mom's parents, this has always been the old home place. As Gramps aged, he set up a trust with my dad, his only child. Were you insinuating you might want to sell?" Trying for casual, Myra took a drink.

When Zeke continued his silent regard of her, she gestured with her free hand. "I'd be willing to go to the bank and see what they'd allow me for a loan to buy you out."

"You? I thought you couldn't wait to get back to your teaching career."

She shrugged lightly, not wanting to give away how badly she wanted to own this ranch. "Having lived here three and a half years, I've discovered I have a knack for ranching. It's probably too late to get a teaching spot. Schools start soon."

"I wasn't thinking of selling. But if not teaching, what will you do?"

Myra shrugged again. "Maybe one of the bigger ranches needs a cowhand."

Zeke toyed with his cup, then grinned. "On my drive here, on the other side of a town called Miles City, I saw a sign on a fence post. At the time it made me laugh. 'Housekeeper wanted. Must be able to drive a tractor and work cattle.' Maybe you'd do."

She got up and started gathering their dirty dishes.

"So, no comment?"

"Miles City isn't Snowy Owl Crossing. And I'd be leery of a job with that description. The term *house-keeper* could entail more side activities than I'd care to take on."

"Like what? Oh…oh! I get you." He blushed. "I'm not usually that slow on the uptake."

It was her turn to stammer in embarrassment. "Uh, I actually meant it might mean the rancher also needed a nanny to take care of his kids."

"Yikes! Are you kidding me?"

"No. At the grange hall it's not uncommon to hear of some cowboy-rancher's wife he met on the rodeo circuit finding ranch life not so glamorous after they have a couple of kids."

"It does seem life out here might be lonely. How close is the nearest neighbor?" he asked, sliding from his chair to bring his dishes to where she stood loading the dishwasher.

"A…a mile or so from here." Myra straightened. Their arms brushed, surprising her because she hadn't realized he'd gotten so close. She stepped back and almost fell over the open dishwasher door.

"Hey, hey. Careful." Zeke grabbed her upper arm to keep her from taking a spill.

Caught between his close, warm body and the dishwasher, her breath hitched and her pulse quickened. She breathed a sigh of relief when he let go of her arm and moved aside.

Her cell phone rang. Myra recognized her neighboring rancher's number. "Hank, hi," she said, stepping away from the sink. "Is everything okay at the Bar W?"

"It's good. I thought I'd check on you. I was in town picking up supplies and I heard a rumor you were leaving. I'm running trucks to market in a few days if the snow melts—and the weathermen predict it will. Do you still need space for your stock?"

Myra pinched the bridge of her nose. She should've known her business would be all over town. The café wasn't empty when she talked to her friends. And gossip was a mainstay of any small town. "I… We still need a truck. I helped the ranch's new owner trail cow-calf pairs down to our grass pasture today. Are any of the Jarvis boys home? Lieutenant Maxwell is going to need help sorting, and certainly help sending cows through chutes for vaccinating, parasite treatment and pregnancy testing."

"Lieutenant Maxwell? Is that the soldier hero who saved Eric's life? Your grandpa Cal mentioned him."

"He's one and the same. Dad gave him the Flying Owl." She made an effort to not sound distressed.

"Hot damn! Where does that leave you, Myra?"

"I'm still figuring that out. About the Jarvis boys...?"

"Two are off at college, and I guess you didn't hear that Gordy, the high school junior, broke his leg playing football. He's in a cast."

"Damn." Myra frowned at Zeke, who'd finished loading the dishwasher and leaned against the sink cabinet watching her.

"The yearlings have to be weaned for market," she went on. "I can do that since some of the money from the sale is slated to pay off the last of Gramps's banknote. When will you have room on a semi?"

"Day after tomorrow. I can be there to load up by nine."

"Okay. Oh, and Hank, I drove down a couple of Bar W heifers and calves, and a few of Ralston's that mixed in with my herd. Working in snow I figured it'd be easiest to bring them all in."

"Dave rented my truck for tomorrow. I'll ask if he'll send a cowhand over while you're cutting."

They reiterated a time for loading and said goodbye. Myra tossed her phone on the counter. "What was that all about?" Zeke asked.

Myra put soap in the dishwasher and started it running. "It means you're stuck with me for a few more days at least. Unless you can pull a cowboy out of your hat. There are calves to get to market and bills to pay. Hank only charges for the gas it costs to drive from here to the stockyards. You won't get a better deal in your lifetime. Plus, greenhorn that you are, you need to see and help with a process that gets done every year."

"Okay. But does that mean you have to forgo finding a teaching job?"

"I told you, it's probably too late now to secure a fall opening."

"You did. You also offered to buy me out. Greenhorn I may be, but I'm not ready to sell. Not until I know if I have what it takes to be a rancher. Just so we're clear, I had what it took to be a Green Beret."

"Touché." She opened the fridge and pulled out some fresh lettuce from the keeper, crossed the room and set it in Orion's bowl. She rubbed his ears and the pig all but smiled.

"Is he full grown?" Zeke asked.

Myra shook her head. "He weighs about fourteen pounds. Jewell says the full-grown micromini probably ends up twenty pounds."

"Do you have a dog to help herd cattle and the like?"

"Not now. Gramps had a beautiful border collie. Lucy gave out before he did, and he'd had her for so many years he couldn't fathom loving another dog.

He made fun of Orion when I brought him home. But it wasn't long before I noticed him talking to the pig. And Orion liked to sit with Gramps in his recliner." She smiled at the memory.

Zeke smiled back. "Look, if you're not champing at the bit to get to bed, can we talk bookkeeping? I already know from listening to you speak with the neighbor that I have a lot to absorb about what goes on outside. But if I don't understand the economics I'll be sunk before I start."

"It's a boring subject, but if we brew another pot of strong coffee I'll give you some hard facts and walk you through the software I use."

"We'll have to load that onto my laptop, I guess."

"Good idea," Myra said, dumping what little coffee remained in the old pot. Then she prepared a new one. "In the meantime, I'll get my laptop. We can work at the kitchen table. There's a desk in the third bedroom, but it shares space with all of my dollhouse materials and jigsaws and stuff."

"About those dollhouses...?" Zeke's voice trailed off, but his question hung between them.

Myra sifted a hand through her hair. "I'll deliver the finished ones to another member of the Artsy Ladies before I leave. I don't know what I'll do with the half-completed projects, or the unused material and equipment. But never fear, I'll clear everything of mine out."

His forehead wrinkled. "I'm afraid I'm still in the dark here. Who are the Artsy Ladies?"

"Some of us formed a group to sell crafts and hopefully save the snowy owls for which the town is named. They've always nested in timberland running through Canada and the US. The owls are sacred to our local Native Americans, too."

"Okay, I get that," Zeke said.

"They're gorgeous. Wait until you see them in flight, or in their nests if you ride up to the woods. Sorry, I'm getting off track. About the dollhouses... Our veterinarian was born and raised in Snowy Owl Crossing. She first noticed a decline in the owl population when she came home to open her vet practice. Right after I moved here to help Gramps, she organized a committee to look into securing a state wildlife refuge for the birds. It takes money to fight for anything like that. Asking for donations to buy expensive land went nowhere in a bad economy. So some of us decided to hold a Thanksgiving bazaar and all sell crafts. Profits above material costs go to fund our effort. We named our group the Artsy Ladies."

"I counted a dozen dollhouses. There's that big a demand for them?"

"You'd be surprised. People come from miles around to buy them and the other handmade wares."

Zeke looked skeptical.

The coffeepot gurgled. "If the houses bug you, I'll make time to haul them away. I'm sure someone can store them until the bazaar."

He held up a hand. "It's okay. I didn't understand.

Why don't I pour our coffee while you get the computer."

"Okay, but prepare to be bored. People born to ranching, like my dad, keep a lot of these facts and figures in their heads. As a math major, I'm different. I like spreadsheets." She left and came back with a laptop. "Even Gramps said keeping a spreadsheet helped us not to overspend. But so you know, some years you make a profit and some you go in the hole. It's imperative to be on good terms with your local banker, who'll float loans to tide you over in bad years. Notes you pay back in a year when stock prices are up and you haven't been plagued by a horrid winter or summer drought." Myra fired up the computer just as the lights flickered.

Zeke shot a glance at the ceiling lights.

"Don't worry, we have a generator if the power goes out. Lanterns and flashlights, too."

He pulled a chair around to her side of the table and sat.

His body heat warmed Myra, but left her stumbling over giving him basic costs for cows, feed, bull, labor, transportation, vet and other supplies. "In a fantastic year still only eighty percent of our cows wean calves. Heifer calves weigh less than steers, which bring less money. See this column. For last year I adjusted the amount we earned in stock sales. This year I'll do the same when we ship." She discreetly edged her chair away from his.

Seeming not to notice, he said, "Hmm. You broke

even the prior year, but lost money last year. Is that typical?"

She waved her hand to indicate that it varied. "It's better than average for a small operation. A big cattle ranch like Dad's can run four or five years in a row on borrowed money and then have a huge windfall. In an up year you buy equipment or roof the barn. And there goes the profit."

"At the risk of sounding obtuse, why keep on keeping on?"

She sat back and shut down the program. "I guess it's for love of the land. There's not much open land left. I can't explain it, but ranching is a job that gives you a sense of freedom. Isn't that what you fought for? I know it's why Eric went into the army."

Zeke reached up to massage his wounded shoulder. He didn't answer her question.

"That's enough lessons for tonight." Feeling too close to him for comfort, Myra abruptly got up, closed the laptop and carried her cup to the sink. "I see it's still snowing," she said, looking out the kitchen window. "It's lessened some, but not totally. So it's time to take another batch of hay to the cows."

"Really?" Zeke frowned.

"Snow and cold pulls weight off an animal fast. In winter or like with this early snow, it's day and night feeding. Cattle raising is almost always a seven-day-a-week job, Zeke. There's also night work during calving. Grab your coat, and if you don't own a hat with earflaps, there are extras on the rack by the front door."

Myra went to the front door and pulled on her boots, jacket and hat. She picked up a big flashlight and led the way to the barn.

Zeke, who'd had to rush to keep up, didn't say anything until after they'd loaded the trailer again and he sat shivering on the hay. "If I wasn't here," he called to be heard above the tractor noise, "would you be doing this alone?"

Myra briefly glanced back. "Yes. I've gone solo the last two years, once Gramps's arthritis got so bad he couldn't take the cold." From her companion's pensive expression, she actually wondered if he might seriously be contemplating returning his gift. If that happened, she needed to phone her father in the morning, to be square with him. He needed to know if Zeke didn't want the ranch that she did. She didn't expect to be willed any part of Rolling Acres, so the Flying Owl was it for her. Eric would benefit from her parents' holdings. Most ranches could only support one family. If one sibling had to buy out the interests of others, it put a hardship on the one left. Sometimes that person couldn't afford to get married and raise a family.

That made her wonder if Zeke Maxwell had a steady girlfriend or even a wife stashed away in Boston or some other port of call. If so, that person most definitely wasn't a ranch woman, or he'd have said so—wouldn't he?

Because all things to do with Lieutenant Maxwell gave her heartburn, Myra stopped thinking about him. Instead, she concentrated on signs that told her she was still on the right path to reach the herd.

It was spitting snow when the first bunch of cows came into sight. Stopping, Myra let the tractor idle and passed Zeke the cutters. "Will you toss this mob some hay, please?"

"How much?" He rose stiffly.

"I could say as much as they'll eat. But until we see what all is left tomorrow, we won't know if we gave them too much or not enough. Just free a bale and scatter hay as I drive along."

Zeke cut the first bale open. "Are these different cows than those we already fed? I thought we'd be tossing hay in the same places."

"You should try to feed in different spots so the manure doesn't get so deep in one area. Saves you from having to spread fertilizer around when the snow melts, plus it gives cows a clean table to eat, so to speak. If we had to have an early snowfall, this is a good area for the herd. There are plenty of draws and shrubs to shelter them from the wind. And the stream's not in danger of freezing over. Water and feed are the two essentials. After you separate the cows from the yearlings and Hank transports them, you'll drive these cows and the bull down to the pastures nearer the barn. I'll try to show you those pens tomorrow."

"When do you move them back up here?" he asked

right before she revved the tractor and they headed to the next grouping of cows huddled against the biting wind.

"After these heifers drop their calves in the spring. Usually that's March and April. I suppose I can make a chore list," she called back to him, trying not to sound exasperated. But the man was a total novice. What had her father been thinking? Had he been blinded by the fact Zeke had put himself in harm's way to save Eric that he gave no thought to what might befall the Flying Owl? That kind of selfless heroism did deserve recognition, but darn, couldn't her dad have called in some markers and found Zeke a job in Billings or maybe with the Stock Association? Her grandfather and her dad had both once been officers.

Zeke remained strangely silent throughout the rest of the hay distribution. Perhaps he was too cold to talk. The snow petered out. As they drove home, the sky cleared to patchy clouds. The silvery moon popped in and out of the clouds. Those were the quiet beauties that never failed to touch Myra's heart. She wondered what was going through Zeke's mind. He never said a word.

It was well past midnight when she once again unhitched the trailer and stored the tractor in its shed.

Zeke broke his silence. "I'd think times like this would be when you'd want to have a dog. What if you run into trouble out there in the dead of night?"

She cocked her head and guided him to the house. Stamping snow off her boots at the door, she said, "I have my cell phone and there's good service all over this ranch. But if you want a dog, Zeke," she said, opening the door and shedding her hat and jacket inside, "I know Jewell would be more than happy to hook you up with a healthy pet. I can ask her to drop by tomorrow or the next day. We need vaccine for the heifers. If you want my advice, don't let her get you a puppy. You're going to have plenty to learn about the ranch, which won't leave time to train a puppy."

He nodded. "How much sleep do you get?" he asked tiredly.

Myra took pity on him because he did look beat. "I know I tagged you to fix breakfast, but how about if tomorrow I handle that? In fall and winter we eat breakfast around six. Spring and summer earlier."

"I'll set my cell-phone alarm. Is there a towel I can use in the bathroom?"

"Yep. And the bedding is fresh. It's all new, actually. Courtesy of my mom. They stayed here for Gramps's funeral."

Zeke returned his borrowed hat to the rack, excused himself and made a beeline for his bedroom.

Myra was weary, too. Probably she was more tired for still laboring under the shocking news that she needed to turn over her beloved ranch to a stranger. To a man who, however heroic he might have been on the battlefield, was green as a gourd about cattle ranching. Going to the kitchen, she picked up Orion, whispered her thoughts to him and carried him to her room.

LATE THOUGH IT WAS, Zeke needed to shower. He hoped the sound wouldn't keep Myra awake.

Letting hot water beat down on his back and the sore shoulder that still bore scars from his surgeries, his mind drifted. Myra Odell of the curling blond hair and somber, whiskey-colored eyes, was a dynamo. She was nothing like her sibling. When he'd acquired Eric on his combat team, the kid had been fresh-faced and kind of unsure about everything. He'd never have made a career soldier.

Zeke shut off the water and toweled dry. He thought about Myra going out in the snowy evening to load a trailer and haul hay into a stark, cloudy night. Eric hadn't shirked any duty to which he'd been assigned, but he hated night patrol. He went out of his way to trade night duty for any number of undesirable tasks. Maybe that all stemmed from growing up feeding cattle on nights like tonight.

Checking his clothes as he emptied his duffels and hung things in the closet, he noted that while he'd brought long-sleeved shirts and knit Henleys, he didn't own anything flannel. He made a mental note to buy flannel shirts, long underwear and a Sherpa-lined jacket like Myra wore. August had yet to end and both times he'd ridden out with her he'd frozen his fanny.

He fell into bed, wondering if he did have what it'd take to be a rancher. His twin had called this a sweetheart deal. Even he'd considered it a windfall when the papers from Jack Odell had arrived. Now he wasn't sure.

As he lay on his back, staring up into total blackness, it crossed his mind that he could sell the cows, cattle or whatever one called them. And use his army disability pay to live out his days here rocking on the back porch he'd glimpsed. From his drive up, he could see that the mountain range behind the property held a certain gray and purple majesty.

Forget it. The still-rational part of his brain reminded him how stir-crazy he'd been during his recovery and later in Boston when he hadn't found a job. He wasn't cut out to do nothing. So what were his options? No clear idea came to mind because the warmth of the soft bed and the day's unfamiliar exercise overtook him and he slid into sleep.

LIGHT POURING INTO the bedroom woke Zeke. At first he felt disoriented, until the room coalesced around him and he remembered having come to the ranch. The Montana ranch he now owned.

Even as he kicked off the covers and sat up, his phone alarm chimed. And he smelled something cooking. Sausage, maybe.

Climbing from the bed caused pain in more areas than his injured elbow and shoulder, and left him feeling as if he'd aged overnight. It had to have a lot to do with manhandling hay bales, or perhaps bouncing around on a tractor-pulled flatbed. That last trip out to the herd had been an especially rough ride.

How had he gotten so out of shape in ten months? The six he'd spent in VA surgeries and rehab, and the four he'd spent pounding the streets in Boston job hunting? Before that, he'd jogged Afghan hills carrying a loaded M16 and a fifty-pound pack.

Zeke told himself to stop being wussy. After dressing, he made the bed, and after washing his face, left his room—only to fall over Myra's pig. The creature was chasing a rubber ball down the hall. To keep from stepping on the pig, he lurched to the side, but slammed into the door frame. It shook the house and hurt his right arm—thankfully, not his healing left one. All the same, it prompted a colorful array of swearwords.

When he regained his balance and glanced up, Myra stood in the kitchen doorway, spatula in hand.

"What in the world happened?"

"I tripped over your silly pig."

"Sorry. I let him out to exercise when I know he can't go outside. Will you put him in his pen? I have sausage and potatoes warming in the oven. Now that you're up I'll fix the pancakes."

She disappeared from the doorway, her voice floating back to Zeke. He gingerly picked up the round little pig and was surprised when the animal snuggled under his unshaven jaw. Zeke hadn't expected a pig to act like a puppy or for those ears to be so soft.

Feeling a bit awkward, Zeke scooped up the ball, too, and did as Myra asked, carrying pig and ball to the kitchen pen, where he deposited them.

"Thanks. I'll fill you a plate and you can wash up. I'm happy to report yesterday's storm has passed. Can you hear the snow melting off the eaves? A weak sun is rising. Unfortunately it'll make everything slushy and slick."

"What's on our agenda for today? If the snow is melting, does that mean we don't have to haul hay out to the cows?"

"That depends on how strong the sunlight gets. There's still grass in the hills. There's also more shade, and the cattle may stay in the shelter of coulee brush. I'll check to see if better weather is predicted. If so, we can take out a few cakes of protein supplement to tide them over until the grass is visible again."

Zeke dried his hands on the kitchen towel she handed him. "Okay," he said agreeably, taking the warm plate of food from her.

"I'll bring the coffee carafe to the table so we don't have to hop up and down."

Zeke watched her dump a teacup full of lettuce, carrot and an apple slice into the pig's heavy metal bowl before she brought her plate and the coffeepot to the table.

"Is that all you feed…what did you call him?"

"Orion. And yes," she said, settling down after pouring them both coffee. "He's a miniature. I'm not fattening him up for market. A pig will eat all day if you let them. Jewell said it's no different for ones bred as house pets. He eats scraps in small portions. I have to keep his water bowl full always. And so you know, while we're here, never give him salty treats, avocado or chocolate. That's why I have child locks on the bottom kitchen cabinets. If he's loose he opens cupboards."

"I wondered about that yesterday." Zeke looked up from his plate. "Does he sleep in the pen at night?"

"I have a dog crate in my bedroom with his night blanket."

Zeke shook his head and tucked into his food.

"If you get a dog before I leave here, you'll have to feed him in the barn. Orion would gorge himself on dog food, which is way too rich for a mini pig."

Swallowing the last bit of sausage, Zeke picked up his coffee. "I'm still not clear on what all you say is on today's agenda. I recall you told your neighbor we'd get stock ready for him to take to market. Do all ranchers work together?"

"I'll start with basics about our community. The reservation borders town on the east. Sioux, mostly. It's a community in itself, similar to Snowy Owl Crossing. They farm, ranch and guide hunters and fishermen. Like local ranches, the Flying Owl is a cow-calf operation. We get calves in the spring and sell them in the fall." She paused until she saw Zeke nod as if he followed her explanation.

"Calves are ear-tagged at birth to make sure they don't get separated from mothers. Pairs are sorted and calves branded before we move the herd to summer range. I've found it's easier to keep heifers with calves to eventually be sold in an area with access to a bull so they'll produce again. Those that didn't calve this year spend time with a rented bull in summer. Hopefully to produce calves. That's what'll happen to some of the ones we fed yesterday. Have I stopped making sense? You look mystified."

He placed his knife and fork across his empty plate. "It's a lot to take in. Are there books that teach cattle ranching?"

"Books?"

Zeke gestured with his cup. "Yes, in boot camp we were issued technical manuals explaining much of what a new recruit needed to know."

"I suppose there are books. Aren't there books written on practically everything?"

"Yes, but if you didn't learn all the stuff you spout off the top of your head from a book," he said, frustrated, "how is it you know so much?"

"I was born on a ranch," she pointed out, standing to collect both of their plates. "Summers from my earliest memory I spent right here tagging after Gramps. Oh, sure, Gram taught me canning, jam making and cooking. But I learned all I've ever needed to know about running a ranch from helping Gramps and Dad do the work."

"Okay, so listen. I'm having some thoughts here. Yesterday you said it's too late for you to get a teaching job this fall. What would you charge to stay here and work for me until a math job comes your way? I can follow you around and learn what I need to know to keep this ranch running like it does now."

The dishes clattered in the sink where Myra dropped them. She spun toward him, her mouth agape. "Wor… work…for you?"

Zeke sucked his bottom lip between his teeth then released it. "Didn't mean to take you by surprise. I do own this ranch now," he said gently. "If it's a title you want, how about we call you the ranch manager until I get up to speed?"

Myra's cell rang, and she snatched it off the counter. "It's, uh, my dad. I'm sure he's calling to see if I'm headed to Rolling Acres. I only spoke to Eric last night. I'll be right back."

Zeke heard her say hello as she walked down the hall. Then her bedroom door slammed and he was left in a kitchen devoid of noise except for Orion rooting for food in his almost empty dish. Bending, Zeke rubbed the pig's large pink ears. "Shocked her I did, Piggy Pal. It sounded like a good idea to me." He finished his coffee, replaced the pot on the burner and put the breakfast dishes in the dishwasher. Myra still hadn't returned, so he went to shave. Although, if it was as cold out today as yesterday, maybe he should grow a beard. But he didn't like them because he'd been required to have one for so long. He'd needed one in Afghanistan to blend in with locals. Not blending in could have gotten him killed. Once he separated from the military, he'd stayed clean shaven, and considered it a luxury. Passing a hand over his prickly cheeks, he detoured back to his room.

Chapter Three

Myra said hello, but didn't acknowledge that she knew it was her father calling. She was still majorly upset with him. It felt right to give her bedroom door a hard push.

"Myra, it's Dad. Your mother asked me to call to see if you'd be home for lunch. We thought you'd be under way already."

Pacing around the bedroom that had been hers off and on for many years, Myra weighed her answer. "Actually, I won't be home for lunch or anytime soon."

"Why? Eric said you had more snow than we did, but I saw on the morning news that the highway is clear. You shouldn't have trouble driving."

"The weather has improved. But, Dad, you turned the Flying Owl over to a total novice. I can't walk away and let the ranch fall into ruin."

"What do you mean? It's not a working ranch anymore. Your grandfather told me he was trapped under a mountain of medical bills after Gram died. That's why he sold what was left of his herd and offered a chunk of pasture to a neighbor."

"What are you talking about?"

"I told him to sell the whole shebang and come live with us, but he refused. When you went to help out, I didn't press further. So up to now I've ignored your mom's unhappiness over the way you put your career on a back burner. Frankly, with Eric in a war zone and making sure Rolling Acres stayed in the black, not needing to worry about my dad's health and well-being took a load off me. But, honey, you can stop feeling responsible for the Flying Owl. I paid the estate tax and the last payment on Dad's banknote. Giving the property to Lieutenant Maxwell frees us all up."

"You paid Gramps's banknote? Why? I'm about to ship last year's calves. That revenue is earmarked to cover the note and sustain the ranch until we sell next year's calves."

"Come on, Myra. How many pregnant cows did Dad own? Twenty? Although I can't fathom why he didn't sell the lot. His asthma and arthritis were so bad when we talked shortly before he passed away, he admitted he hadn't walked out to the barn in almost a year."

"He didn't need to, Dad. I managed the ranch. I grew his herd. He had around a hundred head when I moved here. We didn't sell any. This year I'll be shipping almost that many calves. Our overall herd stands at close to three hundred."

There was a long silence. Enough for Myra to think she'd lost the connection. Suddenly her father yelped an explosive "Why am I only hearing about this now? Isn't that something you should have told me at Dad's funeral?"

"You didn't ask." Myra crossed to her bedroom window. "As I recall, you guys were in a rush to leave and barely stayed for the reception my friend from the café in town helped prepare."

"I'm sorry about that, honey. You know Rolling Acres was in the middle of calving. With Eric and me at the funeral, it only left two ranch hands to handle a four-man task."

"You didn't hear me say I was in the middle of calving, too? Thank goodness two of my neighbors helped out, which is what neighbors in Snowy Owl Crossing do."

"Honey, I didn't call to argue. I honestly had no idea Dad didn't sell off his herd. But I'm good with you keeping the funds from your stock sale to tide you over until you find a teaching job. Instead of staying with us, you may want to rent an apartment in Billings or Missoula, whichever city you think offers the best opportunity for you. Of course your mom and I would rather you be in Billings. That way you can come on holidays to visit. Oh, your mom is just saying come stay over summer breaks, too, until you find some significant someone, get married and start a home of your own."

Myra recognized the smile in his voice that surely

came from her parents' long-standing wish for her to get married. She wasn't in any mood to humor them. "You still aren't hearing me, Dad. I'm not leaving here. Not yet. I love this ranch. I realize we all owe former Lieutenant Maxwell a debt of gratitude. But he knows zero, zippo, not one thing about cattle. What happens to the Flying Owl, not if but when he flounders? When he realizes he's in over his head, I want to be here to carry on. Then I'll do my level best to convince Nate Gooding at the bank to lend me money to buy Maxwell out."

"That's preposterous, Myra. Do you have any idea what that land is worth? The property taxes alone are partly why I decided to gift the ranch to Eric's friend."

"And it never entered your mind to ask if I was interested in keeping the ranch? Aren't Eric and I the only two in line to inherit from you and Mom? I assume he'll take over Rolling Acres. I thought this was my legacy."

"But…but you went to college when your brother chose the military. Before his obligation was up, he saw it was a mistake. He told us he'd be returning to the ranch. At the risk of sounding old-school, Myra, ranches belong in the hands of a competent man."

She'd heard this before, but it still irritated her. "I can't believe you said that. And man though he is, Zeke Maxwell is about as far from being a competent rancher as I've ever seen. The one thing in his favor so far, he's begun to see it himself. This morning he offered me a job managing the Flying Owl.

At the time I wasn't sure I wanted to work for him. Now I think I'll stay and hope by spring our city boy tires of Snowy Owl Crossing's isolation. Sorry, Dad, I've gotta run. Hank Watson is trucking our calves to market tomorrow, so I've a full day's weaning ahead of me."

Hearing her dad sputter as she removed the phone from her ear, Myra disconnected. Fully expecting a callback from her mother, she tossed her phone down on her nightstand and charged out of the room.

She almost bowled Zeke over as she rushed into the living room. He was bent down peering inside one of her completed dollhouses.

"Sorry I spent so much time gabbing with Dad," she said brightly. "Grab your gear. Time's a'wasting. We need to get busy sorting calves."

"You look flushed. Is everything all right?" Zeke hurried after her, pausing to pluck his coat from the rack where he'd hung it by hers the night before.

"I'm fine, just running late." She stepped out onto the porch and pulled on her boots.

Zeke followed her out and shut the door. "Will I need the hat with earflaps again?" he asked, watching Myra set a gray cowboy hat atop her taffy-colored waves.

"Separating calves from their mothers is sweaty work. You can probably get by wearing your baseball cap. Most ranchers favor a cowboy hat." She left the porch and was met by a cold blast of wind. "It's gonna be chilly when we begin. You won't want to let body heat seep out through the top of your head. In this country it's always smart to start the day wearing a hat."

He went back inside and came out with his baseball cap.

Pulling on her well-worn leather gloves, Myra spared a moment trying to decide which part in today's process Zeke would find hardest or would least like. Aware she probably hadn't heard the last from her folks, the sooner Zeke got the message he wasn't cut out to be a rancher, the quicker she could buy him out. The bank ought to grant her a loan, especially once she proved she had taken on the ranch in a downturn and set it on a profitable course.

Was she being too mean? Engineering chores to help Zeke fail? No, she decided. Not if he figured out on his own that he was a fish out of water.

Zeke caught up. "I assume we're taking the littler animals away from the bigger, older ones. Do we do that by hand or on horseback? I've only seen something like that in Western movies. Cowboys always rope the calves. Of course, I've never handled a rope for that purpose."

"For what purpose have you handled a rope?" His statement shook Myra from her own thoughts. She hoped he wasn't going to say he'd hung anyone. Most of what she knew about Green Berets came from having rented a couple of violent war movies for her grandfather.

"We used ropes for scaling cliffs, or sometimes to assist a buddy up into a chopper."

"Ah." *Thank goodness.* "Well, for this task I'm not riding. I don't want to tear up the grass since we'll bring the mama cows back to the corral to feed once they're vaccinated and checked for new pregnancies." She climbed up to the second railing on the fence that surrounded the milling pairs. "See those two smaller corrals?" She let Zeke climb up beside her before pointing.

"I like using two smaller corrals to separate yearling steers from heifers before we drive them into Hank's semi. Steers weigh more and so earn more at the feedlot. And some heifers we keep, but we need an accurate count." She angled a glance at the man whose shoulder brushed hers. "You do know the difference between a steer and a heifer by looking at them, don't you?"

His mouth thinned to a droll line. "I realize you think I'm a total dunce. I was about twelve when I learned all about the birds and bees."

One quick perusal of his handsome face and she didn't doubt his declaration. She imagined he'd always had girls shamelessly chasing him. How else did city kids learn about mating? Girls like her, raised on ranches, took anything related to birds and bees in stride. She didn't blush at comments that she'd seen send her city college friends into red-faced giggles.

"Good enough," she said. "I'll start out driving a calf toward you. And you'll plant yourself between the two small corrals. If I send you a steer, shoo him into the larger of the two pens. Scram heifers into the smaller one."

Zeke jumped down off the fence. "I'm glad you didn't say left or right, because then I'd have to ask if I'd be facing you or facing the pens."

"You'll want to keep your back to the railing between the little corrals as much as possible. Not all mama cows will be happy to have us taking away their offspring. They've been known to head butt, kick or bite."

"Sounds grim. And you do this every year?"

"Twice a year. The first time is after calving ends. You'll sort mamas and babies and deliver them to the same range we brought these pairs down from yesterday."

"I doubt I can find my way back to that spot. Listen, I hate to pressure you, but have you had time to give any thought to my job offer?"

Myra climbed down and opened the gate, giving him room to pass. "I am considering it. I mentioned it to my dad. My parents will fuss. They sent me to college to… It doesn't matter." She waved a hand as if to erase the comment. "Let's get started."

"Now you have me curious as to why they'd be keener on you attending college than I sense you were to go," he said and cocked his head toward her as he wiggled his fingers into his own gloves.

From the trouble he was having, Myra thought his gloves probably hadn't dried overnight. Wet gloves could be miserable. *He'd learn.* "My mother's not the biggest fan of ranching that ever lived," Myra murmured. "She grew up on Rolling Acres and wanted to leave and see the world. Her senior year of high school she went to a grange dance, met my dad and they fell in love. I've always suspected she wanted me to live her fantasy. Relocate to a city, meet and marry a doctor or lawyer...anyone but a rancher. She still loves my dad to pieces, but she's always told Eric and me that ranch life is too hard. Remember I said you'll get few days off. And forget vacations. But I'm not like my mom. I'm a fan of ranching."

"Why did you go to college, then?"

"Don't most kids want to please their parents? Dad expected Eric to follow in his footsteps. They argued when he joined the ROTC. I thought one of us shouldn't disappoint them. Now Eric's back to help Dad. It turned out he didn't like being in the army any better than I liked being a teacher. Funny how life intervenes. Did you always want a military career?" It was a casual question asked as they made their way around the inside perimeter of the corral.

Zeke laughed. "Sure, after vowing I'd be a policeman, a firefighter or a pro baseball player." He sidestepped a cow patty. "Having a twin breeds early competition. Growing up, we each swore to become what the other claimed he wanted. We fought when we played over who got to be the firefighter or cop. In high school and college we both played baseball. I quit the team my junior year and hung out with some guys in the National Guard. Seth took a science class that turned him on to minerals. For the first time in our lives we went our separate ways."

"You must not have had pressure from your folks. What business were they in?" Myra immediately wished she could take back the question. She didn't want to know personal stuff about the man she wished would go away.

"In a way Mom influenced Seth some. Instilled in him a desire to see the world. She ran a travel agency for twenty years. Mom was forever flying off to one part of the world or another. Dad was an insurance agent, able to work from home. He mostly oversaw us and ran the house."

Unable to drop the subject, Myra asked, "Are you close to your brother now?"

"We're reconnecting. We got the need for competition out of our systems. By the way, I invited Seth to the ranch. But I looked in that third bedroom and it resembles a carpentry shop."

"It kind of is, with my dollhouse patterns, material, jigsaws and Dremel tools. I sand wood and cut doors and windows in there, but if I stay on I can move them. When's he coming?"

"I don't know. He gave me a list of gems he plans to acquire in various countries prior to attending some major gem show."

"Okay. Sounds as if I have time to clear out my stuff." Moving into the herd, Myra drew Zeke's attention to cows and calves with brands other than the winged owl. "We have to hold those pairs aside. If one gets by you, we'll finish cutting then drive him back out. It's possible Dave Ralston will be by to collect his stock this morning. Hank said Dave's scheduled to take his calves to market today."

"Let's get to it. I'm cold just standing around." Zeke shrugged his shoulders as if to make his point.

"You have to be quick on your feet. You'll open the proper gate when a steer or heifer comes close, and shut the gate fast once the calf is inside."

"Will they try to come back out?"

"Yes. If their mama bawls enough."

"All right. I'll have to learn as we go."

He didn't know the half of it. She felt sorry for him, but why should she go easy on him? Her goal was to make him see he wasn't cut out to be a ranch owner.

She chose a steer that wasn't too far away from Zeke, let out a yell and slapped the surprised yearling on his rump. Startled, the animal bolted right toward Zeke. The man proved to be agile, sidestepping to open the gate, and they had their first steer penned.

"Good job," she called, although she hadn't intended to give him encouragement. Selecting a skittish young heifer, Myra repeated the process. She noticed at once that Zeke had more trouble opening the left-hand gate. Eric had said Zeke had undergone multiple surgeries on that arm. Myra expected him to complain or ask her to go easy on his injury. But he didn't.

She could make it harder on him if she chose to

drive a series of heifers toward him one after another. But she wouldn't. She wasn't spiteful. It'd be different if he was totally able-bodied. What didn't help was how able-bodied he looked. Tall, pleasingly muscular. Long legs fit nicely in blue jeans. No cowboy boots, but boots. Dang, he could pass for a rancher. That alone probably softened her feelings. Softened her to where she sent him two or three steers for every one heifer, giving him time between to massage his left arm.

She was about to ask Zeke if he wanted to swap jobs when the mother cow of the last steer they'd sorted bawled, pawed the ground and with head down, charged Zeke. He had turned away to shut the gate.

"Zeke!" Myra shouted. But he didn't react in time. The cow's wide head slammed Zeke on his lower back, striking his shapely butt. As the cow's head came up, Zeke flew through the air.

Myra winced at the impact, as if that helped absorb the hit. Of course it did nothing.

Because the angry cow didn't appear ready to give up and trot away, Myra stripped off her belt and darted around other pairs. She smacked the errant animal lightly with the leather strap before mama cow could launch another attack on the man slowly picking himself up off the wet grass.

"Are you okay?" Myra asked after the offending mother left Zeke and plodded to the fence in search of her missing youngster. She continued to be vocal.

Chuckling, Zeke brushed blades of grass and mud off the knees of his grass-stained jeans. "You did warn me. We'd had such success I guess I got too cocky."

"You can't let down your guard," Myra chided gently and glanced up as a red truck hauling a triple horse trailer pulled down the lane to stop outside the corral. The slant R logo was on the driver's door, which swung open to reveal a compact man in his midfifties.

"Dave Ralston's here," Myra told Zeke. "I wondered if he might show up today. That semi will be filled with his calves headed to market. He can transport his two cows and the calves that are mixed in with ours, too. Uh, yours."

"You don't have to keep correcting yourself," Zeke said, straightening to limp over to greet a neighbor he had yet to meet. "I think technically these are your cows, cattle, stock. Whatever you call them," he added lamely to Myra, who matched his stride.

"Pairs," she said firmly. "Dave, hi. I'm glad you're here to get your animals. I've had trouble keeping one of your steers from being sent to the breakout corral. He's a curious little fellow." Because Dave glanced at Zeke, she hurriedly introduced the men.

They shook hands and Dave cast an eye around the property. "Hank told me Jack Odell up and gave you this ranch, sonny. You're a lucky duck if ever one lived. You're sittin' on a gold mine here."

Myra's stomach dropped. She tried to discreetly

jab her elbow into Dave's side. "He doesn't mean that literally," she rushed to inform Zeke. "Granted there are abandoned gold mines out on BLM land. Occasionally we see in the news where someone running cattle on a leased pasture falls through rotten boards covering some old mine or another. I've never run across any on Gramps's property."

"What's BLM land?" Zeke asked.

"Government owned. It's under the control of the Bureau of Land Management. You won't need to deal with them." She continued to glare at Dave.

The older rancher's brow furrowed in a slight frown, but as Myra's steady glare didn't diminish, he shut his mouth.

"Can you back your rig around and drop the ramp?" she queried him.

"Yep. I brought a lariat. Figured if I rope the calves you can help wrestle them into the trailer. Get the calves in and the cows will follow."

"Sounds good. While you turn your truck around, Zeke and I will cut out your two pair."

"Get Hank's, too. He's at my place helping my son load the semi for market."

Myra flashed Dave a thumbs-up as he climbed into the cab.

"I see what you were telling me about neighbors helping neighbors. I hope they'll all accept me," Zeke said, following Myra's lead in separating out the pairs with the Bar W and slant R brands.

Myra pretended she hadn't heard him. She didn't

want Zeke to get buddy-buddy with any of the neighbors. She wanted him to throw in the towel ASAP.

In his younger days Dave Ralston had been a champion calf roper. After he slid out the metal ramp, he came into the pen swinging his rope like the veteran he was. It sang through the air and settled over the head of one of his young steers. Digging in his boot heels, he pulled the stubborn animal out of the enclosure.

"Zeke, I'll shove the calf from behind, if you'll close the gate after us."

He hurried to comply, but froze when Myra stepped right in a gooey brown pile on her way to pushing the animal up the ramp.

"You must not have grown up around cows." Dave grinned down at Zeke from the trailer entrance. Freeing his rope, he jumped down. "Better get boots you only wear when you work stock. Guess Myra didn't tell you these small mounds of cow pucky are nothing compared to what you'll wade through when you start jamming mama cows through the chute for pregnancy testing, vaccinations and parasite treatments."

Zeke gave an offhanded shrug. "I ran into my share of chicken and goat droppings in Afghanistan. I felt bad Myra didn't see it in time to avoid landing in it."

"Afghanistan, huh? Is how they portrayed our role in *Zero Dark Thirty* for real?"

"Dunno. I never saw the movie. I tend to prefer

Westerns. Is what they show of a cowboy's life accurate?"

Dave uttered a deep belly laugh as he opened the gate, swung his rope again and this time captured the calf with the Bar W brand. "I 'spect the majority of Westerns get gussied up so the studio's star or even stuntmen and -women don't break something and sue the film backers." Shortening the rope, he marched the calf out of the pen.

"Figured that might be the case. You're handy with that rope." This time Zeke helped wrestle the calf up the ramp, leaving Myra to close the gate.

And he was careful to step over the aromatic pile that sat squarely at the base of the ramp.

"I started roping an old stump in front of our house from the time I was knee-high to a jackrabbit," Ralston said. "You can probably learn if you put your mind to it and practice."

Myra shaded her eyes and snagged Dave's attention. "You'll have to show Zeke how to fasten the calf to the railings inside the horse trailer. He's new to all of this."

"'Pears to me he's a smart fellow," Dave responded, flipping his rope off the second calf as Zeke prodded it on into the trailer. "A guy who defended our freedom in a wild-and-woolly war zone can probably see how you secured the first calf. Don't be so hard on him, Myra."

She dropped her hand, turned and stalked into the pen, careful to bite back sarcasm that would expose her real feelings. Working alone, she cut the third calf out of the larger herd and chased it along the fence to where Dave had only to reach over the railing and drop a loop around the bawling youngster's head. The mama issued a series of angry snorts. She chased after her calf, so it was a simple matter of making sure she didn't plunge off the ramp as she followed her baby up and into the trailer.

With the neighbors' stock all loaded, Myra went back to culling her calves. She looked around for Zeke and saw him standing by the truck jawboning with Dave. Since this was a task she'd done by herself for the past two years, she herded a yearling right up to a gate, opened it and quickly shoved the animal through. It was definitely more time-consuming doing it without Zeke's help. But she wasn't about to tell him that.

And what were they talking about? Ralston liked to gab. She wished he'd shut up and leave. Not only because she needed Zeke's assistance but because keeping him from making friends would ensure his isolation. If she remained his primary contact, it'd drive home the knowledge that whenever she left he'd be on his own.

Her friends had suggested he'd throw in the towel sooner rather than later. But there he and Dave were, yakking, gesturing, grinning like best buds.

Indeed, he seemed in good spirits when he wandered back after Dave drove away.

"I can see how this job would be easier if the person doing it knew how to rope these little buggers," Zeke said. "Dave said he'll teach me the basics, and all it'll take for me to get proficient is practice. Isn't that cool?"

"Huh," she grunted, shoving another heifer into the correct pen. "Roping is harder than it looks. I never saw the need to waste time learning."

"You don't think it'd be better to be yanking calves around from the front end? I saw what you stepped in when you pushed that one from behind."

She shut the gate and leveled a look at him. "If your aim is to avoid landing in manure, you don't want to be on a working cattle ranch."

He bent his head and tipped his baseball cap forward. "Dave said he was surprised to see you sticking around to give me pointers."

Her jaw hardened. "Really? Did he say why?"

"Well, he said you were third or fourth generation to run the Flying Owl. He said it jokingly but sort of insinuated everybody around here believed that before you turned loose of the land, a coroner would have to pry the deed out of your cold, dead hands."

Shock rippled through Myra. Zeke was clearly waiting for her to deny what may not have really sounded like a joke to him. For a second she debated telling the truth. How her heart broke when her father phoned to say he'd gifted the ranch to someone without one shred of ranch know-how. But what good would it do? Zeke had the right to send her packing.

And she cared too much for the future of the Flying Owl to turn her back on it.

"Dave is quite a joker. He probably thought I could hear him. My name isn't and never has been on the ranch deed. Gramps and Dad put the property in a cotrust after Gram died. Listen, all this palavering is getting us nowhere. We have a lot of calves left to sort out."

Zeke pulled back his sleeve and checked his watch. "Isn't it lunchtime? At least, Dave said he was going home to have lunch before he drove his calves to market."

"I'd hoped to get halfway finished before we broke for lunch. But if you're dying to eat, I guess we can put in a longer afternoon."

"How many more to make half?" he asked, sparing a look around the pen.

"Twenty should do it. Hey, I forgot that maybe you're hurting from the head butting you took. We can take a break if you need to rub on some liniment."

"Are you having me on? Isn't that a horse treatment?"

"It works for people's bruised, sore muscles, too. Really, I swear I'm not giving you hokey advice."

"Well, I do hurt, so I might try it. I figured by morning I'd be black-and-blue in a spot that might leave me standing up to eat for a few days." He gingerly rubbed his back pocket but laughed all the same.

"Okay, you've convinced me to break for lunch. Gramps said the sooner you get liniment rubbed on an injury the faster it heals. He used it liberally on his arthritic wrists and knees. I'm sure there's a giant bottle under the sink in your bathroom. You take care of your owie and I'll fix tomato soup and grilled-cheese sandwiches."

"You're on, even though I haven't called any injury an owie in thirty years."

Myra had left the enclosure and turned to study him. "So how old does that make you?"

"I'm thirty-one." He made sure the gate was latched. "I frankly don't recall anyone in my family using the term *owie*."

"Don't get all bent out of shape about it, Maxwell. It's not an assault on your masculinity." She laughed as she dashed up the porch steps and toed off her boots. "We can refer to it as a pain in the butt, if you prefer. I mean, that is the part of your anatomy the cow hit, right?"

"You're rougher than some of my recruits. I'm not going to dignify that with a yes or no. Let's refrain from talking about it at all."

"I wasn't planning on calling the story in to the *Snowy Owl Weekly Gazette*. For the record," Myra said as she hung up her jacket and tossed her hat on the hat rack by the door, "you aren't the first rancher to take a head butt from a mother cow in an uncomfortable spot, and I doubt you'll be the last. Prepare yourself to have it happen again. And you may not have a soft grass landing next time."

Zeke hesitated in hanging up his bomber jacket.

"Hey, did you just call me a rancher?" His smile carved a dimple in one cheek. "That's the nicest compliment you've paid me since I got here. Give me ten minutes to find that liniment. I'll even brew the coffee for lunch." He whistled, crossing the living room.

Myra wanted to call him and take it back. Zeke Maxwell was nowhere near having earned the title. On the other hand, no one else had heard her slip of the tongue. And the smile her words sparked was pretty terrific. So much so, her own smile lingered while she flitted about the kitchen talking to Orion prior to heating soup and preparing cheese sandwiches.

She couldn't remember ever having a man's simple smile make her stomach flutter. Or maybe she was just hungrier than she thought.

Chapter Four

Myra took a minute to give Orion some snuggle love, freshen his water and bring him a veggie snack before she washed her hands and assembled everything for lunch.

Tomato soup steamed on the stove, and she put two cheese sandwiches in the electric fry pan. Suddenly she smelled the pungent odor of liniment, warring with the more savory scents. Startled, she spun toward the door. Even though she knew Zeke planned to treat his bruises, tears unexpectedly filled her eyes.

In two giant steps, Zeke grabbed her and gripped her arms. "What's the matter, Myra? Did you burn yourself? Run cold water over the area. I'll watch the food."

"I didn't burn myself. Sorry, it's the liniment." She smudged the heel of her palm over her weepy eyes.

Zeke took a step back from her sheepishly. "I should apologize. That stuff has helped, but it sure stinks."

Myra shook her head. "It isn't the liniment smell, Zeke. Or I suppose it is. I should've been prepared, but it took me by surprise. I turned expecting to see Gramps."

Zeke slid his arms around her back and pulled her to his chest. Her tears covered his shirtfront. His hug consoled her, but she shouldn't let him be this nice. Still, she sniffled into his shirt pocket. "He's only been gone six months. Oh, I know I'm being foolish." Biting her upper lip, she pushed out of his hold. "I need to flip the sandwiches or they'll burn."

Zeke let her go. "It's nothing to apologize for. I lost men in my unit. Two in particular were close friends—I can't tell you how many times I'd hear a laugh or look around the mess tent expecting to see them." His brow furrowed.

"That must have been more than hard. I've only had to deal with the deaths of my grandparents. All four lived long lives. My good friend Lila Jenkins lost her dad in a terrible mining accident when she was twelve. And four years ago her husband was killed in a different type of mine. I can't imagine how haunting that has to be."

Zeke rubbed the back of his neck. "Yeah. The living are left to mourn. Hey, can we talk about something else?"

Myra nodded. "The soup is ready. If you'll pour it into the bowls on the table I'll bring our sandwiches." She didn't look at him, still reeling from how easily she'd been comforted by him. Eric had been right, Zeke was a nice man. She'd felt her nerves tingle. This wasn't good. She needed to watch herself around him. It wouldn't do to lose her focus on getting him to quit the ranch.

"Your pig is acting funny," Zeke said as Myra set a grilled-cheese sandwich on his plate. His chair was closest to Orion's pen. The pig was running back and forth, making snorty noises and banging his nose against the wooden baby gate.

"I wonder if he's looking for Gramps, too. House pigs are super social. And like I told you, Gramps made liberal use of liniment. So Orion knows that scent."

Nothing could have surprised Myra more than to see Zeke lean over the pen, pick up Orion and set him on his lap. He let the pig settle, then as if it was no big deal, went back to eating his soup.

Myra smiled. "Most people would think they had to go wash after touching a pig."

He hiked a shoulder. "Afghan families live, eat and sleep with bigger pigs, goats, chickens and sometimes even milk cows. I got used to it from the times elders invited me to eat with their families. Orion hasn't been outside. Which brings me to one real concern. I hope he doesn't pee on me."

Myra tipped back her head and laughed. "Mini pigs are clean, but they are pigs and still like to root in dirt. Orion uses a litter box I keep on the back porch. It's why he has the doggie door."

"That's a relief. He seems friendly. Guess I won't get a dog as long as you're here. Speaking of which. After Dave gave a bit of insight into the next steps I have to take with those mama cows, I know I need help. A lot of help," he muttered before biting into his sandwich.

"Even I need help with that chore," Myra acknowledged. She pushed aside her bowl. "I've given this arrangement a lot of thought. If we continue to work well together, and unless you hate the solitude of a Montana winter and call it quits, I'll stay until spring. But I don't want any title like manager." She scowled a bit. "I prefer if we call it a friend helping a friend." She almost gagged on the word *friend*.

Zeke set down his sandwich. "Just knowing you'll be here is a huge relief. For the record, I'm not a quitter."

Myra's heart sank and she quickly tucked into her sandwich.

"You don't sound as if you want to consider this a job. Is it crass to talk about money? I have my military pension. But even if I buy all the food and pay utilities, you'll need money for…uh…personal stuff."

"About that. My dad said I should take the revenue from the sale of the yearlings. He says he thought Gramps had sold all of his stock and some land to pay Gram's medical bills before I came to help him. I shouldn't be surprised, I guess. Dad and Gramps were two of a kind when it came to privacy." She crumbled the toasty edge of her sandwich.

Zeke ate, letting Myra talk.

"Something else I didn't know," she said. "In order to clear the deed for you, Dad paid the banknote I planned to retire with the current stock sale. So, here's the thing, Gramps and I operated from a single ranch account. I figured on Hank having the feedlot owner do a direct deposit to that account as usual. All deposits, withdrawals and expenses get logged in the spreadsheet we went over last night. I can share the document online with you so we both see income and outgo. If either of us buy groceries or stuff at the feed store, we post it."

"That's generous of you, Myra. I don't know that I feel right about using that money. The fact your folks signed over this ranch to me was a gift I never expected. I can already see you earned what'll come from this sale."

Talking about her parents handing Zeke the ranch made Myra pissy. She wasn't as generous as her folks. And therein lay the problem. She hopped up and carried her dishes to the sink. "I need to make something clear," she said. "Everything I'm doing to teach you what goes on here, I'm doing because I love the Flying Owl. I can't bear the thought of it going under." She was prepared to say more, but the house phone rang, startling them both. "Dang, I hope it's not my mom. She's been calling to pressure me to move home." Myra hesitated, but went to the old wall phone that rarely got used.

"Hello." She spoke tentatively.

"Myra? It's Tawana."

Myra relaxed. Tawana, a Native American woman, was a close friend and another valuable member of the Artsy Ladies group. Tawana blurted out her sorrow over hearing news about Myra losing the ranch. "I couldn't believe it when Lila told me."

"It's true. But I've made a deal with the new owner to stay on for a while. At least until spring." She peered through lowered eyelashes at Zeke, who'd set Orion back in his pen. He washed his hands at the sink and began putting dishes in the dishwasher. "The good news is I'll be here for the Thanksgiving bazaar. Hey, Tawana, can we talk later? I came in for lunch, but I have to go out again. We have calves to cut so Hank can haul them to market tomorrow."

"Sure. I'm happy to hear you aren't leaving ASAP. Call me when you have time. I worried when I kept getting voice mail on your cell. Oh, wait, I almost forgot…the first batch of snowy owls are back. I've been on the lookout for them. There are five I've seen building nests in Leland Conrad's fir trees."

"Conrad? I know his forest, but I don't know him well. He's kind of a grouch, isn't he? Will he let the owls stay on his property, or will he drive them away?"

"He's not a bad guy. The problem I see is that he is currently trying to sell all of his holdings so he can retire. He's never married. According to Jewell, he's estranged from a nephew he raised. But you don't have time for us to get into his history. I phoned Leland. He's okay with the owls and promises he won't disrupt their nesting. However, if a buyer shows up, he won't make leaving the owls alone part of the deal. That worries me."

"Yes. Maybe Jewell can talk to him. She's persuasive."

"I'll call her. If you have time to ride out there, Myra, they're a sight to behold."

"I may. If we get time I should show them to Zeke."

"Who?" Tawana sounded puzzled.

"Zeke Maxwell. Former Lieutenant Maxwell, the Flying Owl's new owner."

"Oh, right. Okay, I'll let you go. I'm typing up minutes from last night's tribal meeting."

"Say, while I have you on the phone, do you know if anyone's looking for work? After we ship calves tomorrow it's time to take care of the cows. We definitely need some competent extra hands."

"You're in luck. This morning Eddie Four Bear and Aaron Younger stopped by my office to see if I knew of any work. They were helping wean calves on a ranch out by Wolf Point. If you need more guys, Eddie probably knows who else is available."

"We could use three on the chutes. I have Eddie's number. I'll call him. I trust him to pick up vaccine kits from Jewell, too. Save me running into town. Thanks, Tawana."

"Always glad to help our men find work. One more thing… I cut out some new vests last weekend. The beading looks good. I think our customers will really like them."

"They always do. No one ever quibbles over price

for one of your vests. I'll be anxious to see them. Anyway, I've really gotta run. See you."

The two signed off. "That was Tawana White Feather," she told Zeke, who quirked an eyebrow when she faced him. "Sorry to ask her about worker availability without first discussing it with you. But the next part of the process with the cows is a dirty job. It's impossible to do without hiring help, and well worth it."

"I'll leave those decisions to you, Myra. Dave didn't make this part sound fun. So, does this woman you talked to run an employment agency?"

"No. She works in the reservation tribal office. Tawana is a council member and a most talented crafter. She makes leather vests with intricate beadwork. They sell like hotcakes."

"Um. I heard you say I need to see something. Did you mean her vests? They don't sound like something men would wear. I mean, if they're beaded."

"You'll have to see them to judge. Her brother wore one at his wedding and looked sharp. But I wasn't talking about you seeing her vests. I was talking about the snowy owls! Tawana said some of the birds have come back. We were worried they wouldn't return this year."

"Really? How would you know one bird from another?"

"Jewell tagged some of the young ones with neon-pink bands. There are experts who do satellite tracking in other parts of the country, but we couldn't afford GPS transmitters."

"Damn, you guys are really serious about owls."

"You bet. Tawana and others on the reservation are huge advocates of saving the snowy owls."

"Why are they showing up here now? If they fly south for the winter, it's a little late."

"Actually, some go north to the Arctic for the winter, some go as far south as Bermuda. And some don't migrate at all. Our flock seems to like to winter here. Jewell's been studying them the longest. She says they follow the migration of lemmings, which is their main source of food. Frankly we worried that our milder winter last year may have caused them to leave permanently. Tawana's sighting proves some are back."

"Are you pulling my leg? I didn't think lemmings were real. I've always put them in the fake category like going snipe hunting."

"Lemmings are real, you goofus. They're rodents. And snowy owls are good-sized. They can carry off a duck or other waterfowl, too. But it's getting late. Let's go finish our chores. If we have enough daylight left afterward, it'd be a treat to ride out so you can see why so many of us are doing everything possible to save these birds."

"Okay, but I hope you won't hold it against me if I don't get worked up about them. I just don't see the big deal."

Myra didn't say what was on her mind. Not caring about the fate of the snowy owls was strike two against Zeke. Strike one was the fact he fell into owning a ranch she loved. She had little doubt that before she left here there'd be a strike three against him.

The sun shone a bit stronger as the afternoon wore on. Melting snow left the grassy pastures as slick as working on grease. But Myra couldn't find fault with the amount of work Zeke did. She could tell when his weak left side started to bother him a lot, and yet he didn't beg off helping, nor did he shirk in any fashion.

"Did you already tell me why we didn't wean all of the young heifers?" he asked when Myra moved to the gate and declared their job done.

"We hold the sturdiest ones back as breeders. Every year you'll have older cows needing to be sold to a slaughterhouse because they've stopped producing. You rebuild a herd by adding more than you sell. In any cycle you'll weigh the worth, like…do you need the money from the fall sale more than you need to expand your herd?"

"That seems an impossible question for a new-bie like me."

"That is a problem with not having grown up on a ranch."

Zeke eyed her as if expecting her to say more. She didn't, instead opening the gate and shooing aside a cow that tried to escape. She gestured for Zeke to follow her out.

"What now?" he asked as he found bare ground to stamp snow and mud off his boots.

"We have an hour or so of daylight left. Not adequate to decide if the alfalfa fields are dry enough to cut. There won't be time to start that for a few days anyway. So I'm going to ride out to have a look at the owls. If you'd rather stay here, that's fine. You may not want to sit a saddle if you still hurt where the cow head butted you. Grab some rest. I'll be back in time to start supper."

"Do you not want me to tag along?"

"It's not that. I've seen you shifting your weight uncomfortably. If you want to go, Ember can use the exercise."

"I do. Lead on. Are the birds on Flying Owl land? I heard you mention to your friend that the owls nest in some other guy's trees."

"Leland Conrad. I don't know him well. I thought he was kind of a recluse. Gramps talked to him at cattle meetings or at the grange hall. Leland never stayed long and he didn't shoot the breeze over pot-luck tables like other neighbors do. But Tawana said he's not so bad."

They entered the barn and each took the horse they'd ridden the night before.

Once Zeke had saddled Ember, she handed him a set of binoculars and took another set for herself. "These are to better see the owls."

"I figured as much. I'll close the barn door," he said, looping the binoculars' strap over his neck once they led the horses out.

Myra vaulted easily into Cayenne's saddle, then waited for Zeke to mount up.

The horses were frisky, glad to be out and wanting to run.

Zeke held Ember in check, likely because he had no idea which direction they were going.

After they cleared the house and cantered into vast, empty land, Myra let Cayenne move faster.

Zeke did the same to stay abreast of her.

"This is Flying Owl land," she said. "We rotate growing wheat, alfalfa and milo. We reseed our pastures in native grasses every year. Leased pasture on BLM land reseeds itself on the wind. Grass is better for adding weight on cattle. Prairie grass is rich in nutrients. It's also cheaper in time and money than hay."

"At the risk of sounding stupid, why don't you let your pastures reseed on the wind?"

"Zeke, no question is stupid. Running a profitable cattle ranch takes know-how. For us Montanans success hinges on raising healthy calves we can sell for more than it costs to raise them. With our brutal winters, by November cattle have eaten all visible grass. The wind doesn't reseed fast enough for all our needs. That's why we haul hay. You'll do that for four or five months along with supplementary grains bought at the feed store. Right after calving, just before the green grass returns in spring, we feed our stock our richest baled alfalfa. That keeps cows from stripping the new grass down to nubbins." She let out a lengthy sigh.

"I apologize if you've already told me some of that. It sounds familiar. I wonder if I'll ever store in

my head all the information that seems to roll off
your tongue."

"You asked if there was a book on ranching. I'm
sure there is, but ranching in Montana, and even in
our corner of the state, will be different from anywhere else. I said I'd make you a list. Actually, I'll see
if I can carve out time to write descriptions of what
needs doing and when throughout a typical year. It'd
be a general guideline."

"That would be much appreciated."

"We're now on BLM land," she said, switching
subjects.

"Are we in danger of falling in any of those abandoned mines you spoke of?"

"Not here. I've traveled this route many times. All
I know of abandoned mines is from hearing others
talk. I believe they're in the foothills. The gold-mine
collapse that killed my friend Lila's husband is east of
here. That mine operated for years without incident.
From what Gramps said, the company followed a vein
down the mountain, then an upper tunnel crumpled
on top of a new one they'd dug in spokes underneath
the played-out section. It caused a huge collapse. They
never recovered the bodies of twenty or so men. Lila
doesn't talk about it, and if anyone mentions mining
she gets up and leaves."

"It sounds like an awful way to die. I worry about
my brother mining in developing countries. But I assume in the States there are rules governing mines.
Currently Seth's on his second trip to Afghanistan

for lapis. I roamed those mountains and went with demolition crews who mapped natural caves. I hated being underground."

Myra slowed and turned Cayenne east. The new pace made it easier for them to talk even as they continued to climb into an area where snow still lay in patches. "Did you get to see your brother while you served in Afghanistan?" she asked.

"Yes. On his first trip. Eric met him, too. The base commander let Seth and another gem hunter stay with us. I hope he calls me when he leaves there to go to Tanzania. Although he may be safer in Afghanistan. Unfortunately, regions where people dig for precious or even semiprecious gems are often dangerous."

"Do gem hunters get shot at? I can't tell you how glad I am that Eric decided not to continue a military career. When he phoned to say you'd saved him during a gun battle with IED explosives involved, my mother was a basket case."

Zeke frowned. "Gemologists do get shot at. According to Seth, many men have died in a quest for diamonds, rubies, emeralds and sapphires."

Myra turned in her saddle. "I've read in our newspaper where what they call summer gem hunters come to Montana searching for sapphires. I think they're found in or around defunct gold mines."

"Is that so? I wonder if Seth knows that," Zeke murmured.

The terrain got steeper and talk fell off. All at once Myra reined in and looked back down the hill to where Zeke had stopped. "What's wrong?" she called. "Did Ember pull up lame? I should have told you to watch out for gopher holes."

"There's no problem. I stopped to look at the mountain shadows. I've gotta say this is truly God's country." Leaning an arm on his saddle horn, Zeke continued to study the light and dark areas where gold from the late-afternoon sun glittered like a crown atop the highest ridges still fringed with snow.

"I've always thought so," Myra said, following his gaze. "I shouldn't be surprised to see deeper snow up here. We should have worn hats and gloves, I guess."

"It's not too cold." Zeke touched his heels to Ember's flanks and joined Myra on the slope. "I get what you meant when you said living here gives you a sense of freedom. That's partly why I left Boston to come see if your father really wanted to give me a house in these wonderful, wide-open spaces."

Myra touched her heels to Cayenne and moved ahead of Zeke.

He trotted his horse up beside her. "In Boston I'd recently seen a TV interview with John Mayer—you know, the songwriter?"

"Kind of a bad boy, right?"

"So went the rumors. Then he dropped out of the LA scene. I'll sort of paraphrase here, but I read this interview when he said he'd moved to Montana where life wasn't all about ego. He said something that resonated with me—how he'd come to realize he wanted one wife in his lifetime, and one set of kids, and neighbors who liked him for himself. Really profound stuff."

"That's why you left Boston?" Myra sounded amused. "Because of John Mayer?"

"I'm making a mess telling this. There's nothing else a man should want in life but what Mayer said in that interview. A lot of my buddies were on second or third marriages. Many had no spare money because they paid so much in child support."

"So military life equates to the fast trackers in LA? Huh. Eric hardly ever talked to me about his time in the service. However, Mom said when he was home on leave, his uniform was a magnet for women."

"I'm still not being clear. My own military career in no way compares to a rock star's life. After opting for a medical discharge, I expected to go back to Boston and nothing would have changed. But the city had gotten bigger, busier, and my friends had moved on. While I don't think I battled ego, I was restless and out of sorts during my time in Boston. That's why the notion of wide-open spaces appealed to me."

"Now, on that score I understand."

"Whoa! What was that?" Zeke asked, ducking from a traveling shadow overhead that was accompanied by a strange noise: *prek-prek, prek-prek.* He stopped his horse.

"That was a full-grown snowy owl," Myra announced. She, too, halted Cayenne. "We were so involved talking I didn't realize how close we'd gotten to the forest." Raising her binoculars, she trained them on the tallest fir in a group that sat at the edge of a denser grove. "The snowy that cruised over our heads lit almost at the top of that middle tree. It was a female. The male's call is harsher, more like *krek-krek*."

"I'm impressed you know the difference." Zeke lifted his binoculars and spun the dial. "I see a pair," he said excitedly, rocking sideways in his saddle even as the gelding shifted his weight. "Man, their backs blend with the tree bark even though with the field glasses you can see the white face and underbelly."

"Tawana said she counted five. Ah, I've got two in sight. Both in that tree are female. Males are almost pure white. Females have what birders call brown scalloping. The one that flew over us must have been collecting straw or twigs to build a nest. They're night hunters, so it's too early for them to be on the look-out for food."

"I feel foolish for ducking, but that thing is bigger than some of our drones," Zeke said, refocusing his binoculars. "What would you guess their wing-span is?"

"Full-grown, they can span fifty to sixty inches. I only know that from listening to Jewell talk about them. She and Tawana and a few older folks on the reservation are huge advocates. I like seeing owls flying about, though. And I'd hate for their numbers to dwindle. That's what's happening according to the National Wildlife Federation." Even as she finished speaking, another bird left the tree and swooped down less than twenty feet in front of where they sat. The bird picked up a slender tree branch in its beak and soared aloft again.

"Honestly, I didn't expect to be so captivated by them," Zeke said. "They're quite a sight. These owls are the biggest birds I recall seeing in flight—even bigger than the crows in the Afghan cornfields. And when that one lit to get the branch, I managed a good look at its face. I'd swear it smiled."

Myra lowered her binoculars. "Jewell said a lot of people think the dark markings below their beaks and eyes resemble a smile."

"I'm surprised they don't seem to be afraid of us." Zeke again trained his binoculars on the trees.

"They'll be more defensive during nesting season. Adult snowy owls don't have a lot of predators. But they have to guard their eggs against avian thieves, and of course their chicks from foxes, wild dogs and wolves."

Zeke let his binoculars fall the length of the strap. "I see we're losing sunlight. There probably isn't enough light to take a photo with my cell phone if an owl comes as close as that last one did."

"True. And we should go. At this rate it'll be totally dark before we get back to the ranch. Why do you want a picture?"

"To send to Seth and to my mom. She's always regaling us with pictures of parrots in Barbados."

Myra guided Cayenne down the steep slope. As

she passed Zeke, their knees bumped, knocking her foot out of her stirrup.

All at once, nearby—too close for comfort—a timber wolf howled. Then another joined in. Unexpectedly Cayenne reared. With a wild shake of her head, she whistled through her nose and pawed the air, dumping Myra from the saddle.

Losing her grip on the reins, she skid face-first through a wet patch of snow. As she got up on her hands and knees, Cayenne clattered off down the slope.

Zeke lunged for the mare's loose, flying reins, but missed. Another mournful call forced Zeke to keep a tight hold on Ember, then he jumped from his saddle to check on Myra. "Are you hurt?" He knelt close beside her because the fading light made it difficult to see.

"Only my pride," she sputtered, wiping wet snow from her jeans and scrubbing her face. "Did you catch my horse?"

"No. We'd better go after her. Ember is getting antsy and it's too gray to see how near those wolves may be." He helped Myra up.

Myra slipped as she tried to stand.

"Are you sure you're okay?"

"Yes, only a bit shaken. Cayenne's never thrown me before."

"If you're sure you're okay to ride, come on." Zeke nipped her at the waist and boosted her up onto Ember's saddle. "We'll ride double."

"I can sit behind you," Myra said, attempting to swing down again.

"Stay. We've gotta make tracks home and I want to know you're not so woozy you'll fall off." Taking charge, he tightened his grasp of the reins and landed in the saddle behind her.

Myra grabbed the saddle horn to keep from leaning against Zeke, and Ember took off at a trot. Then at Zeke's urging, the nervous gelding moved faster.

Snugged between Zeke's solid thighs and cradled by his arms, Myra relaxed against her will. She'd never ridden double like this before. Somehow her fuzzy mind decided it wasn't a bad way to get down out of the foothills.

"It's really dark now," Zeke said, his breath rustling Myra's hair. "I don't see a moon or stars. Do you think Cayenne will head straight to the ranch?"

"I hope so." Myra turned slightly to look at him. She felt her hair brush his cheek and she froze. She hadn't been this close to a man since moving to Snowy Owl Crossing. At the moment her mind warred with itself. Part of her liked the comfort afforded by Zeke Maxwell's strong arms. Another part of her brain whispered, *But he's the enemy*.

Chapter Five

"The wolves sound more distant," Zeke said. "I had no idea there were any here. Are they a hazard to the herd?"

Myra didn't respond.

He slowed Ember's dash through the dark terrain and shook Myra lightly. "Hey, speak up. Let me know you aren't hurt."

"Sorry, I was back thinking of our conversation about taking photos of the owls before I so unceremoniously got dumped from my horse."

"I'm sure I'll have other opportunities. I hope so, at least. Like I said, Mom always sends me photos of tropical birds."

"I'm surprised you didn't go live with your parents after you got out of the hospital," Myra said. "Seems like you'd be in seventh heaven lying around all day on sandy beaches overrun with bikini babes."

"What, in our short acquaintance, made you form such a low opinion of me?"

She could have said he hadn't seemed to have a problem taking a ranch he hadn't worked for, but

Myra still clung to the hope he'd tire of the hard work and pack it in. And maybe he'd change his mind about fun in the sun during severe Montana winters. "I didn't mean to cast aspersions. I thought that was every guy's dream."

"Can't say I don't admire women in bikinis. But I've never been one to lie around all day doing nothing. And my folks have a one-bedroom bungalow inland from the beach. Honestly, I had enough sun and sand to last me a lifetime in Iraq and Afghanistan."

"Fair enough. I stand corrected. But I still wonder why you ride so well. Boston doesn't strike me as a horse haven. And don't you military guys all travel in Humvees?"

"The one tour I did in Iraq before we pulled out, I was embedded with a friendly nomadic tribe. They liked to make fun of the city guys in my outfit. Once they had their laughs at us, they took us under their wing. Their horses are top-notch."

"Well, that makes sense. Oh, look, there's the ranch." Myra sat upright and the top of her head struck the underside of Zeke's chin.

"Ouch, don't knock me out."

"Sorry. I was trying to see Cayenne."

"I think that's her darker outline by the barn." Zeke pointed over Myra's shoulder.

"That's a relief. I would feel terrible if anything happened to her."

As they approached, the mare lifted her head and

whinnied. For a minute it seemed as if she'd take off running again.

"Let me off to calm her," Myra said. "She's still spooked."

Zeke reined in, swung out of the saddle and reached up to lift Myra down. If not for the hold he maintained on her waist, she'd have fallen again.

"Heavens," she exclaimed. "I hurt my knees more than I thought." She hobbled over to grab Cayenne's bridle then limped on to open the barn door.

"We may both soak up liniment tonight," Zeke joked, following her.

"I hope not. There's a lot of hard work on tap tomorrow."

Zeke stopped her with a hand on her arm. "Let me take care of the horses. You go in and treat your knees. We can do sandwiches or something easy for our meal. No need to fix a full supper."

"I put stew in the Crock-Pot at lunch. All we need to do is make coffee and pop some French bread in the oven for ten minutes or so."

"Great. So what besides shipping calves are we doing tomorrow?" Zeke studied Myra in the brighter light she'd turned on inside the barn.

"I need to call Eddie Four Bear. If he and Aaron Younger can round up a third man, tomorrow afternoon we can vaccinate, spray for parasites and test for pregnancies. Believe me when I tell you that's about the toughest job you'll do outside of calving during wind, rain or a late snowfall." Myra handed over Cayenne's reins and limped off.

In the house, she greeted and fed Orion, washed up and started coffee. Then she went to the bedroom in search of her phone. As she'd guessed, her mother had left a stream of messages, all scolding her for choosing to stay at the ranch rather than apply for teaching jobs. Eric had phoned, too. So after she called Eddie Four Bear and got his promise to pick up vaccinations and bring two helpers to the ranch the next day, she dialed her brother's number just to talk.

"Sis, it's about damn time you called home. What's going on? Mom's in a tizzy because Dad said you're staying at the Flying Owl until spring."

Dropping down on the bed, Myra put her phone on speaker while she rolled up her jeans and inspected her knees. Both had begun to bruise, but she'd had worse injuries getting kicked by a cow. "Eric, it seems to have shocked the family to learn I really love this ranch. I know Zeke Maxwell did a heroic thing risking his life to save yours, but he doesn't know the first damn thing about ranching."

"He'll catch on. And truly, Dad had no idea Gramps still had cows. He and Mom both thought all you were doing was taking care of his cooking and laundry."

"I grew the herd," she snapped. "I assumed when Dad checked the ledgers he'd either let me buy the place or give it to me as my inheritance."

"Holy crap, Myra. Who knew that's what you had

in mind? I guess I made a mess for you suggesting to the folks that they give Zeke the ranch."

"Keep this between us, Eric… I swear if you tell the folks or Zeke I'll hurt you. The reason I'm still here is because I'm betting your city boy will take a hike when ranch life gets tough."

"I don't know, Myra. I saw Zeke in action in some bad spots. He's got guts."

"Well, if you're right, after spring calving I'll lick my wounds and leave." She hated that she'd already seen signs Zeke might buckle down and learn ranching. And darn it all, she had to give him extra points for liking snowy owls.

"What about teaching? You have your degree and credentials."

"I never liked teaching math. Don't tell Mom that, either. If things here fall apart, I don't know what I'll do, but I won't teach. That's Mom's dream."

"Damn, sis, now I feel doubly guilty."

"You didn't know. I should have told Dad at Gramps's funeral, but it didn't seem the time to talk about raising cows when we were all grieving."

"No, you're right. And maybe Zeke's not cut out to raise cattle. I'll tell Dad I talked to you and let him deal with Mom. Stay in touch. And for the record, I'm sorry as hell that I screwed up your plans."

"Stop it, Eric." Myra felt tears punch the back of her eyes. "I can't fault what you did. The guy saved your life."

They said their goodbyes, then Myra dried her

eyes, treated her knees and was in the kitchen setting the table when Zeke came in from the barn.

He went straight to his bedroom.

She put bread in the oven, and as soon as she heard Zeke come out of his room, she dished up their stew. It surprised her how normal she was able to act, given the turmoil in her heart after her confession to Eric.

"Did you reach that Eddie guy?" Zeke asked. He peered into Orion's pen and made appropriate piggy-talk before taking his seat at the table.

Myra retrieved the piping-hot bread and shut off the oven. "I did. He and friends will be here tomorrow. With their help and Hank's, we should have all the calves loaded and off to market by noon."

"Got it. Hey, this stew hits the spot. I didn't realize how hungry I was."

"Thanks. I like meals I can throw in the Crock-Pot. More often than not, I come in too tired and dirty to feel like cooking."

"Speaking of dirty. I need boots I can leave in the barn. I also need work shirts and a lined jacket. Is there a store in town you can recommend?"

"The Tractor Supply Company."

Zeke stopped with his spoon halfway to his mouth. "You said that with a straight face. Is this some kind of a greenhorn initiation? Or did you make it up because I didn't know lemmings were real?"

Myra frowned. "You've lost me."

"Come on. Clothes at a tractor supply store?"

She ladled out more stew. "First of all, that's the

store name. They're in a lot of Western towns. Ranchers and cowboys tend to like one-stop shopping."

Zeke continued to look mistrustful, but he ladled out more stew and let the conversation drop.

It was fine with Myra. It had been a long day.

Once Zeke finished eating, he carried his dishes to the sink and rinsed them. "What time do we start tomorrow? I'm going to go see if I can connect with my brother in whatever time zone he's in, then hit the sack."

"I'll go out early to check fences. The unexpected snow could've driven those wolves into the foothills. We need to be vigilant until we bring the herd down to winter pasture."

"A short answer would do. Is early five, six or when?"

Myra jerked in her chair feeling as if she'd been smacked down by his sharp tone. He needed to know wolf presence in the area could wreak havoc with any herd. "Six," she said. "No formal breakfast. Make do." *There, if he wanted short and sweet, she'd comply. It'd suit her fine if he didn't learn enough to run a ranch.* She watched him take out his phone and leave the kitchen.

Did that shift in his attitude mean he'd decided to flex his owner muscle? She wasn't sure how she'd feel if he started giving her orders as if she were his employee. Perhaps it'd been nothing. Eric used to accuse her of bossiness. But she had been in charge of this ranch for three and half years. If she got on Zeke's nerves this early in their working relationship, it was going to be a long danged time till spring.

Clearing the dishes and setting up for morning coffee, she let her mind float back to how pleasant she'd found it riding double with Zeke. Was that the source of her hurt pride now? Had she read more into the close way he'd held her? Probably it was no more than what he'd said—he didn't want her falling off the horse.

To think of something other than Zeke, she rechecked her tender knees then went out on the back porch to put new litter in Orion's box. He followed. Still too restless for bed, she picked up the pig and carried him into the living room. She hadn't worked on a dollhouse since Zeke's arrival, and she had one ready for shutters. That wouldn't be a noisy task. Another house needed to be roofed, but that entailed hammering.

With Orion yawning on her lap, Myra lost herself in applying dark blue hinged shutters to the windows of a two-story house. She'd set down her tools to admire her handiwork when her cell phone rang. Afraid it might be her mother, she scooped up Orion, switched off the light and escaped to her bedroom before she answered.

"Myra, hi. Jewell here. I was about to hang up."

"Sorry it took me so long to answer. I was in the middle of cleaning up from working on a dollhouse."

"Ooh, can't wait to see the new batch. Listen, I wanted to check with you. Eddie Four Bear stopped by. He said you asked him to pick up vaccine kits. I gave him a hundred. If that's not enough I can drop more off tomorrow. I have a call to make at Ralston's. Lou's buckskin picked up a stone. Dave dug it out, but Lou thinks it's infected. She talked him into paying me to take a look."

Myra chuckled. "We all know how tight that man is with money."

"Yeah. I'm so glad my father was never like that. So, about the vaccine…"

"I only need eighty or so. But extras will keep in the fridge. I could have had a few heifers stray. Some of Hank's and Dave's showed up with my pairs."

"How's it going with you-know-who? Ralston stopped at the café today. He told Lila's mom he'd met Zeke Maxwell and thinks he's a nice guy."

"He's…okay."

"Dave referred to him as the Flying Owl's new owner. Eddie said you made a deal with Maxwell to stay on through spring calving."

"That's right."

"Won't that make it twice as hard to leave? Not that we don't all want you here as long as possible, but I know how you love running the Flying Owl. I'm thinking of you, Myra."

She set Orion in his cage and he burrowed into his favorite quilt. Myra closed the cage door and flopped onto the bed. "It's because I love the ranch. In a weak moment I volunteered to stay and help out. Jewell, the man is a total tenderfoot! At least he knows his way around horses. I offered to ask the bank for a loan to buy him out. He said he wasn't interested. I can only hope he'll change his mind."

"What's he like? Is he a frog or a prince?"

Her friend's question stopped Myra cold. If she said frog she'd be lying. If she said prince that'd be all over town by morning. "What are my other options? I could say he's a rat, but it's not his fault my folks gave him the ranch." She blew out a breath. "Up to now he hasn't shirked, but I know he's had multiple surgeries to rebuild his left shoulder and elbow."

"All the Artsy Ladies want to know is if he's single and hot!"

"He's single, though he could have a girlfriend stashed someplace. He has a twin. A gemologist. Zeke invited him to visit. If he shows up before spring I have to clean my craft stuff out of the third bedroom. But sooner or later I'll have to do that anyway."

"You still haven't said what he looks like. If we're going to find out we'll have to come help you clean that room," Jewell said around a laugh. "Why don't you drag him to the dance next Saturday? It's the last potluck of the year at the grange hall, remember. Unless he's totally gross, that is."

Again sidestepping the question, Myra said, "Did Tawana tell you the snowy owls are back? I took Zeke out to see them this evening."

"I haven't talked to Tawana. And Eddie didn't mention it. Did you see some of my banded ones?"

"Not the one I got the best look at. We counted

three. Two females and a male. There may have been more. They're nesting in Leland Conrad's timber."

"Thanks for the heads-up. The early snowfall in Canada must have driven their food source down. Since I don't have to bring you vaccine, I'll run out there tomorrow. I can get there using my Jeep, right?"

"We rode and angled across BLM land. There's probably a road through Leland's ranch. That'd be quicker."

"Oh, I'm so excited. They need a protected habitat, but I haven't heard back from my inquiry to the government's Natural Resource Committee."

"That's another reason I hate the thought of leaving, Jewell. We've all worked so hard to secure a preserve. I want to see it through."

"Maybe you shouldn't be so helpful to Maxwell. If he flounders, won't he be more likely to chuck it all?"

"I don't see it as helping him so much as making sure the Flying Owl thrives."

"You're in a pickle. I have a call coming in on my emergency line. We'll touch base later. Think about coming to the dance. We ladies will put our heads together and come up with a plan to discourage him from staying."

"I'll see if I can get away. My to-do list is a mile long. Bye, Jewell."

After hanging up, Myra rummaged in her drawer and pulled out a notepad. If she listed all of the chores that had to be done, and roughly which months Zeke would need to plan on doing them, just looking at a list could be enough to convince him to go away.

In his room, Zeke sat on his bed. He had only removed his boots. Seth hadn't answered, so he'd left a message. He had no idea where his brother was or what time zone he was in.

He heard Myra moving around the other part of the house. First in the kitchen, then out on the back porch and later in the living room. He'd gotten up and peeked out his door. Seeing her bent over one of her unfinished dollhouses, he debated going out. Then thought better of it. Until tonight when her horse had gotten away from her and they'd had to ride for several miles together on Ember, Zeke hadn't thought of Myra as a woman. Not in the sense of an attractive one.

First she'd merely been a buddy's sister. Not really a know-it-all, but certainly impatient— with him at least. That was prior to feeling her slender back against his chest, her hips flush between his thighs. But what most messed with his equilibrium had been the apple scent of her hair as it blew into his face. All day they'd both worked like demons to separate calves from their mothers. The sun had only come out a few times to warm the air. But it'd been sweaty work.

Somehow Myra had managed to still smell like a woman.

His last steady girl had broken it off with him while he was in rehab. It surprised him that he hadn't been overly sad to hear she'd found someone else. A dentist. Zeke could picture Stacy with a safe, boring guy. He'd sent her a card saying he was happy for her. And he was. At the time, in his condition, he'd only needed nurses in his life. It helped if they were pretty, but he hadn't grown attached to any one in particular.

Now Myra Odell had gotten under his skin. The discovery shocked him. He didn't view it as altogether good news, either. He had a feeling if her parents had any inclination as to the thoughts running amok in his head, they'd kick his butt off the ranch in short order. And damn it all, he liked it here.

Why, he couldn't say. The work wasn't fun. Cows were dirty. But Myra spoke of ranching in such glowing terms. The notion of calling himself a bona fide rancher one of these days, and having people like Dave Ralston see him as one, was appealing. And how could it hurt to have a woman like Myra at his side—in his corner.

Bolting off his bed, Zeke stripped out of his clothes and hurried into the shower—a cold one. Letting water rain down on his face and aching muscles, his wishful-thinking side argued with his good-guy side—which said he should scrap those libidinous thoughts.

He'd toweled off and burrowed beneath the covers when his cell phone rang. Answering quickly and hoping it hadn't disturbed Myra, he knew it either had to be Eric or Seth. No one else called him these days. Well, his mom, but she was an early-to-bed, early-to-rise person.

"What's up, bro? I just checked into my hotel in Nairobi."

"What are you doing in Kenya?" Zeke sat up.

"A dealer who wants my stash of lapis is here. If I can unload it for a good price, there's also a western bank in town and I can deposit to my Boston account before I hook up with my guide to travel into the hills of Tanzania."

"Now I'll worry this dealer will knock you in the head and steal your stones."

"Nah. I've done business with him before. It's after midnight here. You so rarely call, I figured I should ring you back."

"I just wanted to talk. But we can catch up later. Will you let me know you're still alive when you get to Tanzania?"

His brother laughed. "Has becoming a landowner turned you into a mother hen?"

"Maybe. I met a neighbor who is the fourth generation in his family to run his ranch. And Myra— she's currently running this one—her dad was born in this house. Oh, today she took me out to see snowy owls. They apparently return to nest in the hills year after year."

"Oh yeah?"

"Yeah. Our roots are shallow, Seth. Jeez, I'll let you go. I'm not making sense."

"Stay a minute. You glossed over something I

find interesting. Why is this Myra person running the ranch? I thought you said she was going back to teaching."

Zeke weighed how much he should share with his twin, who often seemed to read his mind. "She handled the ranch for her grandfather when he was ill. She didn't really have a teaching job waiting, and schools are starting soon. I'm not sure how much you know about raising cows. I don't know diddly-squat. I asked her to stay on until I understand more. She agreed to show me the ropes until spring. That's when the next crop of calves are born."

"You two are sharing a house?"

Zeke took a deep breath. Leave it to Seth to hone in on the one thing people might see as an issue. "Yeah. So what? It has three bedrooms. In fact, the house is old and needs updating. Especially the kitchen. I don't have a lot of free time, but I need to put in a new sink and a coat of paint at least. Any chance you can come help soon?"

"Good try at distracting me. Is she pretty?"

"I guess you don't mean the kitchen," Zeke said drily. "Uh, yeah, she's pretty. Not in a glitzy movie-star way, but wholesome."

"Dude, you need lessons in common sense and tact. I've never met a woman who'd be pleased to be described as wholesome. It's like saying she's healthy and sound as a horse."

"Goodbye, Seth. You need sleep. Your thinking is skewed. But remember to let me know you're safe at your next port of call." Zeke quickly disconnected. Setting his phone on the nightstand, he turned out the lamp and slid down in his bed. Mulling over what his brother had said—well, Myra had thick, dark blond hair, golden skin and really expressive amber eyes. Yeah, maybe *wholesome* didn't do her justice. But if he had admitted to Seth how attractive he found her, he'd be letting himself in for constant ribbing. And that he could do without.

THE HOUSE WAS dark and silent in the morning when Myra made her way to the kitchen. She set Orion in his pen and tended to his food before she washed her hands and started the coffee.

It didn't surprise her that she was up before Zeke. He'd taken a late-night call—the ringing of his phone had awakened Orion. She hadn't a clue who might call him so late at night. She hadn't let herself wonder about his friends. *Women or men.*

Myra mixed a handful of blueberries in a cup of yogurt and ate it while the coffee perked. She tossed the cup in the trash and listened for any noise from Zeke's quarters. Hearing none, she poured a thermal mug full of coffee then set down a matching mug for him before heading out.

She had Cayenne saddled when the barn door slid open and in rushed a rumpled Zeke. He was trying to put on his jacket while holding his travel mug between his teeth. "My alarm didn't go off," he said, sounding garbled.

"I thought maybe you decided you didn't want to ride fence."

He shook his head. "Haven't I made clear I want to see all that goes on around here?"

"I guess so. Here, I'll take your cup while you saddle Ember."

Zeke passed her his mug. It didn't take him long to have his horse ready to go. "What's in your saddle-bags? Granola bars, I hope," he joked.

"Didn't you eat anything?"

"Nope. So, no breakfast bars?"

"I have wire ties, a staple gun with heavy staples and a hammer. We'll be checking a wire fence stapled to wood posts. Most repairs are simple. Like a staple pulled loose or a broken strand of wire. It's rarely a whole section down."

"Barbed wire?" he asked, closing the barn door before mounting up.

Myra handed him back his coffee. "Gramps installed seven-foot woven wire. Holds in the cattle, keeps out deer and elk. Not a lot of barbed wire used around here. Some use low-voltage electric fences. They're costlier but deter wildlife."

"Do they all keep out wolves?"

She shrugged. "Wolves are clever. If they frighten the cows, the herd can trample a fence for them."

They rode in silence, drinking their coffee as they watched the sun come up and spread peachy fingers of light over the land. With the snow mostly melted, much of the land looked green and pristine.

It took two hours to circle the largest of the ranch's enclosed pastures.

"We rode all that long way and you put in only three staples and wired one broken strand together," Zeke said on the journey home. "Is that usual?"

"I call it successful. It's better not to find places where cows broke out, or predators got in. And we're back in time to meet Hank. That's his big truck rolling in," Myra said, urging Cayenne into a canter.

She greeted the neighbor and introduced Zeke. "If you guys want to pop inside for a drink while you get acquainted, I'll put the horses away."

"I'm for that. I went out without breakfast, so I'm going to buy a microwave," Zeke said, taking the coffee mug Myra handed him. "You want anything?" he asked her.

"No thanks. I'll take water out to where we'll start working with the hcifers after Hank has the calves loaded."

The men turned away, chatting. Myra suffered a moment's pang at how quickly Zeke made friends with her neighbors.

They weren't gone long. She'd unsaddled and run a brush over the horses, fed them grain and filled the sprayer, when she heard their voices. She'd packed a cooler with bottled water from the barn fridge and now wheeled it out to the far side of the weaning pen. Already Hank had backed up to the outer gate. He and Zeke were driving calves up the ramp.

Myra walked over with her clipboard.

"I counted sixteen already in," Hank told her.

This was a chore she'd normally done with him, so he knew her routine. It was good when his tally matched the one she took at weaning. Today it did.

With doors and ramp secured, Hank shook hands with Zeke. "Nice to meet you, neighbor," he said as he climbed into his truck. Before he pulled away, a battered red pickup drove in.

It stopped and three young men emerged. One hailed Myra, and he retrieved a carton from the pickup's bed.

Myra recognized two of the three. "Eddie, this is Zeke Maxwell, new owner here." She rushed over those words that still tasted bitter on her tongue. "Eddie Four Bear and Aaron Younger," she told Zeke.

Eddie wore his black hair long and in one braid that hung to his waist. Aaron's fell straight to his shoulders.

"Myra and Zeke, this is Luke Elkhorn. He's my cousin," Eddie said. "He worked with me and Aaron all spring and summer. He's a good guy."

"Welcome." Myra shook hands with the dark-eyed kid. "We aren't taking you out of school to do this job, are we?" *He looked so young*.

The boy smiled. "I'm nineteen."

"Yeah, he's got a baby face," Aaron teased. And it went that way between the friends until they reached the chutes. For Zeke's and Luke's benefit, Myra went over the process. The other two had assisted her in prior years.

"We talked about who'd do what," Eddie said. "Aaron and me will trade off pregnancy testing and spraying for mites. Luke will pull 'em through the chute and into the open pen if you vaccinate, Myra. Unless Zeke's doing that." He jammed a worn cowboy hat on his head and quirked an eyebrow at Zeke, who held up both arms and backed away.

Myra jumped in. "Zeke is new to ranching. He'll shove heifers into the chute to start. Maybe this afternoon he and Luke can trade off."

Eddie seemed to want to comment but didn't.

Myra motioned to Aaron. "I filled the sprayer. Will you bring it from the barn?"

He left and came back shortly, and Myra pronounced them ready. "Zeke, you've gotta keep heifers moving into the first chute. Cows who have gone through this before may be cantankerous. Twist their tail to make them move, but watch out you don't get kicked."

They each took their stations. She didn't have a lot of time to explain things to Zeke. But it was a self-explanatory process. Zeke shoved a heifer in the chute. Myra vaccinated. It bellowed and the shock drove the cow into chute two, where Aaron doused her with pesticide. Eddie hand-examined the birth canal in chute three, gave Myra a thumbs-up or thumbs-down, then Luke wrestled the unhappy animal into the open pen.

Soon the air filled with grunting, swearing and bawling. Spray churned up mud under everyone's feet, along with plenty of poop mixed with urine. Myra marked her clipboard for each pregnant heifer between readying shots.

They slipped, slid and cursed through lunchtime. By midafternoon they were three-fourths finished. Myra straightened. "Time for another water break."

Zeke left the corral and strode toward the house. Myra watched him as she drank her water.

They were ready to begin again, but Zeke hadn't returned. Then he came out of the house dressed in clean cammo pants and a different shirt. He climbed in his pickup and roared off.

"Where do you s'pose he's goin'?" Eddie asked.

"Was he carrying duffel bags?" Myra murmured.

The others shook their heads. Not having an explanation and shorthanded, they set back to work. Luke took over for Zeke. Aaron and Eddie switched jobs, so Aaron drove finished heifers into the pens. At the end of another hour, tempers were short and they were all hot and splattered with gunk, most of which smelled awful.

Myra's cell rang. She was surprised to see Lila's number. "Hi, Lila. Can I call you later? I'm in the middle of a dirty chore."

"Sure, but I called to tell you we got a look at Zeke Maxwell. He bought a camera, a microwave and wandered around town. Then he bought three pair of boots, some shirts, a hat, a jacket and some paint. Now he's at Cody's Bar on his second beer. Jewell and I popped over. Outside of his looking grim, Jewell said you neglected to say the guy's hotter than a firecracker."

"He's AWOL and left me to pick up the slack," Myra said tartly. "Unless he's leaving town—and it doesn't sound like it if he bought new gear—I guarantee, hot or not, he'll get an earful from me when he wanders back to the Flying Owl. Thanks for the heads-up. Later, Lila, okay?"

Chapter Six

Eddie, who only heard Myra's side of the conversation, spoke flatly. "A couple of owners I worked for refused to get their hands dirty. Not any around Snowy Owl Crossing, but two dudes outside Sheridan, Wyoming."

"Zeke has the option of hiring everything done," Myra said, making a face. "I've deliberately given him scuzzy chores, hoping he'll decide to toss the ranch back in my dad's lap. Or at least sell it to me. When he took off I thought maybe my ploy had worked, but it doesn't sound like it."

"Tawana told us your dad gave away the ranch," Aaron said. "I wish somebody would give me a place like this one. I'd gladly do all the dirty work by my lonesome."

Eddie concurred.

"Yes, but you guys have done most of these type chores since you were kids. Zeke grew up in a city. To be honest, he's not done badly until he skipped out today. And his military record is exemplary, according to my brother, whose life he saved."

"Sounds to me like you can't decide if you want to convince him to give up or not." Eddie paused in his present task of spraying for parasites to point that out to Myra.

She shoved another heifer into the chute, barely avoiding being kicked for her effort. "Maybe I'm conflicted because he got injured carrying Eric out of harm's way."

That seemed to say it all to Myra's helpers. They bent to their tasks and in another hour had completed the unpleasant job.

"Seventy-four heifers are going to have another calf," Myra said with satisfaction after she washed off with the hose and picked up her clipboard.

"That's a prolific bull you have," Aaron noted with a big grin.

Myra nodded. "Gramps chose well with that one. Maybe Zeke won't need to rent a bull to help out. If all the young heifers I kept get with calf, the herd will grow. Hey, guys, you all did a great job. Let's go to the barn and I'll get your pay." She grabbed the cooler handle after each of them took another water bottle.

"There will be growth unless you lose a lot in spring calving," Eddie noted as he rolled the sprayer to the barn. "It could cost Zeke a lot to hire help to handle the calving."

"I did say I'd stay on through spring." Myra opened the barn door. "Of course, that could all change."

"You mean if he flakes off again like he did this afternoon?" Aaron asked.

She shrugged and noticed that Luke hung back, listening but not talking.

Myra went into her office and unlocked her desk. "I need everyone's social security number. Eddie, are you at the same hourly fee as last year?" she asked, taking out a calculator and checkbook.

"Same. Or if you prefer a daily flat fee, Myra, divide it three ways."

"I've always paid hourly. And since we finished in record time and I didn't provide lunch, I'll add a small bonus for each of you." Listing the numbers they gave her, she bent over the checkbook and began to write.

Aaron spoke. "The new owner lets you make that kind of decision?"

She frowned as she tore out the first check and passed it to Eddie. "The bonus is coming out of Zeke's share of the cost."

They laughed and continued to make jokes until Myra handed Luke the last check and the guys got ready to leave. "I like working close to home," Eddie said, pausing as they trooped to the door. "You can give Zeke my phone number in case you take off and he's in need of help."

Aaron poked him in the ribs. "It's because Eddie's got a romance going with Lana Elkhorn. If he runs off to Wyoming next spring, she might find a new boyfriend."

Myra smiled. She'd seen in the past how Aaron and Eddie loved to needle each other. "I'm making Zeke a schedule of ranch jobs and approximate dates. I'll be sure to list all of your phone numbers if you care to leave them. Eddie, I have yours."

Aaron and Luke turned back to the desk and wrote on a notepad Myra set out.

"Tell him about the bonus, too," Luke said, shyly chiming in for the first time. "What I made today pays tuition for a quarter at an online college."

That comment had his buddies ribbing him about being a nerd. Luke took it in stride, Myra noticed as they said goodbye.

Filthy-dirty and tired, she hurriedly put away the checkbook, locked the desk and crossed to the house, anxious to shower off the grime. She shed her boots at the door to be cleaned later. The clothes she had on would take two washings. She wondered what Zeke had done with his things. He had worked long enough to get plenty grungy.

Stepping into a hot shower, she almost purred with joy. Because she'd been splattered from head to toe, she washed her hair first then scrubbed every point on her body that had been exposed. When finished, she wrapped a towel around her head and cleaned the shower stall.

She changed into a sweat suit and heavy socks in case she had to go outside again for any reason, then ran a brush through her hair, electing to let it dry naturally while she started the washer.

Grabbing the net laundry bag, she'd barely stepped into the living room when the front door swung open and Zeke entered carrying some big plastic sacks and two, gallon-size paint cans. He dropped the sacks and shut the door before he noticed Myra.

She scowled at him. "I understand you had a fine time in town, taking photographs, shopping and slugging down two beers at Cody's Bar."

He set the paint down with a thump and aimlessly rubbed the back of his neck. "I'm not used to everyone knowing and blabbing my private business."

"Yes, well, welcome to a small town. Just so you know, ranchers don't usually walk out in the middle of an all-important job. Especially if you're paying help to get it done in one day."

He slowly lifted his hand from his neck and without flinching from her stony gaze, said, "Myra, look—I apologize." Closing his eyes, Zeke ran a thumb and finger over his eyebrows. "You won't understand."

"Try me." She stood her ground.

"Fine! Bawling cows, slippery mud, the awful smell coupled with the noise from metal on metal as cows crashed against the chute—what I started to see wasn't muddy cows, but men covered in blood, like I was back in Afghanistan on a mission going bad."

Myra's jaw dropped. "Heavens, Zeke. Why didn't you say something sooner?"

"I never had a flashback before. I was afraid I was totally losing my grip," he said, avoiding her eyes.

Myra moved forward and curled her fingers around his arm. "I would've understood. We all would have, even though there's no way any of us can half imagine what it must have been like over there."

"I just needed to get away," he mumbled, covering her hand, then as quickly pulling away.

"Did I hurt your injured arm?" she asked, fully withdrawing her touch.

Zeke reconnected, catching both her hands. "No. No. Stay. So…uh…probably everybody in town thinks I'm a bum, huh? Come to think of it…how did anyone know who I was?"

Myra couldn't help feeling guilty. "We don't get many newcomers. When Dad said he'd given you the Flying Owl, I told all of my friends. I wasn't happy, but I'd never deliberately hurt you, Zeke. In fact, have I thrown too much at you too fast? Are you feeling better? Will it happen again?" Feeling herself babble, she took a breath. "I can handle harvesting alfalfa alone if you need time off to see a VA doctor. I'm not sure where the nearest clinic is, but Eric will know."

"Myra, stop. It's okay." Zeke brought her close against him. "The feeling passed before I got to town. I figured since I was there I should make the most of having bailed on you. I bought a microwave and paint for the kitchen. Later, I'll get a new sink and countertops."

"The kitchen?" Myra found it impossible to jump from concern for his well-being to talk of painting the kitchen. Especially when the lazy way he rubbed his thumbs over the backs of her hands sent tingles up her arms—and made her want to hug him. So she did. She slid her arms around his waist. Her head fit snugly under his chin. With an ear pressed to his chest, she was calmed by the steady beat of his heart. Until suddenly it sped, thumping louder. He must be uncomfortable.

Guilt filled her again. "Sorry." She leaned back. "I…uh…hugged Eric every chance I got after he returned. But you're not Eric."

"No," Zeke murmured. "But hugs are fine." He lifted a hand to stroke her damp strands. "Your hair's wet. It still smells like apples. I noticed that before."

"My shampoo." Myra let go. "What did you say about painting the kitchen?" Fully disengaged, she stepped away and rubbed her arms.

Zeke quickly picked up the bags he'd dropped. "I'll go put these new clothes away, then I'll start painting while you work on your dollhouses."

"I've got to put my clothes from today into the wash now. Yours have to be yucky, too. Get them and I'll toss them all in." She couldn't believe she'd gone so swiftly from being wrapped in his arms and feeling almost giddy to talking about mundane things like laundry. What a day.

"I PLANNED TO THROW what I wore today away. It's disgusting to think of the mess they can make in a washer."

"Raising cattle for profit is disgusting work. You can't always be throwing away clothes, Zeke. Gramps installed a commercial-grade washer and dryer for Gram. They do a bang-up job of getting clothes clean."

"I asked you to help me learn ranching, not be

my housekeeper." He left her and the paint cans and headed for his room.

"For Pete's sake, we both live here. Chores overlap. Stop being stubborn."

Zeke paused outside his bedroom. He knew exactly why he was being stubborn. It'd felt all too good touching her and having her arms around him. It'd be way too easy to take things further. He hadn't had a woman in his life for some time. But he wasn't immune, and Myra fit a lot of things on his list of likes. Considering all he owed her folks, taking advantage of their forced proximity was no way to pay back the family's generosity. He'd do well to remember that. "I'll get the clothes if you quit being bossy."

Myra pitched the net bag toward him. "Stuff your things in there while I go feed Orion."

Turning, Zeke watched her stomp into the kitchen, and he felt like a hound dog. *Or should that be horndog?* That was really what drove him to act like a jerk. Maybe he should tell her to leave. How costly would it be to hire Eddie or Aaron on a monthly basis? They'd sounded as if they hired out. On the other hand, they'd acted on Myra's directions. Maybe they'd be good workers, but not effective managers. *Crap!*

Striding back, he yanked up the net bag and almost gagged at the smell. He hurried into his room and found his pants and shirt on the floor of his bathroom, where he'd stripped them off earlier. "Ugh." They made the whole room stink. Doing his best to hold his breath, he opened the bag and dumped his stuff inside. He left the room again and encountered Myra holding Orion in her arms.

Zeke couldn't say how it happened, but suddenly he imagined Myra holding a baby instead. *His baby.* A knot formed in his stomach. He let the bag fall, spun on his heel and retreated to his room, accidentally letting his door slam. Then even as he set to work ripping tags off his new shirts and pants, he couldn't shake the image of Myra as a mother. A wife and mother. *Maybe he did need to see a VA doctor.*

He was in the process of arranging his new boots in the bottom of his closet when he heard the washer start. Two pairs had short heels—better for working, the salesman had informed him. One dressier pair made of black snakeskin had higher, slant heels. That was an impulse purchase, as was a black felt Resistol hat. Looking at it here in his bedroom, it seemed like overkill. Yet when he'd faced a whole wall of hats, some handmade, others duded up with feathers or beaded bands, he'd picked a simple one that felt good on his head. Now he questioned whether people would rib him for playing at being a cowboy. Would he feel awkward wearing all this garb out in public? He grimaced and set the hat on his closet shelf.

As he contemplated returning it for a refund, Myra knocked.

"Zeke?"

Still uneasy about discovering his lusty feelings, Zeke debated several seconds before striding over to open the door.

"I have meat loaf baking. I'm considering making corn bread, unless you'd rather fix your biscuits. They were so tasty."

He brightened. "Do you put creamed corn in your corn bread?"

She nodded.

"Then I vote for that. We had a cook when I attended jumpmaster school at Fort Bragg who made corn bread like that. All the guys in the class wanted to kidnap him when they sent us to another unit."

"Jumpmaster? You parachute out of airplanes?"

"Not recently, but yeah, I've made many jumps."

"Nothing about ranching takes that kind of grit," Myra stated emphatically.

Zeke exited his room and closed the door. "Parachuting is a matter of training. I'm sure you didn't come into this world knowing how to vaccinate cattle. Doing that as many times as you did today, all while avoiding getting hooked by horns, takes guts."

Myra shrugged. "I guess it's a matter of perspective. Okay, getting back to supper, I'll make corn bread tonight if you cook tomorrow night. We've got to start cutting alfalfa, get it baled and stored in the barn ASAP. I heard on the weather network that the temperature's going to dip again. Sounds as if winter's coming early. We need to bring the last of the herd down out of the foothills, too."

It was plain to Zeke that if Myra had ever felt uncomfortable about the hug they'd shared, she'd gotten past it. Perhaps she'd only meant it as a sisterly gesture. Maybe she did place him in a category with Eric. He'd never had a sister, so looking at her that way wasn't an option for him. And just now as their shoulders and hips brushed when they went through the kitchen doorway side by side, Zeke's insides vibrated. He turned and went out to his pickup to bring in the microwave. Plainly he had way more work to do to keep his feelings for her platonic.

Still, dinner was pleasant. They were almost finished and Myra's cell phone rang.

"Hank, hi," she said on answering. "So you're back from selling our stock?" She smiled at Zeke. "That's a good total weight." She jumped up and sorted through some papers stacked on the counter and sat back with a pen. "The cost per pound is four cents less than last year, but with the calf weight up it comes out to approximately the same income." She jotted down a figure and shoved it across the table to Zeke.

It didn't mean much to him and was less than he'd made per year in the military. But Myra seemed pleased, so he smiled back at her.

"I did hear the weather report, Hank. I plan to cut alfalfa tomorrow. So your sons combined today and you rented Dave's baler for tomorrow? I'd better give him a call to arrange our time." It sounded as if she was repeating his half of the conversation for Zeke's benefit. "Sure, Zeke and I can help move bales into your hay shed if you reciprocate." She frowned a bit. "Yeah, I know the October potluck dance at the grange is Saturday night. Jewell reminded me.

No, I didn't mention it to Zeke. We'll see how much work we get done since we're all racing against another snowfall."

They talked awhile longer, then Myra swiped off and set her phone with the pen and paper. She began stacking dishes. "It had better be early to bed tonight."

Zeke grabbed another piece of corn bread before she could make off with the pan. He eyed her as he bit into it.

"Why are you giving me that look? Cutting, baling, moving, stacking should all be self-explanatory," she said. "I'll throw our work clothes in the dryer. They're clean and will be ready to wear tomorrow."

He swallowed and wiped his lips. "What about the potluck dance?"

"Ah…that." She carried dishes to the sink. "The cattlemen's association holds them four times a year. If you've seen any old Western movies with barn dances, it's pretty much like that. Women sit around and talk about fashion, kids and food. Men discuss feed and cattle prices, and football. Everybody eats. Some dance, then everyone goes home."

"You don't sound like a fan."

Myra didn't glance up from loading the dishwasher. "They're okay. It'll be my first without Gramps." Her voice wavered.

Before he could help himself, Zeke was at her side, pulling her into his arms. "Damn, I'm always putting my foot in my mouth. I didn't mean to press and make you sad." He rubbed his hands up and down her tense back until she relaxed.

"It's okay." Her voice was muffled against his shirtfront. "Saturday night will be your chance to meet all of your Snowy Owl Crossing neighbors."

"Is that a problem for you?" He reached between them and with a curled forefinger lifted her chin until they gazed into each other's eyes.

"N-no," she said shakily. "The Flying Owl is yours now. These folks are your neighbors. In a few months they'll no longer be mine."

Zeke noticed again how her voice hitched. Remembering what it'd been like for him to say goodbye to the men in his unit—men who'd been closer to him at times than his twin—he thought he knew what Myra might be feeling. She'd worry that Saturday would be her last gathering with her friends. Bothered by the dull sheen in her normally sparkling eyes, Zeke caught her face in both his hands and he kissed her cool, trembling lips. He didn't stop until he felt them warm under his.

When he eased back, Myra's eyes were no longer dull. They were, however, unfocused, disbelieving. Zeke released her and scrubbed a hand over his face. He wasn't sure disbelief was a good sign.

"What was that for?" she asked huskily, turning aside to grip the edge of the sink with both hands.

Zeke wanted to say he'd been thinking about kissing her since they rode home together on Ember after going to see the snowy owls. Instead, he said, "Nothing," and pinched the bridge of his nose. "I made you sad about your grandfather by asking about Saturday's event. Do you want to slap me?" he asked abruptly, tucking his fingertips into his back pockets.

She whipped around. "No. No. Why would I? I'm not a violent person."

He grinned at that. "Could've fooled me. I've seen you shove a thousand-pound heifer into a chute and stick them with a needle full of gunk that made them holler."

"That's different. It's necessary."

"Okay. I'm going to hit the sack now. I hope you don't change your mind about that slap. I could, probably should, apologize. But…kissing you wasn't a hardship, Myra." Leaving it there, he bent, scratched Orion behind the ears and sauntered from the room.

Myra continued to cling to the sink for some time after she heard his bedroom door close. Heavens, she didn't want to slap him. Far from it. And she was glad he hadn't apologized, but she was sorry he'd kissed her out of sympathy for her grandfather. That sucked.

Yes, she'd felt sad, but her reasons were jumbled. She feared neighbors at the event might view her differently now. While there was pain attached to losing Gramps, there was pain, too, in losing the ranch. Mixed in was more than a little chagrin. What was wrong with her that a great-looking single guy like Zeke felt he had to roll out some excuse for kissing her? Moreover, why did she wish a kiss might happen again?

Myra pulled herself together to phone Dave Ralston and set a date for his baler in exchange for helping him stack hay. Once that was done, she picked up Orion, turned out the kitchen light and went to move the clothes to the dryer. She set items already dry by his door before retreating to her room. Did she seem less womanly for working cattle and running a ranch? Should she be mollified that Zeke said kissing her hadn't been a hardship? What did that mean, anyway? *Dang!*

Before getting ready for bed, she took stock of the clothes in her closet. Normally for potlucks she wore the kind of jeans and shirts she worked in. Clean ones, of course. But she did own a couple of skirts.

"Orion," she announced, setting him down on his comfy quilt. "Saturday night you'll see a new me."

But crawling into bed, she was plagued by second thoughts. *Was she going soft on him?* Her good friends in the Artsy Ladies group would give her a hard time if she dressed up. *Did she care?* Far too late into the night she weighed their probable reactions against wanting Zeke to see her as something more than a rancher.

Chapter Seven

Morning brought gray cloudy skies and blustery north winds.

"Do you think it's going to snow?" Zeke asked Myra. He stood at the kitchen window eating his toast.

"I hope not." She peered over his shoulder. "The fields are dry. If we have to bale wet alfalfa, it'll mold before we need it as feed over the winter. Every rancher in the area will be rushing to finish. Our next few days will be busy running from ranch to ranch."

They tidied up, dressed warmly and went to the barn. Myra drove the combine. Zeke rode shotgun. Talk was limited until Myra noticed Zeke's new jacket.

"I'm glad I bought it," he said. "The wool lining blocks this wind."

Their conversation ended. Myra didn't know what she had expected. After the way they'd parted the previous night, she'd been prepared for some discussion of their relationship. Obviously it weighed heavier on her mind than on his. And she should be the one paying attention to duty. It did still grate on her, how yesterday he'd called her bossy after asking for her expertise and opinions. Then he'd kissed her, of all things.

They lumbered up to the field. Myra stopped the combine and explained to Zeke how they cut swaths up and down the long direction.

"Seems easy enough. Show me how to operate this machine," he said.

She did and it surprised her how quickly he caught on. For the first time since he'd set foot on the ranch, Myra felt as if she wasn't needed. She sat in the jump seat doing nothing as he cut two perfectly straight rows. "It's noticeably colder up here," she said, raising her voice to be heard above the noise of the combine engine.

Zeke made another turn. "I can handle this if you have something else that needs doing."

Myra stiffened, feeling dismissed. But that was foolish. "Let me off. I'll go saddle Cayenne and ride out to bring down the rest of the herd."

"Can you do that alone?"

"Of course."

Taking her at her word, he stopped and helped her down. "If you haven't returned by the time I finish, do I drive to the barn?"

"Do you have your phone?" At his nod, she said, "Program in Dave's number. He'll come over or send someone to pick up the combine. Later, we go help Hank."

Myra thought he'd have more questions, but he added the number she gave him and pocketed his phone again.

A brisk ride up to the herd in an even brisker wind cooled her ire and brought clarity to her situation. She'd been running on the false hope that Zeke Maxwell would fail and she'd reclaim the Flying Owl. While he had walked away from one dirty job, he could easily hire these kinds of things in the future. Calving and branding were chores even she brought in help for. And Zeke had a military pension. A one-man operation didn't require as much funding to stay solvent. That was the truth of it.

Tears leaked from her eyes as she chose a cow to tie a cowbell on so the herd would follow. Myra blinked hard, electing to blame the wind for her tears.

It wasn't hard to circle the herd and start them moving. Dumb as people thought cows were, they knew changing seasons. This mature group knew better food and shelter awaited them if they left the foothills. Because it was a mindless task for Myra, she had time to make plans. Fall, regardless of inclement weather, was when work slowed down on the ranch. She'd finish her dollhouses for the bazaar and in her spare time dust off her teaching résumé. She'd need a job. It couldn't hurt to send out feelers to the school where she had taught four years ago, and to a couple of others.

The very notion hurt, but she needed to think about her future.

With a few decisions now made, she reached the pasture with the herd by noon. The cattle seemed eager to crowd into the large fenced area with access to a stream and plentiful grass. Myra leaned out of the saddle to close and lock the gate after the last straggler. She felt a sense of accomplishment as she always did after completing a job. Shifting upright in the saddle, she rode on to the alfalfa field.

Not expecting to see Zeke done with the cutting so soon, it surprised her to find him with Dave Ralston, offloading the baler. The alfalfa had all been cut.

Myra slid off Cayenne. "Hey, I didn't think we were due to get your baler until tomorrow." She aimed her question at Dave.

"Hank's crew finished early, freeing up Foley's combine. Hank said you're gonna help him load bales and stack them in his shed. Looks like everyone sped up because of that weekend storm."

"I figured on waiting until tomorrow to bale here. But if you have a minute to show Zeke how the baler works, I'll go unsaddle Cayenne, grab a bite and head on over to Hank's. Did you stop for lunch?" she asked Zeke.

He shook his head. "I'm not really hungry."

"Don't skip meals. I'll bring you a sandwich and a thermos of coffee." Swinging into the saddle, she turned toward the house and heard Dave say, "That's why we need a woman around, Zeke, old buddy. They keep us healthy. Yeah, yeah… I know there's other reasons," he added with a laugh.

Not wanting to hear how Zeke might answer, Myra kicked Cayenne into a trot.

Once she stalled the mare and fed her and Ember, Myra went into the house to check on Orion while the coffee brewed. Then she assembled sandwiches and put veggies and a whole chicken into the Crock-Pot for supper. Filling a thermos for Zeke and one for herself, she hurried out to the pickup. It wasn't the first time and wouldn't be the last that she'd eaten her midday meal on the way to another job.

Dave's flatbed and her combine were gone when she again drew abreast of the field. Zeke already had two neat rows of bales strung out behind him. Myra wished she had money to buy a hydraulic bale loader. So far no one in the area had sprung for one. They were costly, but hand loading, unloading and racking heavy bales had caused many a rancher to suffer a heart attack. But what did she care? She was leaving.

She flagged Zeke down. "Take a minute to eat. I'll wolf mine down on the way to the Bar W."

"Dave said since your land is flat I can drive the baler back to the barn when I'm done. He'll pick it up tomorrow. I don't think this will take me more than a couple of hours. What should I do then?"

"The clouds have lifted. It's hard to believe reports of a snowstorm. Still, we need to get our bales inside. If you get through, come to Hank's ranch."

"Okay. Where is the Bar W?"

Myra picked up a stick and drew a rough map in the ground. "This is nice soft dirt. If the weather stays like this tomorrow, I'll take a portable pen out for Orion. He can dig while we load bales. This may be the last clear week before spring."

"No kidding? It's still September."

"Some Montana winters last six months. Or like last year only three. But that's rare. Hey, the day's wasting. Call me if you get lost."

Zeke's sharply arched eyebrow signaled his thoughts on that. He followed up by calling out, "I led men on night patrols from one remote Afghan village to another without losing my way. Around land mines," he added. So Myra tossed him a wave and drove off.

THE BAR W RAN a bigger operation than the Flying Owl. Hank's ranch had grown over time with the help of his sons and their wives. They all had homes on the large property. As Myra drove along their winding lane, she could see the family working in the distance. She parked between barns and rummaged in her center console for gloves and a back belt. Luckily she also had a spare, because she hadn't mentioned using a back brace for work with heavy bales to Zeke. She should have given him one early on when they'd hauled hay to the herd.

Work stopped briefly as she joined the Watson family and their one hired hand. Hank drove the tractor pulling a large trailer between bales that sat a dozen feet apart in long rows that disappeared over a gentle rise.

"Where's Zeke?" Hank asked Myra.

"I left him baling our field. Dave dropped off the baler early. Did you hear we're supposed to have snow by the weekend?"

Hank's youngest son, Mark, straightened and adjusted his Stetson. "This wind is cold enough to bring snow, but there're fewer clouds than when we started at dawn."

Myra passed Mark then Hank's older son, Joe, and went by the hired hand with a brief greeting, indicating she'd load the bale beyond him.

Hand loading required a rhythm. Anyone not familiar with the process might think it was some weird ritual dance. As the trailer lumbered past a helper, a bale was loaded, then that person jogged ahead to the next waiting bale and so on until Hank announced the trailer held enough to take to the shed. One by one each helper grabbed a spot on top of the bales and rode in. At the enclosure they worked in tandem, removing bales and ricking them so air circulated to keep the green-cut hay, alfalfa or milo from molding over a long winter.

They were unloading their second batch of bales when Zeke drove in.

"See, I made it with your sketchy directions," he said, tossing Myra a grin.

She ignored his jab and introduced him to the younger Watsons and to Len Carver, a cowboy who shook Zeke's hand before announcing, "I'll let Zeke take my place. I saw a couple of fences that needed mending."

Joe Watson laughed after the cowboy left. "Len hates doing stuff he considers farmwork. He'll choose tackling anything involving horses or cattle first."

"Give the man a break, Joe," Hank chided. "Len's saved us a lot of stock we would've lost without his experience turning a calf coming breech."

"Is that common?" Zeke asked Myra in a low voice after she had him detour past her pickup for the back belt.

"Not common, but it happens. I've been thinking about spring calving. You may want to hire Eddie and Aaron."

"Aren't you staying through spring?" Zeke unzipped his jacket to Velcro the wide belt around his waist. He'd fallen a few steps behind Myra, so he spoke louder.

Apparently overhearing him, Joe Watson fell back, too. "Yeah, Myra, what gives? We were shocked when Dad told us you were leaving. My wife says the bazaar won't earn half as much for the snowy-owl fund without the draw of your dollhouses."

"That reminds me, Myra," Zeke said as he pulled on his gloves, "three snowy owls swooped right down in front of the baler. They all had something in their talons. What a sight. You'll see where I zigzagged instead of baling in a straight line as I watched them."

"You probably opened up a nest of field mice," Myra said.

"The owls are back early," Joe exclaimed. "Damn,

that generally means a bad winter won't be far behind their arrival."

Zeke turned to Joe. "Will the birds go farther south?"

He shrugged. "Myra, maybe you can answer that. You ladies keep better track of the snowy owls than we men do."

"Jewell tracks them. They don't always follow the same migration path. If we can ensure a safe habitat, we hope over time owl families will return each year and their numbers will increase."

"As long as they stick to hunting rodents and don't start making off with my wife's chickens, I'm fine having their numbers grow," Joe growled. He stopped and lifted a bale next to where his father idled with the trailer.

Myra passed Mark and beckoned to Zeke. "You load this bale when Hank pulls up. I'll go to the next one in line. Watch. You'll see how it's done."

Because Zeke worked behind her, Myra didn't notice as the afternoon wore on how much he favored his left arm and shoulder until Mark quietly called it to her attention. "You maybe ought to advise Zeke to take it easy. He's lifting everything with just his right arm. Being new at this, he could've strained his left shoulder. Unless he takes it easy, he might not be able to help bring in your bales tomorrow."

Myra spun around to assess Zeke. "They're *his* bales now," she said. But Mark was right. Zeke was definitely favoring his left side. "It's an injury from

Afghanistan," she noted, frowning. "Eric said Zeke almost lost his arm rescuing guys in his patrol. He had something like eight or more surgeries. But he's a big boy. Surely he knows his limits."

"So the rumors are true. Your new boss really is a hero. Awesome."

It was awesome. Myra wouldn't take anything away from Zeke's heroic actions. But having Mark refer to Zeke as her new boss felt as if he was jabbing a hot poker in her belly. All of the neighbors seemed only too happy to accept Zeke as one of them. That stung most of all.

She'd worked side by side with these guys for three years. Longer if she counted the summers she'd spent tagging after her grandfather doing these same chores. Suddenly, though, she sensed the circle closing her out. The men were quick to joke and chat with Zeke.

By the time the last bale was stored in Hank's shed and dusk had set in, the men grouped together high-fiving each other for a job well done.

They didn't high-five Myra.

Hank stripped off his gloves and shook hay dust from his shirt. "Sarah Jane phoned to let me know supper's almost ready. Zeke, why don't you stay and eat with us. Meet the boys' wives. And we'll set a time to collect at your place tomorrow."

Zeke swiftly turned to Myra.

Having the grace then to look sheepish, Hank cleared his throat. "Of course the invitation extends to you as well, Myra."

"Thanks, but I have a chicken in the Crock-Pot at home."

"Oh, I didn't know that," Zeke said. "I'll take a rain check, Hank."

Myra cut in. "No need. There's no better cook in Snowy Owl Crossing than Sarah Jane. Maybe Lila's mom, but she cooks for a living. Stay, Zeke, and get acquainted."

He chewed his lower lip, seeming torn. Then because Myra told the men she'd see them in the morning and walked away, Joe Watson said in a tone that carried, "Good, it's settled. I'm starved. Let's go eat."

Myra didn't look back. Her pickup lights, once she'd climbed in the cab and turned them on, outlined the men trudging to the big farmhouse on the knoll above the barn.

She didn't blame Hank for shutting her out. She'd long known that cattle ranching was a good-old-boy network. She had wormed her way into acceptance of her grandfather's standing in the community. But tonight had made it plain that she needed to move on. She headed out on the rural road that would take her home. *To her now-temporary home.*

This was far from the first time she'd driven this road after dark and then had to enter a house empty except for Orion. But now it seemed different. Emptier.

She sighed and turned on the living room light. Tonight the home she loved felt lonelier. But the scent of her Crock-Pot chicken reminded her she was hungry and that she'd put in a long day.

As had been her habit prior to Zeke's arrival, she let Orion loose to root around her feet while she sat at the kitchen table checking local news on her laptop, slowly eating her meal. Snow was still predicted for late Saturday or early Sunday. It looked like a big storm. She hoped she had gauged right on winter feed. It was always a guessing game. *But why should she care?*

Closing her laptop, Myra decided to call Eric. As a rule she spoke with someone in her family every few days. Her dad would be busy moving cattle and harvesting hay, and her mom might still be miffed at her. But unless Eric came home dog tired, it was odd he hadn't phoned her. She pressed his automatic link on her phone. He picked up at once.

"How's life at Rolling Acres?" Myra said by way of greeting.

"Hi, sis. What's up? I talked to Zeke at lunch. He said he was running the baler."

Myra stiffened a tad. "He didn't mention talking to you. He's having supper with the Watsons. How are the folks? And you?"

"Good. Dad told Mom to give you some space. You sound down. What's wrong? Why is Zeke at the Watsons' without you?"

Myra didn't hide her despair. She was always honest with her brother. "Each day that goes by, taking me closer to spring when I said I'd leave, is like adding a stickpin in my already breaking heart, Eric. I'm trying to be glad Zeke is willing to learn what it takes to make a go of the ranch. Yet I still wish he'd fail. I know that's horrible but I can't help it. The other day I had hoped he'd quit. He bugged out in the middle of prepping the heifers. Then he came back and doubled down. I know it's nothing, but he's even taken a real interest in the snowy owls." Emotion choked off anything else she might add.

"Zeke said he suffered a minor flashback to the chaos that happened during our ambush. You know I've had a few. He said that was his first. They're scary, Myra."

"I know. I don't want to wish him ill, Eric."

"Have you considered telling him exactly how you feel?"

"I can't. It's not his fault. Hey, I'm sorry for dumping on you. Do me a favor and tell Mom I'm updating my academic résumé. In fact, I'll get to it as soon as I hang up."

"It's probably for the best. I actually sort of hoped you and Zeke would hit it off. Especially after he told me you're taking him to a potluck dance Saturday night."

"At the grange. Everybody goes. It's not like a date, Eric. I can tell you he thinks I'm bossy. I wonder if he got that from you."

"Ouch. Go tweak your résumé. You may feel a whole lot better if you get away from the ranch and find another job."

Myra didn't tell him her heart would never heal. Clearly no one understood how deep her feelings ran when it came to the Flying Owl. "Listen, we're due for snow and so is your area. Winterize. I'll see you after calving, if not before."

"Right. I love you to pieces, Myra. But I owe Zeke my life. He knocked me away and took the percussion from an IED."

"I'm aware of that. It's why I'm still here helping him. Bye, Eric." Myra hit Disconnect before the tears came.

She jumped up and stored the leftovers from the Crock-Pot, cleaned up and put everything in the dishwasher. Her résumé didn't need much updating. Then because it was too early to call it a night, she carried Orion into the living room. Moving the card table that held an unfinished dollhouse in front of her grandfather's recliner, she tucked Orion in beside her and settled down to assemble the roof. The pig was soon snoring away, which helped lift the gloom from her heart. Orion didn't have a care in the world.

She'd installed the gables and was fitting a faux-brick chimney when her cell phone rang. She didn't recognize the number and almost didn't answer, but the caller didn't hang up so she cautiously said, "Hello."

"Myra, it's Zeke. I…uh…don't know where I am. I thought when I left the Bar W fifteen minutes ago I was retracing the route I took to get there. Somehow I got off the paved road. For as long as I've been on this gravel, I know it's not leading to the ranch. I left the map your dad gave me in the pocket of my other jacket. And I never plugged the address into my GPS. Actually…" He hesitated for a protracted moment. "I don't remember the ranch address."

Myra could have just provided it and let it go. But a little demon nudged her. "Gee," she drawled, "since our lane isn't crisscrossed with land mines, I guess you can't navigate your way home now, Lieutenant Maxwell."

The silence lengthened and Myra blanched, concerned she'd lost him. Then, at last, sounding humble, he said, "I deserve that dig. In my defense, there are no stars out tonight to help with coordinates."

"Sorry, I couldn't resist. Here's the address." She gave it and had him read it back. "If I had to guess, I'd say you turned off on one of the reservation roads. If so, you aren't too far away. You should see the house in ten minutes or so. But if you don't, call me back with some landmarks."

He hung up, and Myra didn't know why, but the very fact the man admitted he deserved her needling left her feeling much friendlier toward him.

Chapter Eight

Myra dislodged Orion, who shook his head and snorted a few times at being awakened. Concerned for Zeke and now wishing she hadn't given in to the petty urge to dig him, she carried her pig to a front window and peered into the night.

She shouldn't have acted so cavalier. Getting lost in this expanse of nothingness wasn't anything to take lightly. Last year a tourist had missed a crossroad at night when a winter storm blew in. It wasn't until the family expecting him to meet them in Canada contacted authorities that they found him way off any beaten path, frozen to death.

Relief swept through her as she saw headlights appear at the lane and bob past the barn. She didn't wait for him to shut off his pickup's engine before she threw open the front door and dashed out.

Zeke bounded up on the porch, his smile speaking for both of them. He swept Myra and Orion into a bear hug, surprising her. And he kissed her, which shocked her.

"I'm an idiot," he professed, walking her backward into the house. Reaching behind him, he shut the door, blocking the wind that rattled the remains of a hanging plant. Tightening his arms again, Zeke gazed into Myra's face. "Do you realize you may be the only rancher in this whole corner of the world with lights on this time of night?"

"Ranchers tend to turn in early," she said. "But how does that make you an idiot?"

He let her go and shrugged out of his jacket. "I didn't fill my gas tank when I was in town the other day. And I discovered I don't have a map or a flashlight in my vehicle. I'm damned lucky my cell phone was charged. Probably luckier there's cell service around here."

"That only happened the year before I came to help Gramps. Some of the big ranchers south of here lobbied to get a tower. This used to be no-man's territory. It's still not very populated."

"Tell me about it." As if noticing she held a yawning Orion, Zeke reached out and rubbed the little pig's head. "We should keep a porch light burning as a beacon to lost travelers."

"That's up to you. But electricity is expensive."

"It was really unnerving being out there in total blackness."

"I'm sure it was. Outside of that, did you have a good time with the Watsons?"

"Yeah. They're a lively bunch. You probably know Joe has a microbrewery in his basement. He took me to see his setup. His mother thinks he could have

picked a better hobby, but he claims it keeps him occupied in winter. Sort of like your dollhouses. And
Mark has a room at his house filled with model trains.
They all thought it was odd when I said my hobby is
reading. There wasn't much else to do during down-
time in Afghanistan. Unless you count playing basketball or baseball with village kids."

"I don't think it's odd to like reading."

"Thanks. I know you said you had to come home
because you had food cooking. I wish you'd been able
to stay there for supper."

"Why? Oh, of course, so you'd have been able to
follow me home." She laughed.

"That's not why. It was all couples, making me
the odd man out."

"Joe and Mark married their high school sweet-
hearts. That's common here. But there are singles
around. You'll meet most of them Saturday night at
the grange potluck."

"I didn't mean I missed any old company. I would
have liked sharing the evening with you." He touched
her arm again when he said it.

What was behind his sudden flattery? Myra fought
against a flutter in her belly and recalled her recent
litany of complaints to Eric. The prime one being
how she wished Zeke would opt to leave. Pasting on
a false smile, she said, "Probably you're missing the
woman you left back east."

Zeke looked surprised. "She found a dentist."

"Pardon me?" Myra frowned in confusion.

"To marry."

"Sorry, I shouldn't have said anything." Myra sidled toward her bedroom.

"Don't be sorry. I'm not. They were better suited." A smile played at the edge of his lips. "Stacy would've freaked out if she'd ever stepped in cow poop. And she wouldn't have owned a goldfish, let alone have a pig for a pet."

"Country life isn't for everyone," Myra said then wondered if Zeke found her amusing because she was in direct contrast to his former girlfriend. She'd been so sure all she needed to do was wait him out and he'd tire of living here. *Maybe not.*

"Speaking of country life," she said. "Mark noticed you had trouble loading today. Is your arm bothering you? We've got more days of gathering bales ahead of us."

Zeke automatically rubbed his left shoulder. "The surgeon suggested I join a fitness club for exercise. Hefting bales should be as good and it's cheaper."

His cheerfulness rattled her. Nodding because she'd run out of things to say, she murmured, "Okay, well, I'm turning in. I set up coffee. First one up in the morning can turn it on." She slipped into her room, not waiting to see what Zeke did.

Sleep didn't come quickly. She was bothered by that kiss and a conscience that nagged her for hanging on to resentment. Zeke was trying. In fact, he'd bent over backward. And some part of her that she couldn't control found him attractive. In ways that went beyond physical. Despite injuries, he pitched in. He joked at his own expense. He admitted to liking books—and snowy owls—and Orion. And he was a great kisser. She kept finding things to add to his positive column. His negative one was shrinking. Thankfully, sleep claimed her before she analyzed too closely where those pros and cons might lead her. She might really fall for the guy.

THE SMELL OF fresh coffee drew Myra out of sleep the next morning. Checking her clock, she saw it was six thirty. She'd forgotten to turn on her alarm. Bounding from bed, she hurriedly dressed, collected Orion and practically ran to the kitchen.

"Gosh, how long have you been up?" she asked, seeing Zeke pull a pan of biscuits from the oven.

"Awhile. At supper the Watsons said if it wasn't foggy they'd be here at eight to help haul bales. Hank said that'd give everyone time to finish morning chores."

Myra lifted the curtain to look outside. "It's cloudy, but no fog. That's good. The bales should still be dry enough to house."

They ate breakfast. "I'll put on a new pot so after chores I can pop back in and fill a thermos," Myra said when Zeke carried his dishes to the sink. "And I'll make sandwiches to serve everyone for lunch if you'll drive the tractor and trailer out to the field."

"I can do that. How long do you think it'll take us to finish? Will it be today?"

"I hope so. Tomorrow we'll give Dave Ralston a hand. His winter-wheat field is near his barn. Even after helping him we should get home in time to shower, change and make it to the potluck by seven. I'm taking a big pasta salad that I'll fix tonight."

Zeke kept nodding.

Myra knew it was a lot to take in, but he didn't ask her to repeat anything. And as cold as it was when they went out to make rounds of the cattle, she thought she may need to change what she'd planned to wear. This might not be skirt weather. Especially not short-skirt weather.

THEY GOT A late start moving bales. While checking on the herd, they discovered a broken section of fence. The bull was out. Zeke went back to the barn for tools while Myra corralled the bull in a smaller pen and phoned Hank. "Hi, it's Myra. We'll be delayed. Our bull got out."

"I'm okay with late. I have a heifer that needs doctoring. I'll tell the boys, too."

Myra and Zeke returned to the house as the Watsons drove in at one thirty.

"Why don't you pack up lunch," Zeke said. "I'll bring the tractor and flatbed by here. We can ride to the field together."

"Sounds good. And we can take Orion out to play in that loose dirt, so let's load his pen and haul everything on the flatbed instead of me driving my pickup."

She had everything waiting on the porch when

Zeke pulled up. He left the tractor idling and shot up the steps to help her carry Orion's things out.

"What's that you've got him wrapped in?" he asked, casting a sidelong glance at the bundle in her arms. "He can't do much rooting in a blanket."

"It's his jacket. More like a cape Jewell knit for him." Myra held Orion up for Zeke to see. "It buttons under his belly in two places. And it washes."

"Huh. He looks like a black-and-white bumble-bee with ears."

Myra snuggled the pig and watched Zeke load the pen. "Pay him no mind, Orion. I think you look fashionable. And you can stay warm and have fun."

Laughing, Zeke boosted Myra into the tractor jump seat.

Out at the field the Watsons also poked fun at the pig's jacket.

"Stop, or you'll go hungry," Myra told the boisterous men. Still, once she'd settled Orion, she passed around plastic cups of coffee and wrapped sandwiches. "We can all start work on full bellies," she said.

Not only did they start late, at four, with several rows still to go, the trailer got a flat tire, which had to be repaired.

Pointing to a dusky sky, Myra said, "Hey. If we don't want to make our last run in the dark, we need to get back on task."

Mark shivered and rebuttoned his shearling jacket. "Getting colder, too. We may load out Ralston tomorrow in snow."

His brother took a long gander at the sky. "Not supposed to snow until tomorrow night. I hope everyone going to the potluck has four-wheel drive." Bending, he lifted the first bale in the next row.

They worked steadily to the end of that row and were about to start another when Hank stabbed a finger at the sky. "Will you look at that? Is that a pair of snowies?"

They all stopped and craned their necks, including Zeke, who stilled the tractor.

"It's not dark," Joe said inanely. "I thought they only hunted at night."

Myra scanned the sky and saw the smaller of the two birds dive into the row they'd just left. "Zeke saw them hunting in daylight while he was baling. Maybe they're stocking up because there's a storm coming."

"Could be the same pair," Zeke said, moving the tractor ahead a few feet.

Mark tossed another bale on the trailer and they adjusted their positions. All at once Zeke braked hard, let out a yell and vaulted off the tractor. He leaped over a bale not yet loaded. "The big owl," he shouted. "She's after Orion."

Reacting to his shout, Myra ran after him. She and Zeke reached the makeshift pen inches from a massive bird coming down talons first.

Myra heard Zeke breathing hard and fast. Her heart thundered in her ears amid Orion's frantic squeals. She waved her arms to deflect the owl. The bird kept coming. Up close it didn't look as if it was smiling.

The owl's curved back talons sank into Orion's cape as Zeke grabbed the pig's short front legs. He dodged the flapping wings. The air was a cacophony of screeches, shouts and squeals.

Horrified, Myra saw Zeke and the owl locked in a vicious tug of war. "Lift Orion higher," she yelled. "I'll unbutton his jacket."

Zeke immediately raised his arms, but Myra could tell by his grimace that his once-injured left arm hurt him terribly.

In spite of the determined bird's beating wings tangling in her hair, she ducked and winced, barely avoiding being pecked by the curved beak. Amber eyes she'd once thought beautiful now glowed with menace.

Slow to react to the unfolding scene, Joe and Mark finally joined the fracas. The men waved their Stetsons and made a racket. Grateful, Myra felt the last button slip free of its hole. The force of the release sent Zeke and Orion reeling backward into Mark and Joe. They all sprawled on top of a bale.

The owl issued one last screech. With a forward thrust of her wings, the bird rose above the pen, her only prize Orion's black-and-white knit cloak.

Scraping back her disheveled hair, Myra scrambled to Zeke on her hands and knees. She relieved him of the pig, still squealing because Zeke gripped him so tightly. "Are you all right?" she asked Zeke, her arms and voice shaking. "I'm pretty sure you were in agony while you fought to save Orion." She breathed out a stream of frosty air. "I swear I never dreamed anything like this could happen. Heavens, I can't think straight to properly thank you," she said, cuddling her pet inside her jacket.

"I wish I could've got that on video," Hank said, late crossing the field to join the others. "Unless they see it, nobody will believe what happened. I'll bet no more than two or three minutes passed, but it seemed so much longer."

"Sure did," Zeke said, accepting Joe's hand up from where he lay amid prickly cuttings of alfalfa. He suddenly gripped and rubbed his left elbow, murmuring, "Do you suppose the bird can escape from that knit blanket?"

Myra squinted skyward. "With those talons she'll rip the cloak to shreds."

Mark Watson settled his Stetson again. "In all the years we've lived here, I've never seen a snowy owl that close. Man, Zeke, you leapfrogged over here before I figured out what the hell was going on."

Hank placed a hand on each of his son's shoulders. "We don't want to risk another episode. Myra, you scoot to the house with Piggy. The rest of us will get back to loading bales. That's if Zeke's not too done in to drive the tractor."

"I can do that," Zeke said. "Doubt I can lift a bale. But if you guys load the last two rows, Myra and I can unload in the morning."

"Agreed." Electing to let the men work it out, Myra crooned to Orion on her way to the house. She could tell the fright hadn't left the animal. And her knees still wobbled. Inside the house, she dampened a hand towel and cleaned Orion up before setting him in his kitchen pen. He burrowed under his quilt but poked his nose out when Myra put mixed greens in his metal bowl. "I love the snowy owls," she said, scratching her pet behind his ears. "But I love you more. This was a lesson learned today, and we owe Zeke a ton of thanks for saving you. First Eric, now you," she said, straightening away from the pen.

She remained at the house preparing her pasta salad until she felt Orion had calmed down enough to be left alone.

But before she could go back to the field, the men appeared, all headed toward the barn.

"Is Orion okay?" Zeke called as she came toward him.

"He's fine, thanks to you." She swallowed a lump. "I know some would say he's just a pig. But he's a whole lot more to me."

"I know." Zeke smiled down at her since she'd caught up to his slow-moving tractor. "The little guy is kinda special."

Hearing him say that warmed Myra's heart. But the two of them didn't discuss the incident further that night.

However, the next day when they met at Dave Ralston's to collect his winter hay, Zeke's bravery was a hot topic. He brushed aside the accolades.

Later, as he and Myra returned to the Flying Owl,

Zeke again fussed about how fast information traveled among neighbors.

"Get used to it," Myra advised. "You haven't seen half the gushing. Wait until we get to the potluck. Yikes, is that snow?" she asked, suddenly pointing out the windshield. She drove, but they both leaned forward to peer at the sky.

"Yep," Zeke acknowledged. "We finished at Dave's just in time."

Seeing the fat flakes thicken, Myra mentally scratched any thought of wearing a skirt to the grange hall. Who knew if they'd need to help push friends' or neighbors' vehicles out of snowdrifts?

As if Zeke could hear her thoughts, he asked, "What should a guy wear to this shindig tonight?"

"Dress like a rancher. Didn't you buy new stuff in town?"

"Yeah. I went in for a jacket. A fast-talking salesman sold me fancy boots and a hat. Will people think I'm trying to be cowboy Ken doll?"

Myra sputtered out a laugh. "Sorry, but is there a cowboy Ken doll?"

He shrugged. "I don't know. Seth and I only had G.I. Joe and ninjas."

She spared a glance at him in a cab lit only by green-and-gold dash lights. "Of course you did." His dark buzz cut was growing out, but it accentuated his handsome, rugged features. "Wear the new gear," she said, stopping beside the house.

They went inside through blowing snowflakes and

laughed as they stomped their feet and dusted off each other's hair. "I'll feed Orion then get ready," Myra said. "We should leave in half an hour. I'm allowing extra time because of the snow."

"Gotcha."

Myra heard Zeke's shower running when she passed his room on the way to hers. At her closet she tucked the skirt and blouse she'd put out into a back corner and pulled out her best skinny black jeans. She had a fringed leather jacket—an impulse purchase from last year's bazaar. Until now she'd had nowhere to wear it. But for as many times as she'd attended one of these potlucks without caring what she wore, how dumb was it to be acting all girlie because of Zeke Maxwell?

She did it anyway. She brushed out her ponytail and dressed carefully. The boots she chose had two-inch wedge heels and zipped to her knees. Standing before her mirror, she knew if she indulged in more than her usual lipstick, her friends would tease her unmercifully. Still, she couldn't resist swiping on a light smudge of brown eye shadow. Deep breath and a last fluff of her hair, and out of the room she breezed, then stopped cold.

Zeke paced near the door, turning a black cowboy hat in his hands. He wore black slant-heeled Western boots, pressed blue jeans and a black long-sleeved shirt, open at the throat. It fit him like a glove, showing off his well-honed upper body.

"It's too much, right?" he said. "That's why you're gaping at me."

Myra choked a bit. "I'm thinking no Ken doll I ever remember looked as hot as you."

Zeke definitely blushed.

"Uh… I should have said *fit*," she blurted, charging past him toward the kitchen. "Let me grab my pasta salad from the fridge. Are you driving or am I?" she asked in a rush, trying to cover the compliment.

"I'll drive. And may I say I prefer *hot* over *fit*," he called after her.

She returned carrying a large plastic bowl with a lid. "It was a slip of the tongue. Don't let it go to your head."

Zeke opened the front door and took the bowl. "I can never tell your true feelings about me, because if you give me a compliment it's always backhanded."

They trekked through a dusting of snow to Zeke's pickup. He unlocked the passenger door and steadied Myra as she climbed in, after which he handed her the pasta salad and his hat.

"No comment?" he queried once he was settled behind the wheel.

"Did I take back the praise I heaped on you for saving Orion?"

"No," he admitted, starting the vehicle and turning around.

"Do you mind turning on the heat?"

Reaching out, Zeke twisted a knob, producing a blast of warm air. "Better?"

"Yes, thanks." Myra kept her face turned to the side window.

They fell silent for some fifteen minutes. Then following Myra's directions, Zeke slowed down and got in behind a line of pickups and SUVs. One by one all left the highway to end in a parking lot surrounding a well-lit building. "It's a big Quonset hut," Zeke remarked, shutting off the engine.

"A brilliant design in snow country." Myra passed Zeke his hat and thrust open her door.

"Hold on. I'll come around."

One thing Myra couldn't deny was that Zeke had impeccable manners. He took the bowl for her, then loosely gripped her elbow as she stepped down. And he didn't let go, but rather guided her along the path, which was beginning to get slick from the snow and dropping temperature.

The interior of the building burst with noise—raucous laughter and male, female and children's voices. In the background, sporadic sounds of band members tuning a variety of instruments filled the air.

They'd no more than stepped inside when an older woman whisked the bowl out of Zeke's hands. She bustled to a long table flanking one wall. Across the room, two men, also in Western garb, tapped the first of two beer kegs. Near them and throughout the middle sat smaller tables surrounded by folding chairs.

Zeke barely had time to take it all in when Myra grabbed his hand and pulled him into a good-size coatroom. Shelves above the coats held a plethora of cowboy hats. Bending, Zeke whispered in Myra's ear, "Those pegs on the back wall…are those holstered weapons real?"

"Yes." She hung up her coat. "Many outlying ranchers carry. They've got a greater chance of encountering the wolves we heard in the foothills. Also mountain lions or an occasional rogue moose. You can apply for a permit if you'd like."

He shook his head and shed his outerwear. "I've had quite enough of weapons, thank you."

Myra thought it took a big man to admit that. Again warmth toward him swept through her.

Two older couples entered the coatroom. Myra introduced Zeke, then led him into the great room, where a skinny brown-haired boy ran up and flung his arms around Myra's waist. "Auntie Myra," the kid exclaimed. "Mama sent me to tell you they've got the usual table."

She ruffled the boy's unruly hair. "Zeke, this is Rory Jenkins. His mom is Lila. She works at the café and runs the B and B I told you about."

"Auntie?" Zeke lifted an eyebrow.

"Shh!" Myra touched a finger to her lips. "All of the Artsy Ladies are Rory's aunties." She smiled at the kid.

"Ah. Pleased to meet you." Zeke extended a hand to Rory, who only blinked at Zeke then ran off with a pair of bigger kids.

Myra set off but was startled when she felt Zeke's hand at the small of her back.

Surprised by the possessive sensation of his broad hand, Myra felt heat pooling low in her abdomen. Shaken, she blurted, "You can go find Joe and Mark Watson, or Dave and his son. I'll hunt you up when it's time to go home."

His steps didn't falter. "I've met those guys. I'd like to say hello to your friends." He went with her to where a number of ladies sat around a large table. Chatter ceased as everyone eyed the man all but glued to Myra. She began by introducing Lila's mother, a youngish-looking blonde woman in her late sixties. "You've heard me talk about the crafts and careers of some of the others," she told Zeke. "Tawana, Lila and Jewell, Shelley and Mindy." Myra pointed them out in turn.

The women had all heard about the incident with Orion. They made a big deal about Zeke's part in the rescue. He brushed aside their glowing compliments by singling out Lila and Jewell. "I remember seeing you two at Cody's Bar," he said. "Jewell's a great name for someone with red hair like yours." Smiling, he moved on to acknowledge Shelley and Mindy.

"Shelley teaches ceramics," Myra noted. "Mindy owns the town beauty shop. She makes lovely hair bows and scrunchies that sell like hotcakes at our Thanksgiving bazaar."

Zeke held up his hands in surrender. "I understood fine until you got to scrunchies. I think I'll leave you ladies to your catching up. I saw the Watsons come in." Turning to Myra, he murmured, "Should I come back here to eat with you?"

"You can. Or sometimes the men pick a table so they can discuss cattle futures or the price of tractors and stuff."

He said once more that it was nice to meet everyone, squeezed Myra's shoulder then sauntered off. His gesture caused a flurry of speculation around the table, just as she knew it would. She countered Lila's mother, who said, "That man's a keeper, Myra," by reminding them she was leaving come spring. It cast a pall over the friends until Shelley asked how bazaar projects were going.

As the evening progressed, Myra found herself following Zeke's travels around the hall. He laughed and chatted with most of the local ranchers and their wives. It hurt a little to see how easily he fit in. She longed to be staying. But he hadn't asked her to.

Zeke did eat with a group of men, but wandered back to the women's table when the band struck up their first tune.

It was then Myra learned he loved to dance. And he was good at it. He took a turn around the floor with each of her friends, but spent the rest of the night dancing with her. In his arms she imagined herself a princess. A new feeling for her.

She felt a pang of sorrow when the bandleader announced the last dance. More so because this was her last potluck.

But they collected their coats and her empty dish and said their goodbyes. It was a shock to walk out of the warm hall into a curtain of falling snow.

"Would you like me to drive home?" she asked Zeke. "I know you had a few beers."

"Three over a long evening. But if you want to escort me home and can do it without running off the road in this whiteout, go for it." He handed her the keys.

She reached the main road without incident.

For a few minutes, Zeke seemed tense. "How do you know you're on the road?" he asked.

"See those eight-foot-tall colored poles off to the side?"

Zeke looked.

"Those are snow markers. Every foot up the pole is a different color so you can see how deep the snow is. The top foot is bright red. As long as I've lived here I've never seen it that high. Some old-timers claim they remember when it did."

"Amazing." He leaned back against the seat.

Every time Myra glanced his direction on the slow drive to the ranch, she noticed him smiling. "You seem happy," she finally remarked. "I guess there's no need to ask if you had a good time tonight."

He turned toward her. "I can't tell you when I've enjoyed myself more. I made good friends in the army, but there was always underlying tension. Everybody I've met here is relaxed. For the first time I feel I've found a spot I can call home."

He spoke with such sincerity, Myra didn't doubt he meant the words that struck lances through her heart.

Chapter Nine

A series of storms swept through Snowy Owl Crossing in the next weeks. Weather forecasters advised their listeners to say goodbye to fall and hello to an early winter.

County snowplows maintained the road to and from town, and Zeke helped Myra attach a snow blade to the tractor to clear paths from the barn to all of the holding pens. They also opened a lane to the main road.

"Working together sure makes this easier," she told Zeke. "I did this by myself the last couple of years."

"You mean you didn't call neighbors to help?"

"They would have, but why ask unless it's for something I can't do alone?"

"It's nice to know people are only a phone call away," he said.

"Some winters take more neighbors helping neighbors," Myra responded.

And it seemed she'd no more than made the prediction when needs arose.

In the ensuing weeks, Myra watched Zeke pitch in

anytime a neighboring rancher asked for a hand repairing equipment. It got so friends who'd once called her now phoned Zeke first. Her breath felt constricted as she felt her hold on the Flying Owl lessening.

The simple truth was—in really bad weather ,outdoor activities ground to a halt. Ranchers slogged through essentials like feeding stock twice a day. Otherwise more time was spent indoors.

Myra worked on her dollhouses and kept out of Zeke's way as he moved things around to paint the house. One day he went to town and brought home what he needed to change out the sink and install countertops he'd preordered.

"You're ruining the old-world charm of the house," Myra fretted at supper after he'd shoved the table and chairs aside yet again.

"Ruining?" He glanced up from his plate.

"Yes. There was nothing wrong with how the kitchen looked. I no longer come in this room and picture Gram and Gramps living here." What she meant was that Zeke had put his stamp overtop everything she loved.

"They aren't here any longer," Zeke said quietly. "Fresh paint brightens the rooms. That sink was older than an antique. It was only a matter of time before the pipes rusted through. Then we'd have a flood, which would mean replacing the whole floor. Orion might have drowned," he added, gesturing toward the pen.

His last dire prognostication shut Myra up. She

ate without talking until Zeke broke the silence. "I've heard you rummaging around in the extra bedroom late at night. Are you cutting out a new dollhouse?"

"I'm packing materials. You said your brother might visit. He'll need a bed."

"There's no rush. I talked to Seth at Halloween. He's hunting opals in Australia and plans to winter there, scuba diving with a fellow gem hunter. Our winter is their summer."

"Still, I won't start any new houses. I have ten to sell at the bazaar."

"About those. I looked one over the other day. Have you thought about putting lights in some? If you lit even half, you could sell them for more and it wouldn't cost but pennies to do."

"Lights? Can you show me?"

They cleared the dishes and Zeke brought a dollhouse to the table. "Here, you can add a battery pack and a switch. You have these little lamps already. Run thin wire along the ceiling and add in a micro LED." He showed her how.

"Zeke, that's brilliant. Weather permitting, I'll go buy wiring after feeding stock tomorrow."

"I'll ride along. You can help choose paint for the living room. It's time for that orangutan orange to go."

She scowled. "It makes the room warmer."

"So would gold." He smiled. "Do you have a minute to look at a notebook I started? Joe Watson suggested I list major chores that need doing and when."

"I intended to type something up," Myra said. "All

this bad weather threw me off. But if you write the instructions yourself, they'll probably make more sense later."

He brought out a pocket notebook and Myra had to admit he had neat printing for a man, and he'd absorbed all she'd told him. Things she was sure he hadn't understood. "Looks to me as if you've got everything down. Calving is the next big operation, and you have to experience one season to understand all the steps."

"Believe it or not, cattle ranching is beginning to make sense. I had no idea what to expect when I came here. You're an excellent teacher, Myra. I see why your folks steered you toward a career in education. I actually feel as if I belong now."

She blinked rapidly to hold back a rush of tears. She'd hoped for quite the opposite effect, but was saved any comment because the kitchen lights flickered twice and went out.

"Whoa!" Zeke reached for her and pulled her close. "What now?"

She spoke against his neck. "We give it ten minutes to see if they come back on. If not, we start the generator." She pulled back a bit. "Did you put the LED lantern back after you tore the old sink out?"

"Yes. And I noticed a couple stashed around the house." Zeke let go of her and felt his way along the new countertop. He got out the double mantle lantern and switched it on. "Whew, I'm glad the batteries are good."

"They get replaced every September. That's something you should write in your notebook."

Orion dug under his quilt until he'd covered up, leaving only his snout visible.

"He doesn't like the lantern," Myra said. "I guess because the light is whiter and more intense."

Zeke leaned over the pen and rubbed the pig's ears. "Poor little guy's scared. His heart is beating as fast as when the owl tried to carry him off." He stood up. "Tell me where to access the generator. I'll go start it."

"You know about generators?"

"Oh yeah. That's high on the list of stuff the army teaches."

"It's housed behind the back porch. Take the lantern. You can't miss it. But be careful. It can be cantankerous. Oh, listen to that wind. You'll want your jacket."

"Is there a lantern in the living room? I can bring it back to you so you have a light while I go outside."

"It's in the pocket under the window seat. I'll just get Orion and come with you. We may be without power for some time. That means no TV, no radio, no microwave or dishwasher. The unit isn't strong enough to light the whole house. So depending on what caused the outage, we may be early to bed, late to rise for days."

"Sounds like we need a bigger generator," Zeke grumped.

"Gramps put it on his Christmas wish list every year. Santa never delivered."

"Funny." Zeke held the light aloft while Myra juggled Orion and retrieved the second lantern. "Speaking of Christmas…are you planning to spend the holiday with your folks?"

She straightened, shooting him a look. "No. The last few years I've stayed here with Gramps and mailed their gifts to them. Are you inviting someone to visit you so that you want me gone? A lady, perhaps?"

"Didn't we have this discussion? My last girlfriend married someone else. I ask because Eric said your mom would love if you were home for the holiday. I thought if you'd be gone a week or two, I'd hire Eddie Four Bear to help feed our stock."

"You don't need help with that. Your money is better spent on chores you can't do alone."

Zeke donned his jacket and hat, picked up his lantern and walked out.

Myra shifted back to thinking he wasn't ready to run a ranch. She would leave for a week if she thought it'd hasten him into reaching the same conclusion. But if he had the wherewithal to hire Eddie, she should probably give up. Except she'd committed to staying through spring, and going home would give her mom ample opportunity to guilt her back into teaching. Not that she wasn't considering it. She'd updated her résumé but hadn't sent it out. She listened to her heart, which still disputed Zeke calling the ranch *his* home. Yet as hard as it was to accept, she needed to separate herself from the Flying Owl and find a teaching job.

ZEKE STEPPED OFF the enclosed porch and was hit
with a blast of icy wind. It served him right for acting churlish in there. But dammit, he was doing everything he could to impress Myra. When it came
to the ranch it seemed nothing he did was enough.
Somewhere around the time of the potluck dance
he'd stopped thinking about her leaving, but as yet
he hadn't had the nerve to bring it up. Really, he
hadn't fully figured out in his own mind how that
would work—what it meant. At odd times it popped
into his head that he could offer her a business part-
nership. At others, when they talked and laughed over
meals, or went around the ranch, he imagined a totally
different relationship. Often at night he pictured her
sharing his bed. *Yeah, he definitely needed to start
showing her how he felt. See if she had any thoughts
along those lines.*

But what were those lines? he wondered as he
shone the light over the generator. *Love? Marriage?
Kids?* He wanted all of that in due time. Myra, though,
was hard to read. What if she scoffed at his feelings?
Or what if she just up and left? As independent as she
was, why did she need him? Not to start this damned
generator, apparently.

One good look at it and he saw that to supply electricity to a house this size it would have to be twice as
big. He wondered why Myra's grandfather had muddled along with something so ineffective.

If she hadn't been joking about the man asking
Santa for a new unit, then money must have been

the issue. He hadn't studied the spreadsheet since the first day she'd showed it to him, but if the ranch didn't earn enough for upkeep, or for the owner to take a few days off, or hire help, why pour heart, soul and endless hours into the place? Anyone could see it was what Myra did.

He started the generator, happy to hear it chug to life without coughing or wheezing.

Returning to the house, Zeke had geared up to launch a serious talk with Myra, only to discover she'd fallen asleep with Orion in the recliner. Funny how sleep softened her. Unable to resist because they looked so cute, he got his camera and snapped a photo, then decided he may as well call it a night.

THE POWER OUTAGE lasted five days, causing undue hardship on some neighbors and businesses in town. Myra and Zeke split up many days, each dashing off to assist a neighbor. The dairy farmers were forced to milk cows by hand, as the electric milking machines required too much power for most generators.

The night the power was restored, Zeke volunteered to cook. For the whole week they'd cooked on a hibachi he'd set up on the porch.

"Ow," Zeke yelped in the middle of rolling out the biscuit dough. "My fingers are cracked from milking so many darned cows."

"Hey, you did it, though. You learned the rhythm. Something Eric never got the hang of."

"Really? He must have never pulled goat duty in Afghanistan."

"Did you keep goats on base?" Myra asked, looking up from threading electrical wire through one of her dollhouses as Zeke had shown her.

"At our more remote sites. Village elders tended to cooperate better if we passed around skins of warm goat's milk first."

"Some of the Afghan terrain I've seen in news clips reminds me of here. Empty, wild, yet beautiful."

"It's hard for me to compare the two." Zeke slid the pan of biscuits into the oven then stirred the noodles he had boiling. "There, I was always looking over my shoulder for snipers or checking paths for mines."

Myra spliced wire to a hanging lamp. "Do you think it'll ever be safe?"

"There's always hope. Hey, some little girl is going to be ecstatic with that dollhouse."

Looking satisfied, Myra said, "I hope parents can afford the higher asking price for the lighted houses. Extra money will be welcome. We plan to request an appointment with the federal Natural Resource Committee in Washington so we can discuss the owls in person. We haven't had any luck in three years of petitioning our state house for a snowy-owl refuge. Our group could buy land, but it wouldn't be a recognized preserve. If we can't post it as a refuge it's pointless. And there's a matter of yearly taxes we'd have to pay. We voted to set aside funds to send Jewell and Tawana to DC. So we're all trying to earn more at this year's bazaar."

"It's next weekend, right?" Zeke put the coffee scoop back in the can and turned on the maker. "Do you think I can do my Christmas shopping for my family there?"

Myra tried the dollhouse lights before setting aside her tools. "I heard you ask your mom the other day for gift suggestions. What does she want?"

"She said to save my money. Their beach condo is small."

"Hmm. Maybe crafts made in snowbound rural Montana won't go well in sunny Barbados."

"And Seth's in equally sunny Australia. Although he's there temporarily. I can always buy him travel items."

"You mentioned photographing the snowy owls for your mom. We don't have professional photofinishing here, but you could ask Carl Meyer at the newspaper to print one of your shots to frame."

"What a good idea. I'll take my camera out tomorrow if it doesn't snow."

THE NEXT DAY after they finished feeding the stock, Zeke removed his gloves and tucked them in a back pocket. "If you can get by without me for a while, I'll saddle Ember and ride into the foothills to see if I can scare up an owl to photograph."

"Go ahead. I'm going in to put on a pot of chili for tonight. Then I'll take a load of dollhouses into town while the weather is good. I talked to Lila last night. She said the grange hall is ready for crafters to start setting up."

"Do you need me to help load and unload them?"

"I've always done it alone. I'll take half of them today. Saturday of the sale, if you like, we can ride together and haul the other half. Driving one vehicle makes sense since parking is at a premium."

"I know you've always done things by yourself. But I'm here and I want to help."

Myra cast him a quick glance. "Are you accusing me of stepping on your toes?"

"No, but at first you readily explained everything. Lately, I have to see you tackling something and barge in to offer assistance."

"I told you winter's the time to catch up on small chores. You've insisted on painting and spiffing up the house in spite of the fumes, so if I see something that needs doing outside, I do it. Frankly, half the time I forget you're here."

"Well, thanks a heap. So glad you find me forget-table," Zeke said testily.

Myra huffed out an exasperated growl and stomped toward the house.

Left to grumble alone, Zeke went into the barn and saddled Ember. Not only hadn't he found a good time to bring up to Myra his earlier thoughts about their relationship, it seemed to him as winter dragged on and the holidays approached, she went out of her way to put more space between them.

It was hard to stay irritated riding through a cold, crisp day. Snow sparkled in areas touched by the sun. White peaks rose in the background. Lower down, evergreen trees stood out against the patchwork like lonely sentinels. But they reminded Zeke he felt lonely. Throughout his years in the army he'd almost never spent time alone. Myra thrived on solitude. She also didn't like change—that was evident in her unhappiness over his sprucing up the ranch. Yet she embraced his suggestion of adding lights to her dollhouses. And after he'd seen how the Watsons had strung canvas between trees to shelter part of their stock, she'd seemed pleased when he'd done the same here with a little help from Joe and Mark.

Maybe he was misreading her. Perhaps she thought he should do more on his own.

He went over their earlier exchange. He could have worded his part of their back-and-forth better.

Just as he vowed to make more of an effort to show Myra he could be a real asset, he saw a trio of snowy owls skimming an open field. Reining in Ember, he lifted his camera. For ten minutes or more the birds flew between the field and a nest situated high in a tall pine. Two of the owls wore pink bands. Zeke couldn't wait to tell Myra so she could relay the information to Jewell.

Before the birds flew farther afield, Zeke scrolled back through several of his photos. Excited to see how clear some of the shots were, he turned and rode home. *Home. It had a good ring.*

Myra's pickup was gone. Zeke was disappointed until he recalled her plan to take a load of dollhouses to the grange hall. Then he decided if he hurried he might take advantage of her being in town. He didn't know Carl from the newspaper, but if he could find Myra in Snowy Owl Crossing, she could introduce him. And help him pick out a nice frame for his mom. Unsaddling Ember, he returned the horse to his stall.

Damn—there he went relying on her again.

It wasn't until he was under way that he hit on another idea. He knew Jewell well enough. So rather than track down Myra and expect her to tell her friend about the banded birds, Zeke could find the vet and tell her himself. Maybe if he showed her his photos, he could ask her help in meeting Carl and picking frames. Satisfied he'd solved two issues with one simple solution, he drove straight to Jewell's clinic.

Chapter Ten

Myra backed her pickup close to the side door of the grange hall. She went inside to find help to unload her dollhouses. If she'd waited for Zeke to return from his ride as he'd suggested, he'd be here to help her. Instead, she'd been bent on proving she didn't need assistance from anyone.

She didn't know why she'd acted so snarkily to him. Actually, she did know. Day by day she felt her hold on the Flying Owl slipping away. Zeke took over more and more ranch chores. He had become a reliable part of the larger ranching community. She saw he wasn't going to leave. Nor should he. He fit in.

Once the power had been restored, she had sent out résumés to principals she knew in Billings and Bozeman. She had scrolled through school websites in Great Falls, but they were her last choice. Great Falls and Helena were too big-city. She'd always considered herself a country girl. She *was* a country girl.

Stepping farther inside the hall, she saw it had been transformed by rows of booths all decorated for the fall bazaar. Classes at the local elementary school had decorated with brown-and-orange crepe paper. Stapled around booth openings were turkeys, pilgrims, cornucopias and hundreds of faux oak leaves cut from construction paper.

In past years Myra hadn't given much thought to booth decorations. Looking around today, it hit her hard knowing this was her last year to exhibit. She would never have children of her own here, running around on sale day showing off their own and classmates' decorations. Discovering how deeply she longed to have a child struck out of nowhere. She'd attended friends' weddings—had even been a bridesmaid. Never had she felt anxious that love, marriage, babies and life on the ranch would drift out of her reach.

"Myra, are you all right? Why are you just standing there?" Lila Jenkins stepped out from a booth.

Giving herself a mental shake, Myra waved. "I guess I was taking it all in. The kids who decorated outdid themselves this year. Did Rory's class do your booth?"

"Mine and some others." Lila crossed the room. "You requested shelves, so the committee assigned you a corner booth. Have you brought dollhouses today?"

Myra nodded. "Five. Wait until you see the addition Zeke suggested. Battery-operated lighting. There wasn't time to refit all of them. But they'll sell for more, so it's good to try a few, I guess."

"The committee ran ads in more newspapers this

year. My quilts and your dollhouses were featured because we always sell out."

"Maybe they should have said in the ads this will be my last year." Myra teared up.

Lila hugged her friend. "Don't say that. The Artsy Ladies are praying for a miracle. Come on, let's bring in your houses and I'll help you arrange them. Then if you have time for coffee we can stop by the café. This morning Mom said she hadn't seen you in ages."

Myra swallowed back the pain that accompanied her declaration about this being her last year. "Did the café close during the power outage?"

"We were open thanks to Mom installing a new generator. There weren't a lot of customers, though. Since school was closed, Rory bussed tables. That freed me up to finish handwork on my last couple of kid quilts. Rory wants the one I made with baseballs all over it. Did I tell you he's gone crazy over baseball? Matt and Lori Barnes's son Kemper plays for Little League. Rory so wants to join. But the fees are expensive. And games are in Wolf Point. Getting him to and from would be hard since I'm doing my best to hang on to the bed-and-breakfast and work part-time for Mom."

The women chatted as they went out to Myra's pickup. "I don't know much about Little League. Do they practice a lot?"

"Daily," Lila said, taking the dollhouse Myra handed her. "They practice at our park, but the field isn't right for league games." The women carried houses in, and after settling them, Lila added, "The games also coincide with fishing season."

"Oh no. Fishermen are your best customers." Myra led the way out to get more houses. "Rory's young. Maybe the B and B will pick up to the point you can hire help. Then next year he can join a team."

"He's ten the day before Christmas. Matt Barnes said players really need to get involved in the sport by then, or they lose valuable instruction."

Myra commiserated as they set the last house. Then she said, "Hey, before we go, let me show you the lights." She flicked on one battery pack. Light shone through the windows.

"That is so cool. You must be getting along better with Zeke if he took that kind of interest in your dollhouses."

"He's okay. But I'm sorry he is who he is." Myra shut off the lights. "Let's go. I don't want to talk about Zeke."

Lila nodded. "You head over. I picked up the grange key from Harv Bell, so I need to run it by his office. Tell Mom I'm on my way."

They parted and Myra drove down Main Street and parked beyond the café. She hurried back and went in. "Hi, Doreen," she called when Lila's mother emerged from the kitchen. She relayed Lila's message. "Doesn't look like you're so busy that she and I can't have coffee."

"And a cupcake. I'm trying out new recipes. Rory's

class is going to sell them at the bazaar. Today I have a batch of lemon and a batch of applesauce."

"Applesauce sounds perfect," Myra said, taking the full mug Doreen Mercer passed her. "I'll take that back booth by the window," she announced as Lila breezed in.

Lila brought her mug and two cupcakes over. She stood by while Myra shed her jacket. "Golly, will you look at that," Lila exclaimed, bending nearer the window. "Isn't that your guy, Zeke, walking across the street with Jewell?"

"Can't be," Myra exclaimed, whirling to peer in the direction Lila pointed. "For one thing, he's not my guy. But Zeke went riding." She pressed her nose to the window and was shocked to see that Lila was right. Zeke and Jewell walked side by side, talking, gesturing and, by the look of them, both having a great time.

Emptiness clawed at Myra's stomach, but she did her best to act normally when she again faced Lila. Still, she barely managed a careless shrug. "He must have gotten back early." She deliberately took a bite of her cupcake and drank her coffee without retaining much of what Lila said. Her mind kept seeing Zeke and Jewell looking so happy together. Although why was that surprising? Jewell was gorgeous, smart and athletic. At the potluck Zeke had remarked on her red hair. So, had he kissed her, too? Myra recalled his kisses. And she could still feel the warmth of his proprietary hand on her back as she introduced him around at the potluck.

"Myra, Mom has asked you three times if you liked the applesauce cupcake."

Jerking her head up, Myra realized she'd been lost in memories. "Sorry, it was really good. I guess I have a lot on my mind. Stuff I need to do between now and calving season so I'll be ready to leave. Last week I put out feelers on teaching jobs."

Lila reached across the table and clutched Myra's hand. "No! Why can't you continue working for Zeke like you're doing now?"

"I can't." Myra's throat was too tight to say more. But she probably wouldn't have admitted how jumbled her feelings were. Seeing Zeke with Jewell made her realize how much she'd come to care for him. Maybe more than she cared to own the ranch, and that was scary.

"I hate to eat and run, but with Zeke in town I need to get back and feed the stock. According to the almanac, this is only a short hiatus between storms."

Lila and Doreen said they'd see her again at the bazaar.

As she drove to the ranch, Myra couldn't shake how much Zeke and Jewell looked like a couple.

Two hours later, she had fed the stock and was parking the tractor when Zeke drove in. He stepped from his pickup and called, "Why didn't you wait for me to help? I went by the grange hall and saw the booths. It's quite a production. Your dollhouses look nice."

Myra shrugged and crawled off the tractor to close up the barn.

Zeke fell in step on the way to the house. "When do you want to eat? I bought paint for my bathroom. If there's time I may give it one coat before supper."

"I've got chili in the Crock-Pot. There's French bread to toast. You can eat anytime you wish. I have things to do and plan to eat in my room."

"O…kay." Zeke slowed then turned back.

Presumably to get his paint.

Myra ran into him again when she returned her empty chili bowl to the kitchen. He sat eating at the table. "We should drive separately to the bazaar," she announced.

"Didn't you say parking was a problem?" Zeke frowned at her.

"It can be. But the Artsy Ladies always clean up. And I may want to join them afterward."

"Is something wrong, Myra? You seem out of sorts."

"Nothing's wrong. Did you get your photographs?"

Zeke scooted his chair aside to give her room to pick up Orion. "I did," he said, but didn't elaborate.

And Myra noticed he didn't offer to show her the pictures.

"I brought in the mail," he said. "You have two envelopes from schools. Did you send out résumés?"

"Where is it?" Myra demanded.

"On the credenza by the door."

Myra rushed out of the kitchen. She snatched up the mail and went directly to her bedroom. She had thought any response would come via email. Her heart beat faster as she set Orion in his night cage and sat on her bed to open the first letter. Maybe one or both schools had midyear openings. If so, her tenure at the ranch could end ASAP, and Zeke would hire Eddie and Aaron to help with calving.

The first note came from her former principal's secretary, pointing out that her certification had expired. If she took courses over the summer and reapplied, they'd consider her. The second letter was similar, suggesting she take the courses online. *How could she have forgotten to renew her certification?*

This was so far from what she'd expected she sat with her body numb and her mind racing. At last she folded the letters and put them in a dresser drawer. The thought of returning to school was repugnant. Should she even consider going back to teaching? Shouldn't a teacher—a good one—be excited to learn? Now her situation seemed dire. She couldn't stay at the ranch Zeke owned. And if he and Jewell got cozy, Myra couldn't fathom them being okay with having her sharing this house with Zeke much longer.

She slept fitfully that night. And the snowstorm that blew in overnight didn't help her disposition. They were back to hand feeding cows each morning and evening. That meant working too closely with Zeke.

It was still snowing on Saturday. Myra and her

friends worried the weather would keep people away from the bazaar.

But it didn't.

"Perhaps because winter seems never-ending," Tawana said. "People just needed to get out and shop for Christmas."

"I need gifts for my dad, my brother and Zeke. It's probably cheesy to buy the same for all three, but I think they'd all like those belts you made with eagle beadwork in patches along the leather." Myra handed over her credit card.

"Zeke was here earlier. He bought a beaded vest for his brother."

"Really?" Myra tucked her card away. "When I first mentioned your beaded leather vests to him, he sounded totally uninterested."

"He was in buying mode. I saw him at Jewell's stall for quite a while. Maybe buying some of her knit scarves for his sisters?"

Myra felt herself scowl. "He only has a twin brother. And his mom lives where it's sunny all the time." She didn't mention that Zeke may have tarried with Jewell for a totally different reason. But the stark reminder stole away the joy Myra usually had for the bazaar. It didn't even help to have so many moms rave over her lighted dollhouses. She gave Zeke credit, but all the same it hurt to sell her final house, knowing it would be the last one she'd ever sell here in Snowy Owl Crossing.

After the crowd thinned out, Jewell was noticeably absent from their cleanup crew. And Zeke wasn't helping the men break down the booths. Rather than looking for him, she reluctantly stayed to help count their earnings.

"We made enough to more than fund Tawana and Jewell's trip to DC," Shelley announced once they'd all met up at the café. "Next year's profits will be gravy."

Everyone high-fived. Everyone but Myra. Lila slipped an arm around her shoulders. "No matter where you are, can't you still come back for the bazaar?"

"Definitely," Tawana vouched. "But we hope it works out for you to stay. Even if the worst happens, we'll keep in touch. You'll want to know what's happening with the owls, Myra. This morning Jewell said our snowy population is up a bit. She plans to band more chicks next week. If we can get an appointment with the federal committee, and they authorize a preserve, you'll have to come to the dedication."

"I can't help feeling out of sorts," Myra said. "I'm not good company. I think I'll go on home and start wrapping Christmas gifts. Maybe that will cheer me up. Anyway, my bad mood shouldn't drag you guys down." Before the other ladies could say more, Myra put on her jacket and hat, and left the café.

Again she beat Zeke to the ranch. The gloomy way she felt, she considered retreating to her bedroom to brood. But they needed to eat. And as long as she remained, chores needed doing.

She assembled a casserole she could pop in the oven to bake while they made the evening round of feeding. *They*, provided Zeke came home. He didn't have to. He was a big boy. Nothing was stopping him from spending the night with Jewell. If they fell in love she ought to be happy for her friend. *Then why was it so hard?*

Myra heard the front door open, and for a split second her heart lifted. She recognized Zeke's footfalls. He didn't call out to her, but went straight to his room.

She put the casserole in the oven, but rather than be caught hanging out in the kitchen, she grabbed her outdoor gear and hurried to the barn to load hay bales. Hard work eased her frustration. By the time Zeke came to find her she was almost her normal self.

"Something smelled good in the kitchen," he said, entering the barn as he pulled on his gloves.

"A casserole my gram used to make. I hope it tastes like hers."

"Hey, I saw a lot of people carrying out your dollhouses."

"Your lights were the big hit."

"Next year maybe I can make some basic wood furniture to go with."

Myra plopped a bale close enough to Zeke to cause him to jump back. "I don't know who will construct the houses since I won't be here."

He fell silent and bent to the task of arranging bales.

They got through their rounds with minimal talk.

Only after they were back inside eating supper did Zeke again broach the subject of Christmas. "You haven't mentioned putting up Christmas lights or a tree."

Myra set down a forkful of casserole. "We used to. Everything is stored in the barn. Last year after Gramps died, I had too much to do to decorate."

"Point me to it. I'll decorate," he said. "I did my shopping at the bazaar, so I only need to wrap and mail packages to my family."

"Same for me," Myra admitted. "So you found something suitable for your folks and your brother?"

"I did."

Myra waited for him to say what he found, but he dug into his meal, and when he finished, rinsed his dishes and retired to his room.

THE NEXT DAY he followed through on his promise to decorate. Myra could have helped, but she fought too many conflicting emotions. After the bazaar, time always seemed to speed up. Everyone was ready to say goodbye to Old Man Winter, when spring rains would wash away the snow and bring new grass and baby calves. But for her, looking ahead spelled the end of her life on the ranch. And she honestly had no idea what she was going to do.

Zeke's decorations inside and out left the house looking cheerier.

In the days that led up to Christmas, all of Myra's family phoned trying to talk her into joining them for the holidays. Her mother said, "Honey, we miss you. Come home. I spruced up your room with new bedding in the lavender shades you love."

"I appreciate that, but we've been slammed with snowstorm after snowstorm. The day I mailed your packages was the last day the road to town was open. The room will keep until March. We should be finished calving by then."

"Sweetheart, Eric told us your teaching credentials lapsed. We're sorry that happened while you were helping Gramps out. Can I help?"

"No, but thanks, Mom. Listen, I'll phone you on Christmas." Myra hung up because tears gummed up her throat.

Zeke, who'd been painting moldings, had listened unabashedly to Myra's end of the conversation. Noticing how she clutched the phone and wiped her eyes, he set down his brush and paint can. Crossing the room, he pulled her out of the chair and into his arms. "What's wrong? If you're homesick, I'll get along. I talked to Eddie about helping with calving like you suggested. He said he's available any time I need him." Zeke rubbed his chin over Myra's hair. "I hate seeing you so distraught."

"Don't hold me, Zeke, or I'll totally fall apart." She wedged a space between them.

Zeke might not have let go, if his phone hadn't rung. He wanted to get to the bottom of her woebegone attitude. He'd noticed a change before the bazaar that seemed worse after.

Dashing a kiss over her forehead, he flashed an apologetic look as he dug out his cell phone. "Seth! Hey, bro. Ah, you got my package? Yeah, yours came. It's lucky. Would you believe we have five feet of snow?"

"Wow, it's eighty-five here."

"Sure, rub it in. Eighty-five sounds like an impossible dream." Zeke turned to include Myra in his smile and saw her closing the door to her bedroom.

"Will your snow be gone by April?" Seth asked. "I'll wind down my opal hunt by then. If I book a flight now I can manage a couple of weeks to see your ranch before heading to a little spot in India showing promising rubies."

"Great, that'll be great. Myra cleared her crafts out of the third bedroom, and it's next on my agenda to paint. Your timing is typical. You'll have missed helping me update the house."

"Will your housemate still be there in April? I thought you said she'd be leaving in the spring."

"Well, ah…here's the thing," Zeke said, lowering his voice and moving away from Myra's bedroom door. "Don't come unglued, but if I had my way, Seth, she'd stay."

"What? You devil, you. Are you implying the *M* word?"

"*M* as in *maybe*. I'm not doing a good job of making my feelings known. I can't read how she feels about me. Since we share a house, work and all meals, I'm reluctant to romance her too much. It could easily get out of hand. Then if she didn't want to commit I'd feel like a heel and it could drive her away. I mean, look at all I owe her family."

Seth cleared his throat. "I'm not a good person to give advice in the love game, Zeke. Women always see me as a rolling stone."

"We're something, huh? My travelin' days are over. I love it here. This is exactly where I see myself living for the next forty or fifty years."

Myra's bedroom door opened and she sped past where he stood talking to Seth. He wondered how much of his conversation she'd heard. Should he hope she caught the last part? Everyone around knew how deeply she loved the ranch, but he doubted she had any idea he'd developed the same care for the place. What he hesitated to tell her was how big a part she played in what he liked about work and life here.

"Hey, Seth, I need to get back to painting. I'll give you a holler after we open our gifts, okay? If you're not off surfing, that is. Make your reservations and I'll tell Myra you're coming."

IN THE KITCHEN, Myra picked up Orion and hugged him close. She guessed it was fortuitous she'd come out when she did. Her mother used to say eavesdroppers always got their ears full. But Zeke hadn't exactly been trying to cloak what he was saying to his twin. All her wishful thinking that he'd quit and sell her the ranch was dashed for good. She felt calmer on the outside than on the inside, she knew as she went to the fridge for Orion's lettuce.

Instead of clinging to hope, she should've left the day her dad informed her they'd given the Flying Owl to Eric's savior. Now her affection for the ranch was all mixed up with her confusing affection for Zeke.

She only had a few months left to get through. Hard, though, when she wished for more than Zeke meant by that casual kiss he'd brushed across her forehead right as his brother called. Considering his comment to Seth about the ranch being his forever home, Zeke probably couldn't wait for spring calving to pass so she'd leave the place totally to him.

She sighed and set Orion down to eat his lettuce.

Chapter Eleven

Christmas morning brought the heaviest snowfall yet. Myra had managed to get into town Christmas Eve to attend a candlelight service. Zeke had declined to go. When she left the church, it was bitterly cold and the sky was thick with clouds. No one expected it to snow another two feet during the night, though.

"Jeez," Zeke exclaimed in the morning when they stepped out to go feed the cows. "Merry Christmas... not! Do you think we can get to the barn and on out to the pens?" He waded through snow up to his waist, breaking trail for Myra.

"Luckily the plow is still on the tractor. After we load the hay, if you plow a track, I'll toss bunches over the fence. I think the worst of the storm has passed. At least there are far fewer clouds than when I drove home last night."

"How was the service? I probably should have gone, but I promised my folks a group call with Seth, and we're all in different time zones."

"Did you open your gifts last night?"

"The ones from them. I didn't open the one from you."

"I saw you'd put two under the tree for me," she said. "You shouldn't have when I only bought you one thing. Eric gave me earmuffs. My folks sent a check they designated for an online class to renew my teaching credentials." She wrinkled her nose.

At the barn, Zeke unlocked the door and pulled it back. "Eric said something about your certificate being out of date. But once you said you'd rather work on a ranch than teach. Did you change your mind?"

Myra hooked the trailer on the back of the tractor and began loading bales. "I feel like my life is in flux."

Zeke found the long-handled hook and pulled down bales from the next tall stack. Then he and Myra fell silent while they filled the trailer.

The feeding process took much longer than normal due to the deep snow. They'd returned the equipment to the barn when Zeke said, "Will all of the heifers make it to springtime to have their babies? A half dozen or so look ready to pop now."

"Hey, you're paying attention. We'll need to watch closely during January. None should drop calves until February. We count back to when I put the bull in the heifers' pasture."

Zeke's grin was sheepish. "I'll jot that down in my notebook. I wondered how you were so sure calves arrive at a predetermined period."

They stomped the snow off their boots and entered the warm house. "Sometimes I suspect a bull gets randy through the fence. I've had a couple of mid-January calves."

"You talk so matter-of-factly about the birthing stuff. Dave Ralston offered some insight into how messy it can be. He said his wife and his daughter-in-law both help with their calving. I guess it surprises me that women, uh, get so involved."

Removing two mugs from the cupboard and filling them with hot coffee, Myra also dispatched an eye-roll. "Calves are the lifeblood on a ranch. So Ma, Pa, grandparents and kids help make sure they get a safe start. As for women being involved, who do you think birth children?"

Zeke accepted his mug. "Women, of course. But does seeing the process so up close and personal year after year dampen a woman's enthusiasm to have babies?"

"Not that I've seen. Birth is actually rather amazing, Zeke." Myra put a premade pan of cinnamon rolls in the toaster oven and turned it on.

"So, you want kids?" he asked casually.

"Sure, but I have to find a husband first," she responded drily as she checked the rolls.

"Are you hunting?" Zeke set out plates and forks.

"What kind of question is that? Are *you* hunting for a wife?" She pulled on oven mitts, removed the steaming pan and smacked it down on the table atop a hot pad.

"Well, yeah," he admitted, eyeing her as he sat down.

"Silly me, I should've known," she muttered, picturing him laughing with Jewell. "Hold out your plate," she ordered, slipping a spatula under a big roll. Her remark or maybe her testy tone effectively ended what she judged a pointless conversation.

But as she nibbled at her roll, Myra wondered if Jewell knew Zeke was that serious. At the candlelight service Jewell had only talked about the snowy owls.

"Wanna go open presents?" Zeke asked after they finished eating.

"Sure. But I wish you hadn't bought me two gifts. I didn't get you anything elaborate," she said, clearly fretting.

"Are you always such a worrywart?" Bending, Zeke plugged in the tree lights.

"I never considered myself a worrier. Everyone thinks I'm practical. For sure you're into the commercial aspects of Christmas. You bought more lights."

"Maybe it comes from spending so many years on military bases, missing home at the holidays."

"I never thought of that. Sorry… I didn't even plan a traditional meal."

"It's okay," Zeke said, handing her a package. "Maybe next year."

Knowing she wouldn't be here next year made this exchange of gifts more awkward. "Here, open yours, too." She passed him a gaily wrapped box, realizing he must have wrapped the one he'd handed her. It wasn't in a box, so she could tell immediately it was a picture frame. She tore open the overly taped paper, expecting to see a snowy owl the way Zeke had planned to send his mother. The picture in the lovely frame brought instant tears to her eyes. It was a snapshot of her in her grandfather's chair. She'd fallen asleep while working on a dollhouse. Orion dozed in the crook of her arm. His pink ears touched her chin.

"Why are you crying?" Zeke asked, leaning over to frown at the item. "I thought it came out good."

"It's wonderful," she blubbered, hugging it to her breast.

Zeke smiled and lightly brushed her tears away. Sitting back, he opened his gift. "Hey, this belt is great. I saw them in Tawana's booth and intended to buy one when I went back for Seth's vest. She'd sold all the belts. Thanks." He leaned in again and kissed her cheek. "You have one more gift," he said, setting a soft package in her lap.

Flustered by the intimacy of the moment, Myra quickly ripped into it, figuring to find gloves. Once again Zeke had shocked her. "Ooh, you got Orion a new cape."

"I had Jewell knit it to replace the one the owl made off with. I tried to explain what I wanted when I went over to her booth. This one's woven tighter and closes with Velcro to make it easier to remove if another owl grabs Orion." Zeke gazed expectantly at Myra.

His easy mention of Jewell combined with all the thought he'd put into these gifts left Myra weepy. She burst into tears and didn't want Zeke to console her.

"Myra, honey, what's wrong? Do you hate it? I don't understand."

Getting up, she held the gifts close. "They're too perfect. I...I need to be alone." And she fled to her bedroom, where she sobbed out her sorrow. She wouldn't take Orion out to the fields for another alfalfa harvest, because they'd be gone. Where, she had no idea. The truth of it was that Zeke didn't need her. He had Jewell. The warm way he spoke of her help with the gift drove Myra's pain deeper.

But once she emptied out all her tears, it also served as a catalyst for her to buck up and prepare for her ultimate separation from the ranch, from Zeke and from all of her friends in Snowy Owl Crossing. When she finally left her room, she was able to present to Zeke a new, coolly detached woman.

CHRISTMAS WAS A turning point in the weather, too. Where for months they'd been plagued with ice and snow, rains came to melt the snow and turn everything into mud.

Zeke sensed Myra withdrawing, but he wasn't able to put his finger on why. She still did more than her fair share of chores inside and out. She continued to explain the work that needed to be done in terms he was able to jot down in his notebook. But her usual warmth was missing. And the sparkle he loved. It was as if the long winter had sucked joy out of her. He was afraid to bring it up, afraid he'd make her cry again.

EMERGING FROM THE third week in January where Zeke felt he and Myra were drifting further apart instead of growing closer as he'd envisioned before Christmas, he finally had to ask her. "Myra, you seem preoccupied. What's wrong?"

"I'm busy bringing heavies to the corral by the barn so when calving starts in earnest we'll be ready for any event. Up to now you've seen three calves born, and they were normal. You're about to get baptism by fire."

"Uh. Okay. I assume heavies are the heifers about to give birth."

"Bingo. Give the man a Kewpie doll." Tightening Cayenne's cinch, she rode off.

Zeke wasn't sure if he should get Ember and follow. But he wasn't imagining Myra's frostiness.

Deciding his frustration had gone on long enough, he thought he'd ask Eric what was going on. Myra spoke often with her brother. Perhaps their folks were having some problems at Rolling Acres and she didn't feel right sharing that news. Pulling out his phone, he put distance between himself and the barn, lest Myra return unexpectedly.

"Eric? Hi, it's Zeke. Sorry to bother you on a busy workday, but we haven't touched base in a while. Since we're about to be buried in calving, I assume you are, as well."

"Yeah. It's been a wild January. We're up to our ears in mud. Myra said you are, too. She also said you're turning into a real rancher, Zeke."

"Really? She hasn't been that forthright with me. In fact, that's why I'm calling." Zeke quickly laid out his observations and concerns. He finished and Eric didn't speak.

"Hey, buddy, did I lose you?"

"No. Zeke, listen. You didn't hear this from me, okay? Myra made me promise not to say a word, but you sound as if you care about her."

"I do. I care a lot. Is she ill? Tell me. I want to help."

"She's sick at heart. She wanted the Flying Owl. It rocked her world when our folks signed the ranch over to you. Myra hoped you'd give up and go away, and I think she figured you'd sell to her. I wish I loved this place as much as she loves that one. She knows now it'll never belong to her. If you want my advice, leave her alone to grieve. She promised you she'd stay through calving and she will. Oh, hey, Dad's calling me. I've gotta dash. Keep what I told you between us or she'll wring my neck. Bye."

Zeke found himself holding a dead phone, staring into space. He felt as if he'd been kicked in the gut. Eric's words had landed with more force than when he'd been kicked by the heifer. Now, at least, he had an answer. How had he been so blind? Myra would never fall for him as long as he stood between her and her greater desire to own the ranch. Worse, she didn't need him. She'd handled the Flying Owl fine before he showed up. And she could do it again.

He went to the house for coffee and saw Orion rooting around in his pen. Zeke picked him up. Dang, but he'd let this little fellow become his pet, too. Scratching between Orion's ears, Zeke set him down again. He was the interloper in this household.

In rehab he'd met and gotten to be friends with a colonel who'd lost a leg. Stewart Redding was a former Montana lawyer who went home to rebuild his private practice. Zeke had his number. Stewart said if Zeke ever needed legal advice, to call. He didn't need advice; he needed someone to regift the ranch to Myra.

Before he could have regrets, he phoned the colonel.

Making such an exchange would be far simpler than Zeke imagined. He needed to fax a copy of his deed to Stew along with his address. In two or three weeks, Redding would return the new deed to him by mail. That meant he could stay and help out through calving, and be out of Myra's hair for good soon after.

Zeke worried that he'd had too much time on his hands to reflect and be miserable. The next day he drove to town and went to the library to fax off the deed. A day later, calving hit with a vengeance.

"I don't know where you got off to yesterday," Myra finally snapped after the birth of two healthy calves. "Added to a seven-day-a-week schedule feeding stock, this is a twenty-four-hour-a-day process. I'll take nights because I've done it before and know what problems can crop up. I'll know if the temperature drops to where a cow needs to birth in the barn

instead of in the corral. I suggest you call and ask
Eddie Four Bear or Aaron Younger to work alongside
you six to eight hours a day for the next few weeks.
They're both old hands at this."

"You're saying you haven't taught me enough?"

"You've done great so far, and to date no cow has
abandoned her offspring. You haven't had to watch
me pull a stuck calf or turn one. But…I plan to leave
the day after the last calf drops, so you may want to
dicker a price with the guys to help you ear tag babies. That needs to happen ASAP. And after that, the
branding. Then you'll move the herd up into the foothills to the leased pasture."

Zeke opened his mouth to beg her to stay. A look
on her face stopped him, so he dug out his cell phone.
A few minutes later he garnered Myra's attention.
"Eddie and Aaron have jobs until March. Eddie says
Luke Elkhorn took a semester off to earn money for
tuition. Whaddya think? Eddie vouches for Luke."

"It's your call, Zeke," Myra said, going back to a
cow pacing with her tail stuck straight out behind her,
a sure indication she was in active labor.

FOR THE FIRST three weeks of February, Zeke and
Myra passed one another without speaking, usually
in the kitchen, where one stumbled awake as the other
dumped a thermos and yawned off to bed. A few
times they both fed Orion, which he loved.

Zeke made a point to check the mail every day.
It wasn't hard since Myra caught her sleep then. His

package came from the lawyer on a day he and Luke were kept busier than they'd ever been. Luke had to teach him how to turn a breech calf, then he went home.

Zeke tossed the envelope on his bedroom dresser and piled the remainder of the mail on the kitchen counter. Myra had left him a note saying she'd sent a check for grass seed, and he'd need to pick it up from the feed store.

He asked about it next time he saw her.

"Don't worry about it. You won't seed pens until after you move the herd. And there's still a possibility of a late storm. In fact, the almanac predicts falling temps and maybe a norther by the end of next week. I hope it holds off until then. At that point we should only have a few stragglers to birth. Things are going exceedingly well. You haven't lost a single calf. Better, there are no orphans."

"Luke said the same."

"Yeah, but this morning at dawn I went out to bury some of the clutter that built up from calving. I saw two wolves slinking around, so I set out smudge pots along the pen perimeter. If we burn them a few nights, the wolves will likely give up."

"I had no idea. Are you safe riding out there alone at night?" Zeke circled his fingers around Myra's wrist to keep her from dashing away.

"I'm fine. If you run into wildlife, clap your hands and shout." She freed her arm and left the room, saying she was asleep on her feet.

Thursday of the following week, shortly after daybreak they met again in the kitchen. Zeke asked about the wolves and noted Luke had replenished the firepots.

"I only saw wolves that one time. You probably noticed the herd gathers in the center of the enclosures. All of them except new heifers know when the pots are lit it's time to circle the wagons, so to speak."

"Ah, I'll keep that in mind. Say, Jewell phoned last night to see if we needed her to check any calves. She was at Hank's ranch. He had a sick cow and she brought antibiotics. If we need her, you should give her a shout-out. Tomorrow she and Tawana are going to band owl chicks. But she'd drop by here on her way back to her clinic."

Myra stifled a yawn. "I don't need her for the cows. But give her a call. You probably want to see her."

"Why would I want to see her?" Zeke straightened from dumping used coffee grounds into the garbage can. "Luke said our calves are all healthy. One cow wandered off from her calf, but Luke and I scrammed her back, and she recognized her baby."

"I assumed you two haven't gotten together since you went to town two or three weeks ago. That's a long time to not see your girlfriend." Myra rinsed her thermos, set it upside down on a paper towel to drain and headed off.

"Wait." Zeke scratched his head. "I haven't seen Jewell since I ordered Orion's cape at the bazaar. Uh, well, she did introduce me to Carl Meyer at the newspaper. You mentioned him. Jewell wanted to see my photos of the snowy owls. She asked to buy a few, so I traded her for the knitting."

Myra studied Zeke through sleepy eyes. "Christmas Day you said—" Breaking off, she covered a huge yawn then rubbed the center of her forehead. "Never mind. My brain isn't awake. Let's leave it this way. Unless something drastic happens during your shift today, we don't need Jewell's medical expertise. And if all goes well and we wind down calving by the weekend and I'm out of here, I plan to stop in town and tell everyone goodbye."

"We need to talk first, Myra," Zeke said, starting after her.

She held up a hand. "We'll have to carve out a time later. I know the money from the fall sale is in the ranch account and we haven't resolved a split." She backed through the door. "Truly, Zeke, my brain is mush, and I'm dead on my feet."

He pursed his lips to one side then waved her away. "What I have to talk about is important. Let's wait till we're both awake."

The next morning Zeke rose early, determined to give Myra the deed and tell her of his own plans to leave. Prior to retiring for the night, he'd looked the papers over to be sure everything was in order. He packed most of his clothes in the duffels he'd arrived with. He, not Myra, would be gone by the weekend.

Standing at the kitchen window, he was surprised

to see there'd been a massive shift in weather since he went to bed. Angry black clouds occluded the sky. Obviously the temperature had dropped, because Orion objected to going out on the porch through his doggie door. He'd push his snout out, squeal and return to hide under his quilt.

Aware the pig needed to use his litter box, Zeke picked him up and carried him out. Wind blew sleet into the screened room. Orion took care of business and darted back inside, leaving Zeke alone and shivering.

He dashed back in and had to push hard to shut the outer door. As he turned to the coffeemaker, he noticed a paper on the fridge. It was a note addressed to him.

Zeke, it's 4:00 a.m. The storm I told you the almanac predicted has hit. I went to bring in the last pregnant heifer but I found a portion of fence down and maybe twenty head of stock had wandered out. I saddled Cayenne and drove them all back in and repaired the fence. But the pregnant heifer is still loose somewhere. It's five now. A bit lighter, but colder. I'm afraid freezing rain will cover her tracks. I'm going after her. Heading northeast. Like I said, she's our last to deliver. I'm determined we'll have a perfect record. Myra.

Zeke held the note for a minute. The kitchen clock said almost six o'clock, meaning she'd been gone an hour. Unless she'd returned with the heifer and had her in the barn awaiting the delivery.

Darn the Montana weather. He hadn't needed his heavy jacket the past few days and last night he'd packed it. He debated about fixing coffee to take to Myra. If she was in the cold barn she could use a hot drink. On the other hand—well, he didn't want to think about the other hand.

Hurrying into his room, he unpacked his winter jacket and found his heavy gloves. This day called for a hat with earflaps. The one Myra first loaned him still sat on a shelf above the coatrack. Once suited up for the cold, Zeke battled wind-driven ice to reach the barn.

One look around and he knew Myra hadn't returned. Cayenne's stall was empty. Given the changed weather, he needed to make the early feed run. They'd removed the snowplow from the tractor several weeks ago, but because they still supplemented feeding, the trailer remained hooked up.

Zeke began loading bales, telling himself Myra would be back before he finished rounds. Since coming here, he'd been getting stronger, but he soon discovered that to fill the trailer by himself took a hefty toll on his left arm. Picking up the last bale left him in pain. Perhaps the frigid weather had something to do with his hurting again.

Still no Myra.

The drive out to the big pasture was slow going.

He had to stop the tractor, break open bales and pitch hay into the enclosure at intervals.

It wasn't until he fed and checked on cow-calf pairs in the three smaller corrals that he realized how much time had lapsed. His watch said 9:00 a.m. Four hours had gone by. There was still no sign of Myra.

He returned the equipment to the barn and stood in the doorway gazing toward the northeast. He'd seen her boot tracks at a section of newly repaired fence. In spite of the sleet, a lot of areas remained muddy. Zeke rubbed his aching arm, trying to decide what to do. Now he wished he hadn't let Luke take the day off.

Then all at once he saw Cayenne plodding toward him.

But hold on. Plodding wasn't right. Limping was more like it.

Zeke ran out to meet the horse and saw she was riderless. She had gashes across her knees. Blood dripped down her legs. The saddle sat askew and she kept stepping on one loose rein.

Terror smacked Zeke even as he led the mare into the barn. Obviously something bad had happened to Myra. His mind immediately went to a wolf attack. But would wolves only leave banged-up knees? Had Cayenne stumbled and fallen?

He removed the saddle when he heard a vehicle pull up. Hoping someone was bringing Myra home, Zeke dropped the saddle and ran outside. Jewell emerged from her pickup.

"Hey, Zeke, Tawana and I had to abandon our plan

to band owls today. It's too slick to get up to where they nest." Then she stared at him. "You look awful. Sorry, that's a horrible thing to say by way of greeting, but is something wrong?"

Zeke clasped her arm and yanked her into the barn, showing her Cayenne. He dispensed a short version of Myra's note, then said the horse had come in bloodied and alone.

"So Myra's out in this storm someplace without a way to get home? We need to call around and organize a search party. Usually it takes an hour or so to gather one."

Zeke clapped a palm over her phone. "You take care of Cayenne. I'll saddle Ember and go find her. If I don't pick up her tracks, I'll call you."

"Zeke, that's foolish. Do you have any idea where to look?"

"Her note said she headed northeast. I saw her tracks by the fence. Now I have Cayenne's tracks, which are fresher. I did this kind of thing in the military," he said, cinching the saddle tight before adding a bridle.

"Okay," Jewell said. "But northeast from here are a lot of deep ravines. Take a blanket and water in case she's injured. I'll treat Cayenne until you get back or call. Come to think of it, why hasn't Myra phoned home?"

Zeke frowned as he tied lariats around a blanket bedroll. "Don't dredge up trouble. She's going to be fine," he said harshly, swinging into the saddle.

Jewell placed a hand on the bridle for a moment. "You love her, don't you, Zeke?"

He didn't respond.

"If I'm right, why are you letting her leave? Luke told Tawana that Myra will be gone for good this weekend."

"She's not going anywhere," he stated firmly. "Turn loose, Jewell, so I can bring her home where she belongs."

Offering a self-satisfied smile and a double thumbs-up, Jewell stepped aside and let Zeke leave the barn.

Chapter Twelve

Zeke galloped to where Myra had repaired the fence. The tracks were clear. He turned northeast, but sleet soon hampered his ability to see well. Then Cayenne's tracks intersected larger, deeper ones. This could be where Myra picked up the trail of the pregnant heifer.

Pausing at intervals, he called her name. Ice crystals stung his face as wind drove her name back down his throat. Everything remained eerily quiet.

All at once the terrain got rocky. Tracks disappeared. Farther uphill were scattered trees, but dropping away on his left side were the ravines Jewell warned about. A knot formed in Zeke's belly. He had ridden roughly two miles up a vertical incline without finding Myra. By then he was hoarse from yelling for her.

Reaching a fork in the trail, he dismounted. No tracks. Had he lost them? Had he taken a wrong turn? He remounted, panic gripping his throat.

Suddenly a low-flying snowy owl swooped directly over him sounding the *krek-krek* Myra said was an alarm. Since the bird flew down from the left fork,

Zeke judged it a sign. For all he knew, worse danger lay ahead. Regardless, he urged Ember forward.

Evergreens dotting the granite-pocked slope offered some relief from the diminishing sleet. Zeke had his head tucked into his chest to ward off wind when Ember rounded an abrupt corner and kicked rocks over a precipice. The stones rattled down a shear drop-off, causing Zeke to rein in fast.

Sitting to still his racing heart, he spotted a lone heifer. She wasn't pregnant, which stole hope that this was the heavy Myra mentioned in her note. The silly cow languished out in the weather, bawling at nothing Zeke could see.

Passing by, he looked her over but didn't see any injuries. However, she bore the Flying Owl brand. He renewed his hoarse shouts for Myra.

His first call echoed back from the ravine. A second one resulted in a responding thin cry—or so he thought. A muffled "help" merged with a louder bawl from the heifer, who plodded closer to the rim.

Zeke vaulted from his saddle again. Looping Ember's reins around a spindly pine, he cupped his hands at his mouth and at the cliff he yelled Myra's name. This time he heard an unmistakable response directly below a crumbled area that had fallen away.

His heart thundered as he dropped and lay on his belly. Leaning out as far as he dared, he spotted Myra huddled on a narrow outcrop some ten feet below. Sheltered in her arms was a newborn calf. At first a burst of joy stole his voice.

"Zeke, is it really you?" she shouted. "Thank heaven you saw my note."

"Cayenne came home with bloody knees," he managed to say.

"Oh no, is she badly hurt?"

"Jewell stopped by just as she limped in. She'll be fine."

"Good. The heifer delivered, but didn't accept her baby. I thought she'd follow if I carried her calf. I tried to mount Cayenne, but she stumbled. It was hailing and windy. I didn't realize we were so near the edge."

"Let's see what I can do to get you out of this mess."

"It's a really steep slope. I tried grabbing a bush to climb up, but the granite is as slick as glass."

"I have ropes. If I tie them together they'll reach you." He scooted back, stood up and unwound two lariats he'd tied around the bedroll. His major worry was that his bad left arm lacked the strength to pull her and the calf up.

"Is there a way to send the calf up separately?" he called, looking around to see what he might use for added leverage.

"No. She's just a baby."

"Okay, look, I'll make a loop in one end of this rope and snake it down to you. I'll wrap it around a pine. It's scraggly, but far enough back from the unstable shelf I think it'll hold. You're going to have to climb some if you can, Myra. I hurt my left arm feeding stock earlier. My only power is from my right side."

"Zeke, I'm sorry. Can Jewell round up some guys to help?"

"I didn't get her number. But she wondered why you didn't phone me."

"I dropped my cell trying to get it out of my pocket without losing my grip on the calf. This protrusion isn't very wide."

He heard her concern, which reopened a hole in his stomach. But he'd been in worse fixes in Afghanistan. He would make this rescue. "I'm sending down the rope. Hook it around your waist. When it's tight, hang on and I'll pull."

"Ready," she called a few seconds later, her voice wobbly.

Zeke gritted his teeth and forced his injured left arm to help with a hand-over-hand tug-of-war. At least it felt like a tug-of-war. He braced his feet against the skinny tree, praying it would hold. It was slow going. A strand of the rope frayed and split. In spite of the cold, he began to sweat.

After what seemed an interminable amount of time, he saw Myra's hat peek over the rim and his heart kicked. He wound the thinning rope around his body for added support, gave a giant yank, and like a cork popping out of a bottle, Myra and the calf exploded from the ravine and flattened Zeke.

For a time they all lay panting atop chilly, muddy pine needles.

The heifer plodded up and began licking her calf. Myra set the babe on its feet and threw herself at Zeke, pressing kisses all over his face. "You did it," she babbled. "You saved us. Saving Odells must be your lot in life. You've now rescued both of my parents' kids from sure death. What in the world can they give you this time to show their appreciation? What can I give you?"

Zeke scooted upright and kept kissing Myra. He finally took a breath and held her head still. "This is a helluva time to start this conversation. Seriously, Myra, the only thing you can give me…all that I want is—" he hesitated and brushed a tattered glove over her eyebrows "—is you. I might have lost you today without ever telling you I love you."

Myra stared at him with saucer eyes. "Zeke, when you fell backward did you hit your head on a rock? You're talking nutty. I'm leaving, remember?"

"My head's fine and you're not going anywhere," he said gruffly. He tried to hold her, but was forced to let her wiggle away. Distributing his weight on his good arm, he got up. "This isn't something to settle here. We need to get the cow, calf and us home. Can Ember carry our combined weight?"

"Probably. Let me mount, then hand me the calf. Keep Ember well back from the brink when you climb aboard."

"Definitely. Do you know Jewell's number? We should call and tell her you're okay and she can go home. You and I have business to settle." Zeke passed her his phone.

Taking it, Myra punched in numbers. "Jewell, it's Myra. I got the new calf and Zeke's bringing us home. Is Cayenne okay?" She listened a moment. "Ah, good. No, you don't need to wait if you have another call. Bye." She returned Zeke's phone and swung into the saddle. "Wrap the calf in that bedroll I see on the ground."

He did and handed the bundle to her over the mother's protests. Ember danced around, making Zeke's mounting difficult. He finally managed and the heifer lumbered along beside them. Zeke held Myra close. It felt good. It felt right.

The gelding stepped out briskly. In the improved weather they soon reached the juncture where the two paths merged.

"How did you know which trail to take?" Myra turned slightly toward Zeke.

"I heard a snowy owl. It flew down from the left fork. I took it as a sign—a good omen. I've developed a real liking for snowy owls."

"I'm lucky. The right-hand trail is wider. It leads to the summer pasture. Had you taken it you'd never have found us."

"I wouldn't have quit looking. I meant what I said back there. I love you, Myra." He felt her stiffen. "I haven't known how to tell you."

"What about Jewell?"

"What about her? This isn't the first time you've

mentioned her like she means something to me. I barely know Jewell."

"Lila and I saw you two laughing and talking as you walked along Main Street. And at the bazaar you two went off together."

"I told you she made Orion's cape in exchange for a photo of the owls. That's all it was."

"It doesn't matter. I'm all packed. I'm going home to Rolling Acres later today."

"If anyone leaves the Flying Owl, it'll be me. But I'm not going far. I intended to have this talk in the warmth of the house, but as we're in it now I'll go ahead and tell you I've deeded the ranch to you."

"What?" Myra whirled so fast she almost dropped the calf, who cried and caused the heifer to trot up and bawl her disapproval. "Why, when you've proven yourself in so many ways? Plus, I heard you tell your brother how much you love living here."

"Don't you know you're the biggest part of that? Maybe I should have guessed how much you wanted the ranch. I didn't. Not until I asked Eric if he had any idea why you were so down in the dumps. I swear I had no idea the ranch caused a divide between us that widened day by day."

"I'll kill him. I told Eric not to share that with you or our folks. I confided in him at a low point. I was hurt that the folks didn't discuss it with me. On the other hand I never told them how I felt. I'm so ashamed you found out."

"Don't be. I wormed it out of Eric. Just know it means everything to me to see you happy. Look, we're home." He pointed at the barn. "Let's get the cow and calf in where it's warm. Are you okay to feed them while I take care of Ember?" Myra nodded. "Then we'll go to the house and I'll get you the deed I had drawn up." Reining in, he got off and lifted Myra and the calf down.

"I won't take it, Zeke. How can you possibly love me knowing I wanted you to go away from the beginning? I shoved crappy jobs at you hoping you'd fail."

He leaned over and kissed her lips. Drawing back slowly, he said, "It's the crazy kind of love that got hold of me and won't let go. But in case you think it's all about the ranch, I swear if you sold everything and moved to Timbuktu I'd follow you."

She touched a finger to her mouth, then did the same to his before she tightened her hold on the calf and led the heifer into the barn's interior.

Zeke took care of Ember, checked Cayenne and fed them both. He and Myra completed their chores at the same time.

As they trekked to the house, he casually slipped an arm around her waist and was pleased she didn't shove him away.

"I know you hate what I did to the house," he said, helping her off with her jacket after they went inside.

"It's more that I didn't want to like it. I love the improvements."

Smiling, he guided her to the kitchen, where he'd left the deed. Seating her at the table, he handed her the documents. "Read it all, including the fine print. I'll make some coffee to warm you up."

Myra pushed the packet aside. "This isn't the answer, Zeke. If I accepted this I'd never be happy here. Guilt would eat me up. Undo it."

"Why?"

She clasped her hands. "I'd see you no matter where I turned. Chores went so much easier when we did them together. I'd miss you," she admitted, her voice quivery.

"You'd really miss me?"

"Yes. Do I have to say I've fallen for you, too? I thought you could tell I was eaten up with jealousy thinking you and Jewell were an item."

"Then what does it matter whose name is on the deed? I don't want to get the cart before the horse, but can you picture the Flying Owl belonging to Mr. and Mrs. Maxwell?"

"You want to give it to your parents?"

"No!" Zeke pulled Myra out of her chair and into his arms. "Oh, I see that smile. You're teasing. I get it now. You need me to say, Myra, honey, will you marry me?"

She snuggled against him. "Well, that way we could put the ranch in a trust so it'd be there for the next generation. Be there in the future for our family."

"That crossed my mind a few times, too. I was so afraid you'd turn me down. I was afraid you'd think I wanted you to stay only for the sake of saving the ranch."

Myra clutched the front of Zeke's shirt. "We both almost foolishly let the ranch stand in the way of our love."

"So you'll marry me?"

"Yes." She rose on tiptoe and kissed him.

"How soon?" he asked when they both finally had to breathe. "Seth wants to visit in April. I'd like him to be my best man. Maybe my folks can come. How's April for ranchers? Will your family be able to leave Rolling Acres for a day?"

"May would be better. We'd have calves' tagged and branded, and stock moved to summer pasture. But maybe your brother can't stay that long."

"He'll stay awhile. Didn't you tell me once that people found sapphires in old gold mines around here? On the other hand, I don't want him underfoot. Especially if we're not going away for a honeymoon." Zeke tightened his arms around Myra.

She looped hers around his waist. "Lila runs a B and B. Can we rent your brother a room there?"

"I like how you think. A May wedding, then." They kissed until Orion turned over his empty bowl with a bang and broke them apart.

Laughing, they fed him together.

"You said you only wanted me to be happy," Myra murmured. "Knowing we'll spend all our days and nights together in a place we both love does that."

"For me, too. Let's start calling family and friends to spread our good news."

Myra threw her arms around Zeke's neck. "Growing up I dreamed of an Old West–style wedding. I'd love to put planning ours in the capable hands of the Artsy Ladies."

"Perfect," Zeke agreed, lifting her off her feet.

Epilogue

May in the Crossing brought intermittent blue skies and rain that carpeted the hills in green. May also brought snowy-owl chicks, which Jewell banded in orange to make counting next winter easier. And May brought Myra and Zeke's wedding.

She had requested her mother sew her an ivory satin dress with mutton sleeves. Online she ordered a big-brimmed hat with a pink plume to match a ribbon belt and new cowgirl boots. A nosegay of baby roses rounded out her Old West look. Her matron of honor, Lila, wore a burgundy dress with a bustle. Jewell, Tawana, Shelley and Mindy were rays of sunshine in jonquil yellow.

Zeke and his attendants resembled old-time gamblers in gray pin-striped pants, white shirts, black satin vests, string ties and black elastic armbands.

They held the ceremony at Myra's church. A reception catered by Lila's mom would follow immediately at the grange hall so guests could spread out, talk, laugh, eat, dance and get to know Zeke's family and friends.

Once the church filled, a pianist began to play, and a hush fell over the crowd as Lila started down the aisle on the arm of Zeke's brother, Seth, blond haired and green eyed in contrast to his twin's dark hair and hazel eyes.

Jewell accompanied Myra's brother. Three of Zeke's former military buddies, one using a cane, escorted her other best friends to the front of the church, where the minister and Zeke emerged from a side room. He adjusted his string tie and fidgeted until Seth grinned and nudged him with the ring box—a tanzanite-and-diamond band Seth had helped Zeke pick out.

Myra absorbed everything as she waited with her dad at the back of the sanctuary.

"Honey, you're positively glowing today," he said.

"I'm happier than I've ever been, Daddy."

"The old home place never looked so good, and Zeke's quick to give you all the credit."

"Not true. He remodeled inside the house."

"He meant how you handled stock growth. I'm late saying this, Myra, but I couldn't be more proud of how you revived that ranch. I felt awful for giving it to Zeke after discovering it should have rightfully been yours."

Smiling, Myra slid her arm through his. "But see how well it turned out."

"You have a big heart, girl. You so pleased your mother by asking her to sew your wedding dress. She was afraid you'd never forgive her for nagging you to return to teaching."

Myra straightened his boutonniere. "I should've spoken up. Listen, there's our music. Are you ready to give me away?"

"With my record, should I give anything again?" He paused at the satin runner, his eyes questioning.

"Daddy, I love Zeke. And he loves me. I've never been so sure of anything than I am that marrying him is right."

"I see that by looking at you both," he said and moved them onto a trail of rose petals that led down the aisle to where Zeke greeted Myra with open arms.

* * * * *

MY FUNNY VALENTINE

Debbie Macomber

One

Dianne Williams had the scenario all worked out. She'd be pushing her grocery cart down the aisle of the local grocery store and gazing over the frozen-food section when a tall, dark, handsome man would casually stroll up to her and with a brilliant smile say, "Those low-cal dinners couldn't possibly be for you."

She'd turn to him and suddenly the air would fill with the sounds of a Rimsky-Korsakov symphony, or bells would chime gently in the distance—Dianne didn't have that part completely figured out yet—and in that instant she would know deep in her heart that this was the man she was meant to spend the rest of her life with.

All right, Dianne was willing to admit, the scenario was childish and silly, the kind of fantasy only a teenage girl should dream up. But reentering the dating scene after umpteen years of married life created problems Dianne didn't even want to consider.

Three years earlier, Dianne's husband had left her

and the children to find himself. Instead he found a SYT (sweet young thing), promptly divorced Dianne and moved across the country. It hurt; in fact, it hurt more than anything Dianne had ever known, but she was a survivor, and always had been. Perhaps that was the reason Jack didn't seem to suffer a single pang of guilt about abandoning her to raise Jason and Jill on her own.

Her children, Dianne had discovered, were incredibly resilient. Within a year of their father's departure, they were urging her to date. Their father did, they reminded Dianne with annoying frequency. And if it wasn't her children pushing her toward establishing a new relationship, it was her own dear mother.

When it came to locating Mr. Right for her divorced daughter, Martha Janes knew no equal. For several months, Dianne had been subjected to a long parade of single men. Their unmarried status, however, seemed their sole attribute.

After dinner with the man who lost his toupee on a low-hanging chandelier, Dianne had insisted enough was enough and she would find her own dates.

This proved to be easier said than done. Dianne hadn't gone out once in six months. Now, within the next week, she needed a man. Not just any man, either. One who was tall, dark and handsome. It would be a nice bonus if he was exceptionally wealthy, too, but she didn't have time to be choosy. The Valentine's dinner at the Port Blossom Community Center was Saturday night. *This* Saturday night.

From the moment the notice was posted six weeks earlier, Jason and Jill had insisted she attend. Surely their mother could find a date given that much time! And someone handsome to boot. It seemed a matter of family honor.

Only now the dinner was only days away and Dianne was no closer to achieving her goal.

"I'm home," Jason yelled as he walked into the house. The front door slammed in his wake, hard enough to shake the kitchen windows. He threw his books on the counter, moved directly to the refrigerator, opened the door and stuck the upper half of his fourteen-year-old body inside.

"Help yourself to a snack," Dianne said, smiling and shaking her head.

Jason reappeared with a chicken leg clenched between his teeth like a pirate's cutlass. One hand was filled with a piece of leftover cherry pie while the other held a platter of cold fried chicken.

"How was school?"

He shrugged, set down the pie and removed the chicken leg from his mouth. "Okay, I guess."

Dianne knew what was coming next. It was the same question he'd asked her every afternoon since the notice about the dinner had been posted.

"Do you have a date yet?" He leaned against the counter as his steady gaze pierced her. Her son's eyes could break through the firmest resolve, and cut through layers of deception.

"No date," she answered cheerfully. At least as cheerfully as she could under the circumstances.

"The dinner's this Saturday night."

As if she needed reminding. "I know. Stop worrying, I'll find someone."

"Not just anyone," Jason said emphatically, as though he were speaking to someone with impaired hearing. "He's got to make an impression. Someone decent."

"I know, I know."

"Grandma said she could line you up with—"

"No," Dianne interrupted. "I categorically refuse to go on any more of Grandma's blind dates."

"But you don't have the time to find your own now. It's—"

"I'm working on it," she insisted, although she knew she wasn't working very hard. She *was* trying to find someone to accompany her to the dinner, only she'd never dreamed it would be this difficult.

Until the necessity of attending this affair had been forced upon her, Dianne hadn't been aware of how limited her choices were. In the past couple of years, she'd met few single men, apart from the ones her mother had thrown at her. There were a couple of unmarried men at the office where she was employed part-time as a bookkeeper. Neither, however, was anyone she'd seriously consider dating. They were both too suave, too urbane—too much like Jack. Besides, problems might arise if she were to mingle her social life with her business one.

The front door opened and closed again, a little less noisily this time.

"I'm home!" ten-year-old Jill announced from the entryway. She dropped her books on the floor and marched toward the kitchen. Then she paused on the threshold and planted both hands on her hips as her eyes sought out her brother. "You better not have eaten all the leftover pie. I want some, too, you know."

"Don't grow warts worrying about it," Jason said sarcastically. "There's plenty."

Jill's gaze swiveled from her brother to her mother. The level of severity didn't diminish one bit. Dianne met her daughter's eye and mouthed the words along with her.

"Do you have a date yet?"

Jason answered for Dianne. "No, she doesn't. And she's got five days to come up with a decent guy and all she says is that she's working on it."

"Mom…" Jill's brown eyes filled with concern.

"Children, please."

"Everyone in town's going," Jill claimed, as if Dianne wasn't already aware of that. "You've *got* to be there, you've just got to. I told all my friends you're going."

More pressure! That was the last thing Dianne needed. Nevertheless, she smiled serenely at her two children and assured them they didn't have a thing to worry about.

An hour or so later, while she was making dinner, she could hear Jason and Jill's voices in the living room. They were huddled together in front of the television, their heads close together. Plotting, it looked like, charting her barren love life. Doubtless deciding who their mother should take to the dinner. Probably the guy with the toupee.

"Is something wrong?" Dianne asked, standing in the doorway. It was unusual for them to watch television this time of day, but more unusual for them to be so chummy. The fact that they'd turned on the TV to drown out their conversation hadn't escaped her.

They broke guiltily apart.

"Wrong?" Jason asked, recovering first. "I was just talking to Jill, is all. Do you need me to do something?"

That offer alone was enough evidence to convict them both. "Jill, would you set the table for me?" she asked, her gaze lingering on her two children for another moment before she returned to the kitchen.

Jason and Jill were up to something. Dianne could only guess what. No doubt the plot they were concocting included their grandmother.

Sure enough, while Jill was setting the silverware on the kitchen table, Jason used the phone, stretching the cord as far as it would go and mumbling into the mouthpiece so there was no chance Dianne could overhear his conversation.

Dianne's suspicions were confirmed when her mother arrived shortly after dinner. And within minutes, Jason and Jill had deserted the kitchen, saying they had to get to their homework. Also highly suspicious behavior.

"Do you want some tea, Mom?" Dianne felt obliged to ask, dreading the coming conversation. It didn't take Sherlock Holmes to deduce that her children had called their grandmother hoping she'd find a last-minute date for Dianne.

"Don't go to any trouble."

This was her mother's standard reply. "It's no trouble," Dianne said.

"Then make the tea."

Because of her evening aerobics class—W.A.R. it was called, for Women After Results—Dianne had changed and was prepared to make a hasty exit.

While the water was heating, she took a white ceramic teapot from the cupboard. "Before you ask, and I know you will," she said with strained patience, "I haven't got a date for the Valentine's dinner yet."

Her mother nodded slowly as if Dianne had just announced something of profound importance. Martha was from the old school, and she took her time getting around to whatever was on her mind, usually preceding it with a long list of questions that hinted at the subject. Dianne loved her mother, but there wasn't anyone on this earth who could drive her crazier.

"You've still got your figure," Martha said, her expression serious. "That helps." She stroked her chin a couple of times and nodded. "You've got your father's brown eyes, may he rest in peace, and your hair is nice and thick. You can thank your grandfather for that. He had hair so thick—"

"Ma, did I mention I have an aerobics class tonight?"

Her mother's posture stiffened. "I don't want to bother you."

"It's just that I might have to leave before you say what you're obviously planning to say, and I didn't want to miss the reason for your unexpected visit."

Her mother relaxed, but just a little. "Don't worry. I'll say what must be said and then you can leave. Your mother's words are not as important as your exercise class."

An argument bubbled up like fizz from a can of soda, but Dianne successfully managed to swallow it. Showing any sign of weakness in front of her mother was a major tactical error. Dianne made the tea, then carried the pot over to the table and sat across from Martha.

"Your skin's still as creamy as—"

"Mom," Dianne said, "there's no need to tell me all this. I know my coloring is good. I also know I've still got my figure and that my hair is thick and that you approve of my keeping it long. You don't need to sell me on myself."

"Ah," Martha told her softly, "that's where you're wrong."

Dianne couldn't help it—she rolled her eyes. When Dianne was fifteen her mother would have slapped her hand, but now that she was thirty-three, Martha used more subtle tactics.

Guilt.

"I don't have many years left."

"Mom—"

"No, listen. I'm an old woman now and I have the right to say what I want, especially since the good Lord may choose to call me home at any minute."

Stirring a teaspoon of sugar into her tea offered Dianne a moment to compose herself. Bracing her elbows on the table, she raised the cup to her lips. "Just say it."

Her mother nodded, apparently appeased. "You've lost confidence in yourself."

"That's not true."

Martha's smile was meager at best. "Jack left you, and now you think there must be something wrong with you. But, Dianne, what you don't understand is that he would've gone if you were as beautiful as Marilyn Monroe. Jack's leaving had nothing to do with you and everything to do with Jack."

This conversation was taking a turn Dianne wanted to avoid. Jack was a subject she preferred not to discuss. As far as she could see, there wasn't any reason to peel back the scars and examine the wound at this late date. Jack was gone. She'd accepted it, dealt with it, and gone on with her life. The fact that her mother was even mentioning her ex-husband had taken Dianne by surprise.

"My goodness," Dianne said, checking her watch. "Look at the time—"

"Before you go," her mother said quickly, grabbing her wrist, "I met a nice young man this afternoon in the butcher's shop. Marie Zimmerman told me about him and I went to talk to him myself."

"Mom—"

"Hush and listen. He's divorced, but from what he said it was all his wife's fault. He makes blood sausage and insisted I try some. It was so good it practically melted in my mouth. I never tasted sausage so good. A man who makes sausage like that would be an asset to any family."

Oh, sweet heaven. Her mother already had her married to the guy!

"I told him all about you and he generously offered to take you out."

"Mother, *please.* I've already said I won't go out on any more blind dates."

"Jerome's a nice man. He's—"

"I don't mean to be rude, but I really have to leave now, or I'll be late." Hurriedly, Dianne stood, collected her coat, and called out to her children that she'd be back in an hour.

The kids didn't say a word.

It wasn't until she was in her car that Dianne realized they'd been expecting her to announce that she finally had a date.

Two

"Damn," Dianne muttered, scrambling through her purse for the tenth time. She knew it wasn't going to do the least bit of good, but she felt compelled to continue the search.

"Double damn," she said as she sct the bulky leather handbag on the hood of her car. Raindrops spattered all around her.

Expelling her breath, she stalked back into the Port Blossom Community Center and stood in front of the desk. "I seem to have locked my keys in my car," she told the receptionist. "Along with my cell."

"Oh, dear. Is there someone you can get in touch with?"

"I'm a member of the auto club so I can call them for help. I also want to call home and say I'll be late. So if you'll let me use the phone?"

"Oh, sure." The young woman smiled pleasantly, and lifted the phone onto the counter. "We close in fifteen minutes, you know."

A half hour later, Dianne was leaning impatiently against her car in the community center parking lot when a red tow truck pulled in. It circled the area, then eased into the space next to hers.

The driver, whom Dianne couldn't see in the dark, rolled down his window and stuck out his elbow. "Are you the lady who phoned about locking her keys in the car?"

"No. I'm standing out in the rain wearing a leotard for the fun of it," she muttered.

He chuckled, turned off the engine and hopped out of the driver's seat. "Sounds like this has been one of those days."

She nodded, suddenly feeling a stab of guilt at her churlishness. He seemed so friendly.

"Why don't you climb in my truck where it's nice and warm while I take care of this?" He opened the passenger-side door and gestured for her to enter.

She smiled weakly, and as she climbed in, said, "I didn't mean to snap at you just now."

He flashed her a grin. "No problem." She found herself taking a second look at him. He was wearing gray-striped coveralls and the front was covered with grease stains. His name, Steve, was embroidered in red across the top of his vest pocket. His hair, which was neatly styled, appeared to have been recently cut. His eyes were a warm shade of brown and—she searched for the right word—gentle, she decided.

After ensuring that she was comfortable in his truck, Steve walked around to the driver's side of her compact car and used his flashlight to determine the type of lock.

Dianne lowered the window. "I don't usually do things like this. I've never locked the keys in my car before—I don't know why I did tonight. Stupid."

He returned to the tow truck and opened the passenger door. "No one can be smart all the time," he said cheerfully. "Don't be so hard on yourself." He moved the seat forward a little and reached for a toolbox in the space behind her.

"I've had a lot on my mind lately," she said.

Straightening, he looked at her and nodded sympathetically. He had a nice face too, she noted, easy on the eyes. In fact, he was downright attractive. The coveralls didn't detract from his appeal, but actually suggested a certain ruggedness. He was thoughtful and friendly just when Dianne was beginning to think there wasn't anyone in the world who was. But then, standing in the dark and the rain might make anyone feel friendless, even though Port Blossom was a rural community with a warm, small-town atmosphere.

Steve went back to her car and began to fiddle with the lock. Unable to sit still, Dianne opened the truck door and climbed out. "It's the dinner that's got me so upset."

"The dinner?" Steve glanced up from his work.

"The Valentine's dinner the community center's sponsoring this Saturday night. My children are forcing me to go. I don't know for sure, but I think they've got money riding on it, because they're making it sound like a matter of national importance."

"I see. Why doesn't your husband take you?"

"I'm divorced," she said bluntly. "I suppose no one expects it to happen to them. I assumed after twelve years my marriage was solid, but it wasn't. Jack's remarried now, living in Boston." Dianne had no idea why she was rambling on like this, but once she'd opened her mouth, she couldn't seem to stop. She didn't usually relate the intimate details of her life to a perfect stranger.

"Aren't you cold?"

"I'm fine, thanks." That wasn't entirely true—she was a little chilled—but she was more worried about not having a date for the stupid Valentine's dinner than freezing to death. Briefly she wondered if Jason, Jill and her mother would accept pneumonia as a reasonable excuse for not attending.

"You're sure? You look like you're shivering."

She rubbed her palms together and ignored his question. "That's when my mother suggested Jerome."

"Jerome?"

"She seems to think I need help getting my feet wet."

Steve glanced up at her again, clearly puzzled.

"In the dating world," Dianne explained. "But I've had it with the dates she's arranged."

"Disasters?"

"Encounters of the worst kind. On one of them, the guy set his napkin on fire."

Steve laughed outright at that.

"Hey, it wasn't funny, trust me. I was mortified. He panicked and started waving it around in the air until the maitre d' arrived with a fire extinguisher and chaos broke loose."

Dianne found herself smiling at the memory of the unhappy episode. "Now that I look back on it, it was rather amusing."

Steve's gaze held hers. "I take it there were other disasters?"

"None I'd care to repeat."

"So your mother's up to her tricks again?"

Dianne nodded. "Only this time my kids are involved. Mom stumbled across this butcher who specializes in…well, never mind, that's not important. What is important is if I don't come up with a date in the next day or two, I'm going to be stuck going to this stupid dinner with Jerome."

"It shouldn't be so bad," he said. Dianne could hear the grin in his voice.

"How generous of you to say so." She crossed her arms over her chest. She'd orbited her vehicle twice before she spoke again.

"My kids are even instructing me on the kind of man they want me to date."

"Oh?"

Dianne wasn't sure he'd heard her. Her lock snapped free and he opened the door and retrieved her keys, which were in the ignition. He handed them to her, and with a thank-you, Dianne made a move to climb into her car.

"Jason and Jill—they're my kids—want me to go out with a tall, dark, handsome—" She stopped abruptly, thrusting out her arm as if to keep her balance.

Steve looked at her oddly. "Are you all right?"

Dianne brought her fingertips to her temple and nodded. "I think so..." She inhaled sharply and motioned toward the streetlight. "Would you mind stepping over there for a minute?"

"Me?" He pointed to himself as though he wasn't sure she meant him.

"Please."

He shrugged and did as she requested.

The idea was fast gaining momentum in her mind. He was certainly tall—at least six foot three, which was a nice complement to her own slender five ten. And he was dark—his hair appeared to be a rich shade of mahogany. As for the handsome part, she'd noticed that right off.

"Is something wrong?" he probed.

"No," Dianne said, grinning shyly—although what she was about to propose was anything but shy. "By the way, how old are you? Thirty? Thirty-one?"

"Thirty-five."

"That's good. Perfect." A couple of years older than she was. Yes, the kids would approve of that.

"Good? Perfect?" He seemed to be questioning her sanity.

"Married?" she asked.

"Nope. I never got around to it, but I came close once." His eyes narrowed suspiciously.

"That's even better. I don't suppose you've got a jealous girlfriend—or a mad lover hanging around looking for an excuse to murder someone?"

"Not lately."

Dianne sighed with relief. "Great."

"Your car door's open," he said, gesturing toward it. He seemed eager to be on his way. "All I need to do is write down your auto club number."

"Yes, I know." She stood there, arms folded, studying him in the light. He was even better-looking than she'd first thought. "Do you own a decent suit?"

He chuckled as if the question amused him. "Yes."

"I mean something really nice, not the one you wore to your high-school graduation."

"It's a really nice suit."

Dianne didn't mean to be insulting, but she had to have all her bases covered. "That's good," she said. "How would you like to earn an extra hundred bucks Saturday night?"

"I beg your pardon?"

"I'm offering you a hundred dollars to escort me to the Valentine's dinner here at the center."

Steve stared at her as though he suspected she'd escaped from a mental institution.

"Listen, I know this is a bit unusual," Dianne

rushed on, "but you're perfect. Well, not perfect, but you're exactly the kind of man the kids expect me to date, and frankly I haven't got time to do a whole lot of recruiting. Mr. Right hasn't showed up, if you know what I mean."

"I think I do."

"I need a date for one night. You fit the bill and you could probably use the extra cash. I realize it's not much, but a hundred dollars sounds fair to me. The dinner starts at seven and should be over by nine. I suspect fifty dollars an hour is more than you're earning now."

"Ah…"

"I know what you're thinking, but I promise you I'm not crazy. I've got a gold credit card, and they don't issue those to just anyone."

"What about a library card?"

"That, too, but I do have a book overdue. I was planning to take it back tomorrow." She started searching through her purse to prove she had both cards before she saw that he was teasing her.

"Ms. …"

"Dianne Williams," she said stepping forward to offer him her hand. His long, strong fingers wrapped around hers and he smiled, studying her for perhaps the first time. His eyes softened as he shook her hand. The gesture, though small, reassured Dianne that he was the man she wanted to take her to this silly dinner. Once more she found herself rushing to explain.

"I'm sure this all sounds crazy. I don't blame you

for thinking I'm a nutcase. But I'm not, really I'm not. I attend church every Sunday, do volunteer work at the grade school, and help coach a girls' soccer team in the fall."

"Why'd you pick me?"

"Well, that's a bit complicated, but you have nice eyes, and when you suggested I sit in your truck and get out of the rain—actually it was only drizzling—" she paused and inhaled a deep breath "—I realized you were a generous person, and you just might consider something this..."

"...weird," he finished for her.

Dianne nodded, then looked him directly in the eye. Her defenses were down, and there was nothing left to do but admit the truth.

"I'm desperate. No one but a desperate woman would make this kind of offer."

"Saturday night, you say?"

The way her luck was running, he'd suddenly remember he had urgent plans for the evening. Something important like dusting his bowling trophies.

"From seven to nine. No later, I promise. If you don't think a hundred is enough..."

"A hundred's more than generous."

She sagged with relief. "Does this mean you'll do it?"

Steve shook his head slowly, as though to suggest

he ought to have it examined for even contemplating her proposal.

"All right," he said after a moment. "I never could resist a damsel in distress."

Three

"Hello, everyone!" Dianne sang out as she breezed in the front door. She paused just inside the living room and watched as her mother and her two children stared openly. A sense of quiet astonishment pervaded the room. "Is something wrong?"

"What happened to you?" Jason cried. "You look awful!"

"You look like Little Orphan Annie, dear," her mother said, her hand working a crochet hook so fast the yarn zipped through her fingers.

"I phoned to tell you I'd be late," Dianne reminded them.

"But you didn't say anything about nearly drowning. What happened?"

"I locked my keys in the car—I already explained that."

Jill walked over to her mother, took her hand and led her to the hallway mirror. The image that greeted Dianne was only a little short of shocking. Her long thick hair hung in limp sodden curls over her shoulders. Her mascara, supposedly no-run, had dissolved into black tracks down her cheeks. She was drenched to the skin and looked like a prize the cat had dragged onto the porch.

"Oh, dear," she whispered. Her stomach muscles tightened as she recalled the odd glances Steve had given her, and his comment that it must be "one of those days." No wonder!

"Why don't you go upstairs and take a nice hot shower?" her mother said. "You'll feel worlds better."

Humbled, for more reasons than she cared to admit, Dianne agreed.

As was generally the rule, her mother was right. By the time Dianne reappeared a half hour later, dressed in her terry-cloth robe and fuzzy pink slippers, she felt considerably better.

Making herself a cup of tea, she reviewed the events of the evening. Even if Steve had agreed to attend the Valentine's dinner out of pity, it didn't matter. What did matter was the fact that she had a date. As soon as she told her family, they'd stop hounding her.

"By the way," she said as she carried her tea into the living room, "I have a date for Saturday night."

The room went still. Even the television sound seemed to fade into nothingness. Her two children and her mother did a slow turn, their faces revealing their surprise.

"Don't look so shocked," Dianne said with a light, casual laugh. "I told you before that I was working on it. No one seemed to believe I was capable of finding a date on my own. Well, that isn't the case."

"Who?" Martha demanded, her eyes disbelieving.

"Oh, ye of little faith," Dianne said, feeling only a small twinge of guilt. "His name is Steve Creighton."

"When did you meet him?"

"Ah…" Dianne realized she wasn't prepared for an inquisition. "A few weeks ago. We happened to bump into each other tonight, and he asked if I had a date for the dinner. Naturally I told him I didn't and he suggested we go together."

"Steve Creighton." Her mother repeated the name slowly, rolling the syllables over her tongue, as if trying to remember where she'd last heard it. Then she shook her head and resumed crocheting.

"You never said anything about this guy before." Jason's gaze was slightly accusing. He sat on the carpet, knees tucked under his chin.

"Of course I didn't. If I had, all three of you would be bugging me about him, just the way you are now."

Martha gave her ball of yarn a hard jerk. "How'd you two meet?"

Dianne wasn't ready for this line of questioning. She'd assumed letting her family know she had the necessary escort would've been enough to appease them. Silly of her.

They wanted details. Lots of details, and the only thing Dianne could do was make them up as she went along. She couldn't very well admit she'd only met

Steve that night and was so desperate for a date that she'd offered to pay him to escort her to the dinner.

"We met, ah, a few weeks ago in the grocery store," she explained haltingly, averting her gaze. She prayed that would satisfy their curiosity. But when she paused to sip her tea, the three faces were riveted on her.

"Go on," her mother urged.

"I... I was standing in the frozen-food section and... Steve was there, too, and...he smiled at me and introduced himself."

"What did he say after that?" Jill wanted to know, eager for the particulars. Martha shared her granddaughter's interest. She set her yarn and crochet hook aside, focusing all her attention on Dianne.

"After he introduced himself, he said surely those low-cal dinners couldn't be for me—that I looked perfect just the way I was." The words fell stiffly from her lips. She had to be desperate to divulge her own fantasy to her family like this.

All right, she *was* desperate.

Jill's shoulders rose with an expressive sigh. "How romantic!"

Jason, however, was frowning. "The guy sounds like a flake to me. A real man doesn't walk up to a woman and say something stupid like that."

"Steve's very nice."

"Maybe, but he doesn't sound like he's got all his oars in the water."

"I think he sounds sweet," Jill countered, immediately defending her mother by championing Steve. "If Mom likes him, then he's good enough for me."

"There are a lot of fruitcakes out there." Apparently her mother felt obliged to tell her that.

It was all Dianne could do not to remind her dear, sweet mother that she'd arranged several dates for her with men who fell easily into that category.

"I think we should meet him," Jason said, his eyes darkening with concern. "He might turn out to be a serial murderer or something."

"Jason—" Dianne forced another light laugh "—you're being silly. Besides, you're going to meet him Saturday night."

"By then it'll be too late."

"Jason's got a point, dear," Martha said. "I don't think it would do any harm to introduce your young man to the family before Saturday night."

"I… He's probably busy… He's working all sorts of weird hours and…"

"What does he do?"

"Ah…" She couldn't think fast enough to come up with a lie and had to admit the truth. "He drives a truck."

Her words were followed by a tense silence as her children and mother exchanged meaningful looks. "I've heard stories about truck drivers," Martha said, pinching her lips tightly together. "None I'd care to repeat in front of the children, mind you, but…stories."

"Mother, you're being—"

"Jason's absolutely right. I insist we meet this

Steve. Truck drivers and cowboys simply aren't to be trusted."

Dianne rolled her eyes.

Her mother forgave her by saying, "I don't expect you to know this, Dianne, since you married so young."

"You married Dad when you were eighteen— younger than I was when I got married," Dianne said, not really wanting to argue, but finding herself trapped.

"Yes, but I've lived longer." She waved her crochet hook at Dianne. "A mother knows these things."

"Grandma's right," Jason said, sounding very adult. "We need to meet this Steve before you go out with him."

Dianne threw her hands in the air in frustration. "Hey, I thought you kids were the ones so eager for me to be at this dinner!"

"Yes, but we still have standards," Jill said, now siding with the others.

"I'll see what I can do," Dianne mumbled.

"Invite him over for dinner on Thursday night," her mother said. "I'll make my beef Stroganoff and bring over a fresh apple pie."

"Ah...he might be busy."

"Then tell him Wednesday night," Jason advised in a voice that was hauntingly familiar. It was the same tone Dianne used when she meant business.

With nothing left to do but agree, Dianne said,

"Okay. I'll try for Thursday." Oh, Lord, she thought, what had she got herself into?

She waited until the following afternoon to contact Steve. He'd given her his business card, which she'd tucked into the edging at the bottom of the bulletin board in her kitchen. She wasn't pleased about having to call him. She'd need to offer him more money if he agreed to this dinner. She couldn't very well expect him to come out of the generosity of his heart.

"Port Blossom Towing," a crisp female voice answered.

"Ah…this is Dianne Williams. I'd like to leave a message for Steve Creighton."

"Steve's here." Her words were followed by a click and a ringing sound.

"Steve," he answered distractedly.

"Hello." Dianne found herself at a loss for words. She'd hoped to just leave a message and ask him to return the call at his convenience. Having him there, on the other end of the line, when she wasn't expecting it left her at a disadvantage.

"Is this Dianne?"

"Yes. How'd you know?"

He chuckled softly, and the sound was pleasant and warm. "It's probably best if I don't answer that. Are you checking up to make sure I don't back out of Saturday night? Don't worry, I won't. In fact, I stopped off at the community center this morning and picked up tickets for the dinner."

"Oh, you didn't have to do that, but thanks. I'll reimburse you later."

"Just add it to my tab," he said lightly.

Dianne cringed, then took a breath and said, "Actually, I called to talk to you about my children."

"Your children?"

"Yes," she said. "Jason and Jill, and my mother, too, seem to think it would be a good idea if they met you. I assured them they would on Saturday night, but apparently that isn't good enough."

"I see."

"According to Jason, by then it'll be too late, and you might turn out to be a serial murderer or something. And my mother found the fact that you drive a truck worrisome."

"Do you want me to change jobs, too? I might have a bit of a problem managing all that before Saturday night."

"Of course not. Now, about Thursday—that's when they want you to come for dinner. My mother's offered to fix her Stroganoff and bake a pie. She uses Granny Smith apples," Dianne added, as though that bit of information would convince him to accept.

"Thursday night?"

"I'll give you an additional twenty dollars."

"Twenty dollars?" He sounded insulted, so Dianne raised her offer.

"All right, twenty-five, but that's as high as I can go. I'm living on a budget, you know." This fiasco was quickly running into a big chunk of cash. The dinner tickets were thirty each, and she'd need to reimburse Steve for those. Plus, she owed him a hundred for escorting her to the silly affair, and now an additional twenty-five if he came to dinner with her family.

"For twenty-five you've got yourself a deal," he said at last. "Anything else?"

Dianne closed her eyes. This was the worst part. "Yes," she said, swallowing tightly. The lump in her throat had grown to painful proportions. "There's one other thing. I… I want you to know I don't normally look that bad."

"Hey, I told you before—don't be so hard on yourself. You'd had a rough day."

"It's just that I don't want you to think I'm going to embarrass you at this Valentine's dinner. There may be people there you know, and after I made such a big deal over whether you had a suit and everything, well, I thought you might be more comfortable knowing…" She paused, closed her eyes and then blurted, "I've decided to switch brands of mascara."

His hesitation was only slight. "Thank you for sharing that. I'm sure I'll sleep better now."

Dianne decided to ignore his comment since she'd practically invited it. She didn't understand why she should find herself so tongue-tied with this man, but then again, perhaps she did. She'd made a complete idiot of herself. Paying a man to escort her to a dinner wasn't exactly the type of thing she wanted to list on a résumé.

"Oh, and before I forget," Dianne said, determined to put this unpleasantness behind her, "my mother and the kids asked me several questions about…us. How we met and the like. It might be a good idea if we went over my answers so our stories match."

"You want to meet for coffee later?"

"Ah…when?"

"Say seven, at the Pancake Haven. Don't worry, I'll buy."

Dianne had to bite back her sarcastic response. Instead she murmured, "Okay, but I won't have a lot of time."

"I promise not to keep you any longer than necessary."

Four

"All right," Steve said dubiously, once the waitress had poured them each a cup of coffee. "How'd we meet?"

Dianne told him, lowering her voice when she came to the part about the low-cal frozen dinners. She found it rather humiliating to have to repeat her private fantasy a second time, especially to Steve.

He looked incredulous when she'd finished. "You've got to be kidding."

Dianne took offense at his tone. This was *her* romantic invention he was ridiculing, and she hadn't even mentioned the part about the Rimsky-Korsakov symphony or the chiming bells.

"I didn't have time to think of anything better," Dianne explained irritably. "Jason hit me with the question first thing and I wasn't prepared."

"What did Jason say when you told him that story?"

"He said you sounded like a flake."

"I don't blame him."

Dianne's shoulders sagged with defeat.

"Don't worry about it," Steve assured her, still frowning. "I'll clear everything up when I meet him Thursday night." He said it in a way that suggested the task would be difficult.

"Good—only don't make me look like any more of a fool than I already do."

"I'll try my best," he said with the same dubious inflection he'd used when they'd first sat down.

Dianne sympathized. This entire affair was quickly going from bad to worse, and there was no one to fault but her. Who would've dreamed finding a date for the Valentine's dinner would cause so many problems?

As they sipped their coffee, Dianne studied the man sitting across from her. She was somewhat surprised to discover that Steve Creighton looked even better the second time around. He was dressed in slacks and an Irish cable-knit sweater the color of winter wheat. His smile was a ready one and his eyes, now that she had a chance to see them in the light, were a deep, rich shade of brown like his hair. The impression he'd given her of a considerate, generous man persisted. He must be. No one else would have agreed to this scheme, at least not without a more substantial inducement.

"I'm afraid I might've painted my kids a picture of you that's not quite accurate," Dianne admitted. Both her children had been filled with questions about Steve when they'd returned from school that afternoon. Jason had remained skeptical, but Jill, always a romantic—Dianne couldn't imagine where she'd inherited that!—had bombarded her for details.

"I'll do my best to live up to my image," Steve was quick to assure her.

Placing her elbows on the table, Dianne brushed a thick swatch of hair away from her face and tucked it behind her ear. "Listen, I'm sorry I ever got you involved in this."

"No backing out now—I've laid out cold hard cash for the dinner tickets."

Which was a not-so-subtle reminder that she owed him for those. She dug through her bag and brought out her checkbook. "I'll write you a check for the tickets right now."

"I'm not worried." He dismissed her offer with a wave of his hand.

Nevertheless, Dianne insisted. If she paid him in increments, she wouldn't have to think about how much this fiasco would end up costing her. She had the distinct feeling that by the time the Valentine's dinner was over, she would've spent as much as if she'd taken a Hawaiian vacation. Or gone to Seattle for the weekend, anyway.

After adding her signature, with a flair, to the bottom of the check, she kept her eyes lowered and said, "If I upped the ante ten dollars do you think you could manage to look…besotted?"

"Besotted?" Steve repeated the word as though he'd never heard it before.

"You know, smitten."

"Smitten?"

Again he made it sound as though she were speaking a foreign language. "Attracted," she tried for the third time, loud enough to catch the waitress's attention. The woman appeared and splashed more coffee into their nearly full cups.

"I'm not purposely being dense," he said. "I'm just not sure what you mean."

"Try to look as though you find me attractive," she said, leaning halfway across the table and speaking in a heated whisper.

"I see. So that's what 'besotted' means." He took another sip of his coffee, and Dianne had the feeling he did so in an effort to hide a smile.

"You aren't supposed to find that amusing." She took a gulp of her own drink and nearly scalded her mouth. Under different circumstances she would've grimaced with pain, or at least reached for the water glass. She did none of those things. A woman has her pride.

"Let me see if I understand you correctly," Steve said matter-of-factly. "For an extra ten bucks you want me to look 'smitten.'"

"Yes," Dianne answered with as much dignity as she could muster, which at the moment wasn't a lot.

"I'll do it, of course," Steve said, grinning and making her feel all the more foolish, "only I'm not sure I know how." He straightened, squared his shoulders and momentarily closed his eyes.

"Steve?" Dianne whispered, glancing around, hoping no one was watching them. He seemed to be attempting some form of Eastern meditation. She half expected him to start chanting. "What are you doing?"

"Thinking about how to look smitten."

"Are you making fun of me?"

"Not at all. If you're willing to offer me an extra ten bucks, it must be important to you. I want to do it right."

Dianne thought she'd better tell him. "This isn't for me," she said. "It's for my ten-year-old daughter, who happens to have a romantic nature. Jill was so impressed with the story of how we supposedly met, that I... I was kind of hoping you'd be willing to... you know." Now that she was forced to spell it out, Dianne wasn't certain of anything. But she knew one thing—suggesting he look smitten with her had been a mistake.

"I'll try."

"I'd appreciate it," she said.

"How's this?" Steve cocked his head at a slight angle, then slowly lowered his eyelids until they were half closed. His mouth curved upward in an off-center smile while his shoulders heaved in what Dianne suspected was meant to be a deep sigh of longing. As though in afterthought, he pressed his open hands over his heart while making soft panting sounds.

"Are you doing an imitation of a Saint Bernard?" Dianne snapped, still not sure whether he was laughing at her. "You look like a...a dog. Maybe Jason's right and you really are a flake."

"I was trying to look besotted," Steve said. "I thought that was what you wanted." As if it would improve the image, he cocked his head the other way and repeated the performance.

"You're making fun of me, and I don't appreciate it one bit." Dianne tossed her napkin on the table and stood. "Thursday night, six o'clock, and please don't be late." With that she slipped her purse strap over her shoulder and stalked out of the restaurant.

Steve followed her to her car. "All right, I apologize. I got carried away in there."

Dianne nodded. She'd gone a little overboard herself, but not nearly as much as Steve. Although she claimed she wanted him to give the impression of being attracted to her for Jill's sake, that wasn't entirely true. Steve was handsome and kind, and to have him looking at her with his heart in his eyes was a fantasy that was strictly her own.

Admitting that, even to herself, was a shock. The walls around her battered heart had been reinforced by three years of loneliness. For reasons she couldn't really explain, this tow-truck driver made her feel vulnerable.

"I'm willing to try again if you want," he said. "Only..."

"Yes?" Her car was parked in the rear lot where

the lighting wasn't nearly as good. Steve's face was hidden in the shadows, and she couldn't tell if he was being sincere or not.

"The problem," he replied slowly, "comes from the fact that we haven't kissed. I don't mean to be forward, you understand. You want me to wear a certain look, but it's a little difficult to manufacture without having had any, er, physical closeness."

"I see." Dianne's heart was pounding hard enough to damage her rib cage.

"Are you willing to let me kiss you?"

It was a last resort and she didn't have much choice. But she didn't have anything to lose, either. "If you insist."

With a deep breath, she tilted her head to the right, shut her eyes and puckered up. After waiting what seemed an inordinate amount of time, she opened her eyes. "Is something wrong?"

"I can't do it."

Embarrassed in the extreme, Dianne set her hands on her hips. "What do you mean?"

"You look like you're about to be sacrificed to appease the gods."

"I beg your pardon!" Dianne couldn't believe she was hearing him correctly. Talk about humiliation—she was only doing what he'd suggested.

"I can't kiss a woman who acts like she's about to undergo the most revolting experience of her life."

"You're saying I'm…oh…oh!" Too furious to speak, Dianne gripped Steve by the elbow and jerked him over to where his tow truck was parked, a couple of spaces down from her own car. Hopping onto the running board, she glared down at him. Her higher vantage point made her feel less vulnerable. Her eyes flashed with anger; his were filled with mild curiosity.

"Dianne, what are you doing now?"

"I'll have you know I was quite a kisser in my time."

"I don't doubt it."

"You just did. Now listen and listen well, because I'm only going to say this once." Waving her index finger under his nose, she paused and lowered her hand abruptly. He was right, she hadn't been all that thrilled to fall into this little experiment. A kiss was an innocent-enough exchange, she supposed, but kissing Steve put her on the defensive. And that troubled her.

"Say it."

Self-conscious now, she shifted her gaze and stepped off the running board, feeling ridiculous.

"What was so important that you were waving your finger under my nose?" Steve pressed.

Since she'd made such a fuss, she didn't have any alternative but to finish what she'd begun. "When I was in high school…the boys used to like to kiss me."

"They still would," Steve said softly, "if you'd give them a little encouragement."

She looked up at him and had to blink back unexpected tears. A woman doesn't have her husband walk out on her and not find herself awash in pain and self-doubt. Once she'd been confident; now she was dubious and insecure.

"Here," Steve said, holding her by the shoulders. "Let's try this." Then he gently, sweetly slanted his mouth over hers. Dianne was about to protest when their lips met and the option to refuse was taken from her.

Mindlessly she responded. Her arms slid around his middle and her hands splayed across the hard muscles of his back. And suddenly, emotions that had been simmering just below the surface rose like a tempest within her, and her heart went on a rampage.

Steve buried his hands in her hair, his fingers twisting and tangling in its thickness, bunching it at the back of her head. His mouth was soft, yet possessive. She gave a small, shocked moan when his tongue breached the barrier of her lips, but she adjusted quickly to the deepening quality of his kiss.

Reluctantly, Steve eased his mouth from hers. For a long moment, Dianne didn't open her eyes. When she finally did, she found Steve staring down at her.

He blinked.

She blinked.

Then, in the space of a heartbeat, he lowered his mouth back to hers.

Unable to stop, Dianne sighed deeply and leaned into his strength. Her legs felt like mush and her head was spinning with confusion. Her hands crept up and closed around the folds of his collar.

This kiss was long and thorough. It was the sweetest kiss Dianne had ever known—and the most passionate.

When he lifted his mouth from hers, he smiled tenderly. "I don't believe I'll have any problem looking besotted," he whispered.

Five

"Steve's here!" Jason called, releasing the living-room curtain. "He just pulled into the driveway."

Jill's high-pitched voice echoed her brother's. "He brought his truck. It's red and—"

"—wicked," Jason said, paying Steve's choice of vehicles the highest form of teenage compliment.

"What did I tell you," Dianne's mother said, as she briskly stirred the Stroganoff sauce. "He's driving a truck that's red and wicked." Her voice rose hysterically. "The man's probably a spawn of the devil!"

"Mother, 'wicked' means 'wonderful' to Jason."

"I've never heard anything so absurd in my life."

The doorbell chimed just then. Unfastening the apron from around her waist and tossing it aside, Dianne straightened and walked into the wide entryway. Jason, Jill and her mother followed closely, crowding her.

"Mom, please," Dianne pleaded, "give me some room here. Jason. Jill. Back up a little, would you?"

All three moved several paces back, allowing Dianne some space. But the moment her hand went for the doorknob, they crowded forward again.

"Children, Ma, please!" she whispered frantically. The three were so close to her she could barely breathe.

Reluctantly Jason and Jill shuffled into the living room and slumped onto the sofa near the television set. Martha, however, refused to budge.

The bell chimed a second time, and after glaring at her mother and receiving no response, Dianne opened the door. On the other side of the screen door stood Steve, a huge bouquet of red roses in one hand and a large stuffed bear tucked under his other arm.

Dianne stared as she calculated the cost of long-stemmed roses, and a stuffed animal. She couldn't even afford carnations. And if he felt it necessary to bring along a stuffed bear, why hadn't he chosen a smaller, less costly one?

"May I come in?" he asked after a lengthy pause.

Her mother elbowed Dianne in the ribs and smiled serenely as she unlatched the lock on the screen door.

"You must be Steve. How lovely to meet you," Martha said as graciously as if she'd always thought the world of truck drivers.

Holding the outer door for him, Dianne managed to produce a weak smile as Steve entered her home. Jason and Jill had come back into the hallway to stand next to their grandmother, eyeing Dianne's newfound date with open curiosity. For all her son's concern that

Steve might turn out to be an ax-murderer, one look at the bright-red tow truck and he'd been won over.

"Steve, I'd like you to meet my family," Dianne said, gesturing toward the three.

"So, you're Jason," Steve said, holding out his hand. The two exchanged a hearty handshake. "I'm pleased to meet you. Your mother speaks highly of you."

Jason beamed.

Turning his attention to Jill, Steve held out the oversize teddy bear. "This is for you," he said, giving her the stuffed animal. "I wanted something extra-special for Dianne's daughter, but this was all I could think of. I hope you aren't disappointed."

"I *love* teddy bears!" Jill cried, hugging it tight. "Did Mom tell you that?"

"Nope," Steve said, centering his high-voltage smile on the ten-year-old. "I just guessed."

"Oh, thank you, thank you." Cuddling the bear, Jill raced up the stairs, giddy with delight. "I'm going to put him on my bed right now."

Steve's gaze followed her daughter, and then his eyes briefly linked with Dianne's. In that split second, she let him know she wasn't entirely pleased. He frowned slightly, but recovered before presenting the roses to Dianne's mother.

"For me?" Martha brought her fingertips to her mouth as though shocked by the gesture. "Oh, you shouldn't have! Oh, my heavens, I can't remember the last time a man gave me roses." Reaching for the corner of her apron, she discreetly dabbed her eyes. "This is such a treat."

"Mother, don't you want to put those in water?" Dianne said pointedly.

"Oh, dear, I suppose I should. It was a thoughtful gesture, Steve. Very thoughtful."

"Jason, go help your grandmother."

Her son looked as though he intended to object, but changed his mind and obediently followed Martha into the kitchen.

As soon as they were alone, Dianne turned on Steve. "Don't you think you're laying it on a little thick?" she whispered. She was so furious she was having trouble speaking clearly. "I can't afford all this!"

"Don't worry about it."

"I am worried. In fact I'm experiencing a good deal of distress. At the rate you're spending my money, I'm going to have to go on an installment plan."

"Hush, now, before you attract everyone's attention."

Dianne scowled at him. "I—"

Steve placed his fingers over her lips. "I've learned a very effective way of keeping you quiet—don't force me to use it. Kissing you so soon after my arrival might create the wrong impression."

"You wouldn't dare!"

The way his mouth slanted upward in a slow smile made her afraid he would. "I was only doing my best to act besotted," he said.

"You didn't have to spend this much money doing it. Opening my door, holding out my chair—that's all I wanted. First you roll your eyes like you're going into a coma and pant like a Saint Bernard, then you spend a fortune."

"Dinner's ready," Martha shouted from the kitchen.

With one last angry glare, Dianne led him into the big kitchen. Steve moved behind Dianne's chair and pulled it out for her. "Are you happy now?" he whispered close to her ear as she sat down.

She nodded, thinking it was too little, too late, but she didn't have much of an argument since she'd specifically asked for this.

Soon the five were seated around the wooden table. Dianne's mother said the blessing, and while she did, Dianne offered up a fervent prayer of her own. She wanted Steve to make a good impression—but not too good.

After the buttered noodles and the Stroganoff had been passed around, along with a lettuce-and-cucumber salad and homemade rolls, Jason embarked on the topic that had apparently been troubling him from the first.

"Mom said you met at the grocery store."

Steve nodded. "She was blocking the aisle and I had to ask her to move her cart so I could get to the Hearty Eater Pot Pies."

Jason straightened in his chair, looking more than a little satisfied. "I thought it might be something like that."

"I beg your pardon?" Steve asked, playing innocent.

Her son cleared his throat, glanced carefully around before answering, then lowered his voice. "You should hear Mom's version of how you two met."

"More noodles?" Dianne said, shoving the bowl toward her son.

Jill looked confused. "But didn't you smile at Mom and say she's perfect just the way she is?"

Steve took a moment to compose his thoughts while he buttered his third dinner roll. Dianne recognized that he was doing a balancing act between her two children. If he said he'd commented on the low-cal frozen dinners and her figure, then he risked offending Jason, who seemed to think no man in his right mind would say something like that. On the other hand, if he claimed otherwise, he might wound Jill's romantic little heart.

"I'd be interested in knowing that myself," Martha added, looking pleased that Steve had taken a second helping of her Stroganoff. "Dianne's terribly close-mouthed about these things. She didn't even mention you until the other night."

"To be honest," Steve said, sitting back in his chair, "I don't exactly recall what I said to Dianne. I remember being irritated with her for hogging the aisle, but when I asked her to move, she apologized and immediately pushed her cart out of the way."

Jason nodded, appeased.

"But when I got a good look at her, I couldn't help thinking she was the most beautiful woman I'd seen in a long while."

Jill sighed, mollified.

"I don't recall any of that," Dianne said, reaching for another roll. She tore it apart with a vengeance and smeared butter on both halves before she realized she had an untouched roll balanced on the edge of her plate.

"I was thinking that after dinner I'd take Jason out for a ride in the truck," Steve said when a few minutes had passed.

"You'd do that?" Jason nearly leapt from his chair in his eagerness.

"I was planning to all along," Steve explained. "I thought you'd be more interested in seeing how all the gears worked than in any gift I could bring you."

"I am." Jason was so excited he could barely sit still.

"When Jason and I come back, I'll take you out for a spin, Dianne."

She shook her head. "I'm not interested, thanks."

Three pairs of accusing eyes flashed in her direction. It was as if she'd committed an act of treason.

"I'm sure my daughter didn't mean that," Martha said, smiling sweetly at Steve. "She's been very tired lately and not quite herself."

Bewildered, Dianne stared at her mother.

"Can we go now?" Jason asked, already standing.

"If your mother says it's okay," Steve said, with

a glance at Dianne. She nodded, and Steve finished the last of his roll and stood.

"I'll have apple pie ready for you when you get back," Martha promised, quickly ushering the two out the front door.

As soon as her mother returned to the kitchen, Dianne asked, "What was all that about?"

"What?" her mother demanded, feigning ignorance.

"That I've been very tired and not myself lately?"

"Oh, that," Martha said, clearing the table. "Steve wants to spend a few minutes alone with you. It's only natural. So I had to make some excuse for you."

"Yes, but—"

"Your behavior, my dear, was just short of rude. When a gentleman makes it clear he wants to spend some uninterrupted time in your company, you should welcome the opportunity."

"Mother, I seem to recall your saying Steve was a spawn of the devil, remember?"

"Now that I've met him, I've had a change of heart."

"What about Jerome, the butcher? I thought you were convinced he was the one for me."

"I like Steve better. I can tell he's a good man, and you'd be a fool to let him slip through your fingers by pretending to be indifferent."

"I am indifferent."

With a look of patent disbelief, Martha Janes shook her head. "I saw the way your eyes lit up when Steve walked into the house. You can fool some folks, but you can't pull the wool over your own mother's eyes. You're falling in love with this young man, and frankly, I'm pleased. I like him."

Dianne frowned. If her eyes had lit up when Steve arrived, it was because she was busy trying to figure out a way to repay him for the roses and the teddy bear. What she felt for him wasn't anything romantic. Or was it?

Dear Lord, she couldn't actually be falling for this guy, could she?

The question haunted Dianne as she loaded the dishwasher.

"Steve's real cute," Jill announced. Her daughter would find Attila the Hun cute, too, if he brought her a teddy bear, but Dianne resisted the impulse to say so.

"He looks a little bit like Hugh Jackman, don't you think?" Jill continued.

"I can't say I've noticed." A small lie. Dianne had noticed a lot more about Steve than she was willing to admit. Although she'd issued a fair number of complaints, he really was being a good sport about this. Of course, she was paying him, but he'd gone above and beyond the call of duty. Taking Jason out for a spin in the tow truck was one example, although why anyone would be thrilled to drive around in that contraption was something Dianne didn't understand.

"I do believe Steve Creighton will make you a decent husband," her mother stated thoughtfully as she removed the warm apple pie from the oven. "In fact, I was just thinking how nice it would be to have a summer wedding. It's so much easier to ask relatives to travel when the weather's good. June or July would be perfect."

"Mother, please! Steve and I barely know each other."

"On the contrary," Steve said, sauntering into the kitchen. He stepped behind Dianne's mother and sniffed appreciatively at the aroma wafting from her apple pie. "I happen to be partial to summer weddings myself."

Six

"Don't you think you're overdoing it a bit?" Dianne demanded as Steve eased the big tow truck out of her driveway. She was belted into the seat next to him, feeling trapped—not to mention betrayed by her own family. They had insisted Steve take her out for a spin so the two of them could have some time alone. Steve didn't want to be alone with her, but her family didn't know that.

"Maybe I did come on a little strong," Steve agreed, dazzling her with his smile.

It was better for her equilibrium if she didn't glance his way, Dianne decided. Her eyes would innocently meet his and he'd give her one of those heart-stopping, lopsided smiles, and something inside her would melt. If this continued much longer, she'd be nothing more than a puddle by the end of the evening.

"The flowers and the stuffed animal I can understand," she said stiffly, willing to grant him that much. "You wanted to make a good impression, and that's fine, but the comment about being partial to summer weddings was going too far. It's just the kind of thing my mother was hoping to hear from you."

"You're right."

The fact that he was being so agreeable should have forewarned Dianne that something was amiss. She'd sensed it from the first moment she'd climbed into the truck. He'd closed the door and almost immediately something pulled wire-taut within her. The sensation was peculiar, even wistful—a melancholy pining she'd never felt before.

She squared her shoulders and stared straight ahead, determined not to fall under his spell the way her children and her mother so obviously had.

"As it is, I suspect Mom's been faithfully lighting votive candles every afternoon, asking God to send me a husband. She thinks God needs her help—that's why she goes around arranging dates for me."

"You're right, of course. I should never have made that comment about summer weddings," Steve said, "but I assumed that's just the sort of thing a *besotted* man would say."

Dianne sighed, realizing once again that she didn't have much of an argument. But he was doing everything in his power to make her regret that silly request.

"Hey, where are you taking me?" she asked when he turned off her street onto a main thoroughfare.

Steve turned his smile on her full force and twitched his thick eyebrows a couple of times for effect. "For a short drive. It wouldn't look good if we were to return five minutes after we left the house. Your family—"

"—will be waiting at the front door. They expect me back any minute."

"No, they don't."

"And why don't they?" she asked, growing uneasy. This wasn't supposed to be anything more than a ride around the block, and she'd had to be coerced into even that.

"Because I told your mother we'd be gone for an hour."

"An hour?" Dianne cried, as though he'd just announced he was kidnapping her. "But you can't do that! I mean, what about your time? Surely it's valuable."

"I assumed you'd want to pay me a few extra dollars—after all, I'm doing this to create the right impression. It's what—"

"I know, I know," she interrupted. "You're just acting smitten." The truth of the matter was that Dianne was making a fuss over something that was actually causing her heart to pound hard and fast. The whole idea of being alone with Steve appealed to her too much. *That* was the reason she fought it so hard. Without even trying, he'd managed to cast a spell on her family, and although she hated to admit it, he'd cast one on her, too. Steve Creighton was laughter and magic. Instinctively she knew he wasn't another

Jack. Not the type of man who would walk away from his family.

Dianne frowned as the thought crossed her mind. It would be much easier to deal with the hand life had dealt her if she wasn't forced to associate with men as seemingly wonderful as Steve. It was easier to view all men as insensitive and inconsiderate.

Dianne didn't like that Steve was proving to be otherwise. He was apparently determined to crack the hard shell around her heart, no matter how hard she tried to reinforce it.

"Another thing," she said stiffly, crossing her arms with resolve, but refusing to glance in his direction. "You've got to stop being so free with my money."

"I never expected you to reimburse me for those gifts," he explained quietly.

"I insist on it."

"My, my, aren't we prickly. I bought the flowers and the toy for Jill of my own accord. I don't expect you to pick up the tab," he said again.

Dianne didn't know if she should argue with him or not. Although his tone was soft, a thread of steel ran through his words, just enough to let her know nothing she said was going to change his mind.

"That's not all," she said, deciding to drop that argument for a more urgent one. She probably did sound a bit shrewish, but if he wasn't going to be practical about this, *she'd* have to be.

"You mean there's more?" he cried, pretending to be distressed.

"Steve, please," she said, shocked at how feeble she sounded. She scarcely recognized the voice as her own. "You've got to stop being so...so wonderful," she finally said.

He came to a stop at a red light and turned to her, draping his arm over the back of the seat. "I don't think I heard you right. Would you mind repeating that?"

"You can't continue to be so—" she paused, searching for another word "—charming."

"Charming," he echoed. "Charming?"

"To my children and my mother," she elaborated. "The gifts were one thing. Giving Jason a ride in the tow truck was fine, too, but agreeing with my mother about summer weddings and then playing basketball with Jason—none of that was necessary."

"Personally, I would've thought your mother measuring my chest and arm length so she could knit me a sweater would bother you the most."

"That, too!"

"Could you explain why this is such a problem?"

"Isn't it obvious? If you keep doing that sort of thing, they'll expect me to continue dating you after the Valentine's dinner, and, frankly, I can't afford it."

He chuckled at that as if she was making some kind of joke. Only it wasn't funny. "I happen to live on a budget—"

"I don't think we should concern ourselves with that," he broke in.

"Well, I *am* concerned." She expelled her breath

sharply. "One date! That's all I can afford and that's all I'm interested in. If you continue to be so…so…"

"Wonderful?" he supplied.

"Charming," she corrected, "then I'll have a whole lot to answer for when I don't see you again after Saturday."

"So you want me to limit the charm?"

"Please."

"I'll do my best," he said, and his eyes sparked with laughter, which they seemed to do a good deal of the time. If she hadn't been so flustered, she might have been pleased that he found her so amusing.

"Thank you." She glanced pointedly at her watch. "Shouldn't we head back to the house?"

"No."

"No? I realize you told my mother we'd be gone an hour, but that really is too long and—"

"I'm taking you to Jackson Point."

Dianne's heart reacted instantly, zooming into her throat and then righting itself. Jackson Point overlooked a narrow water passage between the Kitsap Peninsula and Vashon Island. The view, either at night or during the day, was spectacular, but those who came to appreciate it at night were generally more interested in each other than the glittering lights of the island and Seattle farther beyond.

"I'll take the fact that you're not arguing with me as a positive sign," he said.

"I think we should go back to the house," she stated with as much resolve as she could muster. Unfortunately it didn't come out sounding very firm. The last time she'd been to Jackson Point had been a lifetime ago. She'd been a high-school junior and madly in love for the first time. The last time.

"We'll go back in a little while."

"Steve," she cried, fighting the urge to cry, "why are you doing this?"

"Isn't it obvious? I want to kiss you again."

Dianne pushed her hair away from her face with both hands. "I don't think that's such a good idea." Her voice wavered, just like her teenage son's.

Before she could come up with an argument, Steve pulled off the highway and down the narrow road that led to the popular lookout. She hadn't wanted to think about that kiss they'd shared. It had been a mistake. Dianne knew she'd disappointed Steve—not because of the kiss itself, but her reaction to it. He seemed to be waiting for her to admit how deeply it had affected her, but she hadn't given him the satisfaction.

Now, she told herself, he wanted revenge.

Her heart was still hammering when Steve stopped the truck and turned off the engine. The lights across the water sparkled in welcome. The closest lights were from Vashon Island, a sparsely populated place accessible only by ferry. The more distant ones came from West Seattle.

"It's really beautiful," she whispered. Some of the tension eased from her shoulders and she felt herself begin to relax.

"Yes," Steve agreed. He moved closer and placed his arm around her shoulder.

Dianne closed her eyes, knowing she didn't have the power to resist him. He'd been so wonderful with her children and her mother—more than wonderful. Now it seemed to be her turn, and try as she might to avoid it, she found herself a willing victim to his special brand of magic.

"You *are* going to let me kiss you, aren't you?" he whispered close to her ear.

She nodded.

His hands were in her hair as he directed his mouth to hers. The kiss was slow, as though he was afraid of frightening her. His mouth was warm and moist over her own, gentle and persuasive. Dianne could feel her bones start to dissolve and knew that if she was going to walk away from this experience unscathed, she needed to think fast. Unfortunately, her mind was already overloaded.

When at last they drew apart, he dragged in a deep breath. Dianne sank back against the seat and noted that his eyes were still closed. Taking this moment to gather her composure, she scooted as far away from him as she could, pressing the small of her back against the door handle.

"You're very good at this," she said, striving to sound unaffected, and knowing she hadn't succeeded.

He opened his eyes and frowned. "I'll assume that's a compliment."

"Yes. I think you should." Steve was the kind of

man who'd attract attention from women no matter where he went. He wouldn't be interested in a divorcée and a ready-made family, and there was no use trying to convince herself otherwise. The only reason he'd agreed to take her to the Valentine's dinner was because she'd offered to pay him. This was strictly a business arrangement.

His finger lightly grazed the side of her face. His eyes were tender as he studied her, but he said nothing.

"It would probably be a good idea if we talked about Saturday night," she said, doing her best to keep her gaze trained away from him. "There's a lot to discuss and…there isn't much time left."

"All right." His wayward grin told her she hadn't fooled him. He knew exactly what she was up to.

"Since the dinner starts at seven, I suggest you arrive at my house at quarter to."

"Fine."

"We don't need to go to the trouble or the expense of a corsage."

"What are you wearing?"

Dianne hadn't given the matter a second's thought. "Since it's a Valentine's dinner, something red, I suppose. I have a red-and-white striped dress that will do." It was a couple of years old, but this dinner wasn't exactly the fashion event of the year, and she didn't have the money for a new outfit, anyway.

She looked at her watch, although she couldn't possibly read it in the darkness.

"Is that a hint you want to get back to the house?"

"Yes," she said.

Her honesty seemed to amuse him. "That's what I thought." Without argument, he started the engine and put the truck in Reverse.

The minute they turned onto her street, Jason and Jill came vaulting out the front door. Dianne guessed they'd both been staring out the upstairs window, eagerly awaiting her return.

She was wrong. It was Steve they were eager to see.

"Hey, what took you so long?" Jason demanded as Steve climbed out of the truck.

"Grandma's got the apple pie all dished up. Are you ready?" Jill hugged Steve's arm, gazing anxiously up at him.

Dianne watched the unfolding scene with dismay. Steve walked into her house with one arm around Jason and Jill clinging to the other.

It was as if she were invisible. Neither of her children had said a single word to her!

To his credit, Jason paused at the front door. "Mom, you coming?"

"Just bringing up the rear," she muttered.

Jill shook her head, her shoulders lifting, then falling, in a deep sigh. "You'll have to forgive my mother," she told Steve confidingly. "She can be a real slowpoke sometimes."

Seven

"Oh, Mom," Jill said softly. "You look so beautiful."

Dianne examined her reflection in the full-length mirror. At the last moment, she'd been gripped by another bout of insanity. She'd gone out and purchased a new dress.

She couldn't afford it. She couldn't rationalize that expense on top of everything else, but the instant she'd seen the flowered pink creation in the shop window, she'd decided to try it on. That was her first mistake. Correction: that was just one mistake in a long list of recent mistakes where Steve Creighton was concerned.

The dress was probably the most flattering thing she'd ever owned. The price tag had practically caused her to clutch her chest and stagger backward. She hadn't purchased it impulsively. No, she was too smart for that. The fact that she was nearly penniless and it was only the middle of the month didn't help matters. She'd sat down in the coffee shop next door and juggled figures for ten or fifteen minutes before crumpling up the paper and deciding to buy the dress, anyway. It was her birthday, Mother's Day and Christmas gifts to herself all rolled into one.

"I brought my pearls," Martha announced as she bolted breathlessly into Dianne's bedroom. She was late, which wasn't like Martha, but Dianne hadn't been worried. She knew her mother would be there before she had to leave for the dinner.

Martha stopped abruptly, folding her hands prayerfully and nodding with approval. "Oh, Dianne. You look…"

"Beautiful," Jill finished for her grandmother.

"Beautiful," Martha echoed. "I thought you were going to wear the red dress."

"I just happened to be at the mall and stumbled across this." She didn't mention that she'd made the trip into Tacoma for the express purpose of looking for something new to wear.

"Steve's here," Jason yelled from the bottom of the stairs.

"Here are my pearls," Martha said, reverently handing them to her daughter. The pearls were a family heirloom and worn only on the most special occasions.

"Mom, I don't know…"

"Your first official date with Steve," she said as though that event was on a level with God giving Moses the Ten Commandments. Without further ado,

Martha draped the necklace around her daughter's neck. "I insist. Your father insists."

"Mom?" Dianne asked, turning around to search her mother's face. "Have you been talking to Dad again?" Dianne's father had been gone for more than ten years. However, for several years following his death, Martha claimed they carried on regular conversations.

"Not exactly, but I know your father would have insisted, had he been here. Now off with you. It's rude to keep a date waiting."

Preparing to leave her bedroom, Dianne closed her eyes. She was nervous. Which was silly, she told herself. This wasn't a *real* date, since she was paying Steve for the honor of escorting her. She'd reminded herself of that the entire time she was dressing. The only reason they were even attending this Valentine's dinner was because she'd asked him. Not only asked, but offered to pay for everything.

Jill rushed out of the bedroom door and down the stairs. "She's coming and she looks beautiful."

"Your mother always looks beautiful," Dianne heard Steve say matter-of-factly as she descended the steps. Her eyes were on him, standing in the entryway dressed in a dark gray suit, looking tall and debonair.

He glanced up and his gaze found hers. She was gratified to see that his eyes widened briefly.

"I was wrong, she's extra-beautiful tonight," he whispered, but if he was speaking to her children, he wasn't looking at them. In fact, his eyes were riveted on her, which only served to make Dianne more uneasy.

They stood staring at each other like star-crossed lovers until Jill tugged at Steve's arm. "Aren't you going to give my mom the corsage?"

"Oh, yes, here," he said. Apparently he'd forgotten he was holding an octagon-shaped plastic box.

Dianne frowned. They'd agreed earlier that he wasn't going to do this. She was already over her budget, and flowers were a low-priority item, as far as Dianne was concerned.

"It's for the wrist," he explained, opening the box for her. "I thought you said the dress was red, so I'm afraid this might not go with it very well." The corsage was fashioned of three white rosebuds between a froth of red-and-white silk ribbons. Although her dress was several shades of pink, there was a smattering of red in the center of the flowers that matched the color in the ribbon perfectly. It was as if Steve had seen the dress and chosen the flowers to complement it. "It's…"

"Beautiful," Jill supplied once more, smugly pleased with herself.

"Are you ready?" Steve asked.

Jason stepped forward with her wool coat as though he couldn't wait to be rid of her. Steve took the coat from her son's hands and helped Dianne into it, while her son and daughter stood back looking as proud as if they'd arranged the entire affair themselves.

Before she left the house, Dianne gave her children their instructions and kissed them each on the cheek. Jason wasn't much in favor of letting his mother kiss him, but he tolerated it.

Martha continued to stand at the top of the stairs, dabbing her eyes with a tissue and looking down as if the four of them together were the most romantic sight she'd ever witnessed. Dianne sincerely prayed that Steve wouldn't notice.

"I won't be late," Dianne said as Steve opened the front door.

"Don't worry about it," Jason said pointedly. "There's no need to rush home."

"Have a wonderful time," Jill called after them.

The first thing Dianne realized once they were out the door was that Steve's tow truck was missing from her driveway. She looked around, half expecting to find the red monstrosity parked on the street.

With his hand cupping her elbow, he led her instead to a luxury car. "What's this?" she asked, thinking he might have rented it. If he had, she wanted it understood this minute that she had no intention of paying the fee.

"My car."

"Your car?" she asked. He opened the door for her and Dianne slid onto the supple white leather. Towtruck operators obviously made better money than she'd assumed. If she'd known that, she would've offered him seventy-five dollars for this evening instead of a hundred.

Steve walked around the front of the sedan and got into the driver's seat. They chatted on the short ride to the community center, with Dianne making small talk in an effort to cover her nervousness.

The parking lot was nearly full, but Steve found a spot on the side lot next to the sprawling brick building.

"You want to go in?" he asked.

She nodded. Over the years, Dianne had attended a dozen of these affairs. There was no reason to feel nervous. Her friends and neighbors would be there. Naturally there'd be questions about her and Steve, but this time she was prepared.

Steve came around the car, opened her door and helped her out. She saw that he was frowning.

"Is something wrong?" she asked anxiously.

"You look pale."

She was about to reply that it was probably nerves when he said, "Not to worry, I have a cure for that." Before she'd guessed his intention, he leaned forward and brushed his mouth over hers.

He was right. The instant his lips touched hers, hot color exploded in her cheeks. She felt herself swaying toward him, and Steve caught her gently by the shoulders.

"That was a mistake," he whispered once they'd moved apart. "Now the only thing I'm hungry for is you. Forget the dinner."

"I…think we should go inside now," she said,

glancing around the parking lot, praying no one had witnessed the kiss.

Light and laughter spilled out from the wide double doors of the Port Blossom Community Center. The soft strains of a romantic ballad beckoned them in.

Steve took her coat and hung it on the rack in the entry. She waited for him, feeling more jittery than ever. When he'd finished, Steve slipped his arm about her waist and led her into the main room.

"Steve Creighton!" They had scarcely stepped into the room when Steve was greeted by a robust man with a salt-and-pepper beard. Glancing curiously at Dianne, the stranger slapped Steve on the back and said, "It's about time you attended one of our functions."

Steve introduced Dianne to the man, whose name was Sam Horton. The name was vaguely familiar to her, but she couldn't quite place it.

Apparently reading her mind, Steve said, "Sam's the president of the Chamber of Commerce."

"Ah, yes," Dianne said, impressed to meet one of the community's more distinguished members.

"My wife, Renée," Sam said, absently glancing around, "is somewhere in this mass of humanity." Then he turned back to Steve. "Have you two found a table yet? We'd consider it a pleasure to have you join us."

"Dianne?" Steve looked at her.

"That would be very nice, thank you." Wait until her mother heard this. She and Steve dining with the

Chamber of Commerce president! Dianne couldn't help smiling. No doubt her mother would attribute this piece of good luck to the pearls. Sam left to find his wife, in order to introduce her to Dianne.

"Dianne Williams! It's so good to see you." The voice belonged to Beth Martin, who had crossed the room, dragging her husband, Ralph, along with her. Dianne knew Beth from the PTA. They'd worked together on the spring carnival the year before. Actually, Dianne had done most of the work while Beth had done the delegating. The experience had been enough to convince Dianne not to volunteer for this year's event.

Dianne introduced Steve to Beth and Ralph. Dianne felt a small sense of triumph as she noted the way Beth eyed Steve. This man was worth every single penny of the money he was costing her!

The two couples chatted for a few moments, then Steve excused himself. Dianne watched him as he walked through the room, observing how the eyes of several women followed him. He did make a compelling sight, especially in his well-cut suit.

"How long have you known Steve Creighton?" Beth asked the instant Steve was out of earshot. She moved closer to Dianne, as though she was about to hear some well-seasoned gossip.

"A few weeks now." It was clear that Beth was hoping Dianne would elaborate, but Dianne had no intention of doing so.

"Dianne." Shirley Simpson, another PTA friend,

moved to her side. "Is that Steve Creighton you're with?"

"Yes." She'd had no idea Steve was so well known.

"I swear he's the cutest man in town. One look at him and my toes start to curl."

When she'd approached Steve with this proposal, Dianne hadn't a clue she would become the envy of her friends. She really *had* got a bargain.

"Are you sitting with anyone yet?" Shirley asked. Beth bristled as though offended she hadn't thought to ask first.

"Ah, yes. Sam Horton's already invited us, but thanks."

"Sam Horton," Beth repeated and she and Shirley shared a significant look. "My, my, you are traveling in elevated circles these days. Well, more power to you. And good luck with Steve Creighton. I've been saying for ages that it's time someone bagged him. I hope it's you."

"Thanks," Dianne said, feeling more than a little confused by this unexpected turn of events. Everyone knew Steve, right down to her PTA friends. It didn't make a lot of sense.

Steve returned a moment later, carrying two slender flutes of champagne. "I'd like you to meet some friends of mine," he said, leading her across the room to where several couples were standing. The circle immediately opened to include them. Dianne recognized the mayor and a couple of others.

Dianne threw Steve a puzzled look. He certainly

was a social animal, but the people he knew… Still, why should she be surprised? A tow-truck operator would have plenty of opportunity to meet community leaders. And Steve was such a likable man, who obviously made friends easily.

A four-piece band began playing forties' swing, and after the introductions, Dianne found her toe tapping to the music.

"Next year we should make this a dinner-dance," Steve suggested, smiling down on Dianne. He casually put his hand on her shoulder as if he'd been doing that for months.

"Great idea," Port Blossom's mayor said, nodding. "You might bring it up at the March committee meeting."

Dianne frowned, not certain she understood. It was several minutes before she had a chance to ask Steve about the comment.

"I'm on the board of directors for the community center," he explained briefly.

"You are?" Dianne took another sip of her champagne. Some of the details were beginning to get muddled in her mind, and she wasn't sure if it had anything to do with the champagne.

"Does that surprise you?"

"Yes. I thought you had to be, you know, a business owner to be on the board of directors."

Now it was Steve's turn to frown. "I am."

"You are?" Dianne asked. Her hand tightened around the long stem of her glass. "What business?"

"Port Blossom Towing."

That did it. Dianne drank what remained of her champagne in a single gulp. "You mean to say you *own* the company?"

"Yes. Don't tell me you didn't know."

She glared up at him, her eyes narrowed and distrusting. "I didn't."

Eight

Steve Creighton had made a fool of her.

Dianne was so infuriated she couldn't wait to be alone with him so she could give him a piece of her mind. Loudly.

"What's that got to do with anything?" Steve asked.

Dianne continued to glare at him, unable to form any words yet. It wasn't just that he owned the towing company or even that he was a member of the board of directors for the community center. It was the fact that he'd deceived her.

"You should've told me you owned the company!" she hissed.

"I gave you my business card," he said, shrugging.

"You gave me your business card," she mimicked in a furious whisper. "The least you could've done was mention it. I feel like an idiot."

Steve was wearing a perplexed frown, as if he found her response completely unreasonable. "To be honest, I assumed you knew. I wasn't purposely keeping it from you."

That wasn't the only thing disturbing her, but the second concern was even more troubling than the first. "While I'm on the subject, what are you? Some sort of…love god?"

"What?"

"From the moment we arrived all the women I know, and even some I don't, have been crowding around me asking all sorts of leading questions. One friend claims you make her toes curl and another… never mind."

Steve looked exceptionally pleased. "I make her toes curl?"

How like a man to fall for flattery! "That's not the point."

"Then what is?"

"Everyone thinks you and I are an item."

"So? I thought that's what you wanted."

Dianne felt like screaming. "Kindly look at this from my point of view. I'm in one hell of a mess because of you!" He frowned as she went on. "What am I supposed to tell everyone, including my mother and children, once tonight is over?" Why, oh why hadn't she thought of this sooner?

"About what?"

"About you and me," she said slowly, using short words so he'd understand. "I didn't even *want* to attend this dinner. I've lied to my own family and, worse, I'm actually paying a man to escort me. This is probably the lowest point of my life, and all you can do is stand there with a silly grin."

Steve chuckled and his mouth twitched. "This silly grin you find so offensive is my besotted look. I've been practicing it in front of a mirror all week."

Dianne covered her face with her hands. "Now... now I discover that I'm even more of a fool than I realized. You're this upstanding businessman and, worse, a...a playboy."

"I'm not a playboy," he corrected. "And that's a pretty dated term, anyway."

"Maybe—but that's the reputation you seem to have. There isn't a woman at this dinner who doesn't envy me."

All she'd wanted was someone presentable to escort her to this dinner so she could satisfy her children. She lived a quiet, uncomplicated life, and suddenly she was the most gossip-worthy member of tonight's affair.

Sam Horton stepped to the microphone in front of the hall and announced that dinner was about to be served, so would everyone please go to their tables.

"Don't look so discontented," Steve whispered in her ear. He was standing behind her, and his hands rested gently on her shoulders. "The woman who's supposed to be the envy of every other one here shouldn't be frowning. Try smiling."

"I don't think I can," she muttered, fearing she might break down and cry. Being casually held by Steve wasn't helping. She found his touch reassuring and comforting when she didn't want either, at least not from him. She was confused enough. Her head was telling her one thing and her heart another.

"Trust me, Dianne, you're blowing this out of proportion. I didn't mean to deceive you. Let's just enjoy the evening."

"I feel like such a fool," she muttered again. Several people walked past them on their way to the tables, pausing to smile and nod. Dianne did her best to respond appropriately.

"You're not a fool." He slipped his arm around her waist and led her toward the table where Sam and his wife, as well as two other couples Dianne didn't know, were waiting.

Dianne smiled at the others while Steve held out her chair. A gentleman to the very end, she observed wryly. He opened doors and held out chairs for her, and the whole time she was making an idiot of herself in front of the entire community.

As soon as everyone was seated, he introduced Dianne to the two remaining couples—Larry and Louise Lester, who owned a local restaurant, and Dale and Maryanne Atwater. Dale was head of the town's most prominent accounting firm.

The salads were delivered by young men in crisp white jackets. The Lesters and the Atwaters were discussing the weather and other bland subjects. Caught in her own churning thoughts, Dianne ate her salad and tuned them out. When she was least expecting it, she heard her name. She glanced up to find six pairs of eyes studying her. She had no idea why.

She lowered the fork to her salad plate and glanced at Steve, praying he'd know what was going on.

"The two of you make such a handsome couple," Renée Horton said. Her words were casual, but her expression wasn't. Everything about her said she was intensely curious about Steve and Dianne.

"Thank you," Steve answered, then turned to Dianne and gave her what she'd referred to earlier as a silly grin and what he'd said was his besotted look.

"How did you two meet?" Maryanne Atwater asked nonchalantly.

"Ah…" Dianne's mind spun, lost in a haze of half-truths and misconceptions. She didn't know if she dared repeat the story about meeting in the local grocery, but she couldn't think fast enough to come up with anything else. She thought she was prepared, but the moment she was in the spotlight, all her self-confidence deserted her.

"We both happened to be in the grocery store at the same time," Steve explained smoothly. The story had been repeated so often it was beginning to sound like the truth.

"I was blocking Steve's way in the frozen-food section," she said, picking up his version of the story. She felt embarrassed seeing the three other couples listening so intently to their fabrication.

"I asked Dianne to kindly move her cart, and she stopped to apologize for being so thoughtless. Before I knew it, we'd struck up a conversation."

"I was there!" Louise Lester threw her hands wildly in the air, her blue eyes shining. "That was the two of you? I saw the whole thing!" She dabbed the corners of her mouth with her napkin and checked to be sure she had everyone's attention before continuing. "I swear it was the most romantic thing I've ever seen."

"It certainly was," Steve added, smiling over at Dianne, who restrained herself from kicking him in the shin, although it was exactly what he deserved.

"Steve's cart inadvertently bumped into Dianne's," Louise went on, grinning broadly at Steve.

"Inadvertently, Steve?" Sam Horton teased, chuckling loudly enough to attract attention. Crazy though it was, it seemed that everyone in the entire community center had stopped eating in order to hear Louise tell her story.

"At any rate," Louise said, "the two of them stopped to chat, and I swear it was like watching a romantic comedy. Naturally Dianne apologized—she hadn't realized she was blocking the aisle. Then Steve started sorting through the stuff in her cart, teasing her. We all know how Steve enjoys kidding around."

The others shook their heads, their affection for their friend obvious.

"She was buying all these diet dinners," Steve said, ignoring Dianne's glare. "I told her she couldn't possibly be buying them for herself."

The three women at the table sighed audibly. It was

all Dianne could do not to slide off her chair and disappear under the table.

"That's not the best part," Louise said, beaming with pride at the attention she was garnering. A dreamy look stole over her features. "They must've stood and talked for ages. I'd finished my shopping and just happened to stroll past them several minutes later, and they were still there. It was when I was standing in the checkout line that I noticed them coming down the aisle side by side, each pushing a grocery cart. It was so cute, I half expected someone to start playing a violin."

"How sweet," Renée Horton whispered.

"I thought so myself and I mentioned it to Larry once I got home. Remember, honey?"

Larry nodded obligingly. "Louise must've told me that story two or three times that night," her husband reported.

"I just didn't know it was you, Steve. Imagine, out of all the people to run into at the grocery store, I happened to stumble upon you and Dianne the first time you met. Life is so ironic, isn't it?"

"Oh, yes, life is very ironic," Dianne said. Steve sent her a subtle smile, and she couldn't hold back an answering grin.

"It was one of the most beautiful things I've ever seen," Louise finished.

"Can you believe that Louise Lester?" Steve said later. They were sitting in his luxury sedan waiting for their turn to pull out of the crowded parking lot.

"No," Dianne said simply. She'd managed to make it through the rest of the dinner, but it had demanded every ounce of poise and self-control she possessed. From the moment they'd walked in the front door until the time Steve helped her put on her coat at the end of the evening, they'd been the center of attention. And the main topic of conversation.

Like a bumblebee visiting a flower garden, Louise Lester had breezed from one dinner table to the next, spreading the story of how Dianne and Steve had met and how she'd been there to witness every detail.

"I've never been so…" Dianne couldn't think of a word that quite described how she'd felt. "This may have been the worst evening of my life." She slumped against the back of the seat and covered her eyes.

"I thought you had a good time."

"How could I?" she cried, dropping her hand long enough to glare at him. "The first thing I get hit with is that you're some rich playboy."

"Come on, Dianne. Just because I happen to own a business doesn't mean I'm rolling in money."

"Port Blossom Towing is one of the fastest-growing enterprises in Kitsap County," she said, repeating what Sam Horton had been happy to tell her. "What I don't understand is why my mother hasn't heard of you. She's been on the lookout for eligible men for months. It's a miracle she didn't—" Dianne stopped abruptly.

"What?"

"My mother was looking all right, but she was realistic enough to stay in my own social realm. You're a major-league player. The only men my mother knows are in the minors—butchers, teachers, everyday sort of guys."

Now that she thought about it, however, her mother had seemed to recognize Steve's name when Dianne first mentioned it. She probably *had* heard of him, but couldn't remember where.

"Major-league player? That's a ridiculous analogy."

"It isn't. And to think I approached you, offering you money to take me to this dinner." Humiliation washed over her again, then gradually receded. "I have one question—why didn't you already have a date?" The dinner had been only five days away, so surely the most eligible bachelor in town, a man who could have his choice of women, would've had a date!

He shrugged. "I'm not seeing anyone."

"I bet you got a good laugh when I offered to pay you." Not to mention the fact that she'd made such a fuss over his owning a proper suit.

"As a matter of fact, I was flattered."

"No doubt."

"Are you still upset?"

"You could say that, yes." *Upset* was putting it mildly.

Since Dianne's house was only a couple of miles from the community center, she reached for her purse and checkbook. She waited until he pulled into the driveway before writing a check and handing it to him.

"What's this?" Steve asked.

"What I owe you. Since I didn't know the exact cost of Jill's stuffed animal, I made an educated guess. The cost of the roses varies from shop to shop, so I took an average price."

"I don't think you should pay me until the evening's over," he said, opening his car door.

As far as Dianne was concerned, it had been over the minute she'd learned who he was. When he came around to her side of the car and opened her door, she said, "Just what are you planning now?" He led her by the hand to the front of the garage, which was illuminated by a floodlight. They stood facing each other, his hands on her shoulders.

She frowned, gazing up at him. "I fully intend to give you your money's worth," he replied.

"I beg your pardon?"

"Jason, Jill and your mother."

"What about them?"

"They're peering out the front window waiting for me to kiss you, and I'm not going to disappoint them."

"Oh, no, you don't," she objected. But the moment his eyes held hers, all her anger drained away. Then, slowly, as though he recognized the change in her, he lowered his head. Dianne knew he was going to kiss her, and in the same instant she knew she wouldn't do anything to stop him…

Nine

"You have the check?" Dianne asked once her head was clear enough for her to think again. It was a struggle to pull herself free from the magic Steve wove so easily around her.

Steve pulled the check she'd written from his suit pocket. Then, without ceremony, he tore it in two. "I never intended to accept a penny."

"You have to! We agreed—"

"I want to see you again," he said, clasping her shoulders firmly and looking intently at her.

Dianne was struck dumb. If he'd announced he was an alien, visiting from the planet Mars, he couldn't have surprised her more. Not knowing what to say, she eyed him speculatively. "You're kidding, aren't you?"

A smile flitted across his lips as though he'd anticipated her reaction. The left side of his mouth rose slightly higher in that lazy, off-center grin of his. "I've never been more serious in my life."

Now that the shock had worn off, it took Dianne all of one second to decide. "Naturally, I'm flattered—but no."

"No?" Steve was clearly taken aback, and he needed a second or two to compose himself. "Why not?"

"After tonight you need to ask?"

"Apparently so," he said, stepping away from her a little. He paused and shoved his fingers through his hair with enough force to make Dianne flinch. "I can't believe you," he muttered. "The first time we kissed I realized we had something special. I thought you felt it, too."

Dianne couldn't deny it, but she wasn't about to admit it, either. She lowered her gaze, refusing to meet the hungry intensity of his eyes.

When she didn't respond, Steve continued, "I have no intention of letting you out of my life. In case you haven't figured it out yet—and obviously you haven't—I'm crazy about you, Dianne."

Unexpected tears clouded her vision as she gazed up at him. She rubbed her hands against her eyes and sniffled. This wasn't supposed to be happening. She wanted the break to be clean and final. No discussion. No tears.

Steve was handsome and ambitious, intelligent and charming. If anyone deserved an SYT, it was this oh-so-eligible bachelor. She'd been married, and her life was complicated by two children and a manipulative mother.

"Say something," he demanded. "Don't just stand there looking at me with tears in your eyes."

"Th-these aren't tears. They're..." Dianne couldn't finish as fresh tears scalded her eyes.

"Tomorrow afternoon," he said, his voice gentle. "I'll stop by the house, and you and the kids and I can all go to a movie. You can bring your mother, too, if you want."

Dianne managed to swallow a sob. "That's the lowest, meanest thing you've ever suggested."

He frowned. "Taking you and the kids to a movie?"

"Y-yes. You're using my own children against me and that's—"

"Low and mean," he finished, scowling more fiercely. "All right, if you don't want to involve Jason and Jill, then just the two of us will go."

"I already said no."

"Why?"

Her shoulders trembled slightly as she smeared the moisture across her cheek. "I'm divorced." She said it as if it had been a well-kept secret and no one but her mother and children were aware of it.

"So?" He was still scowling.

"I have children."

"I know that, too. You're not making a lot of sense, Dianne."

"It's not that—exactly. You can date any woman you want."

"I want to date *you*."

"No!" She was trembling from the inside out. She

tried to compose herself, but it was hopeless with Steve standing so close, looking as though he was going to reach for her and kiss her again.

When she was reasonably sure she wouldn't crumble under the force of her fascination with him, she looked him in the eye. "I'm flattered, really I am, but it wouldn't work."

"You don't know that."

"But I do, I do. We're not even in the same league, you and I, and this whole thing has got completely out of hand." She stood a little straighter, as though the extra inch in height would help. "The deal was I pay you to escort me to the Valentine's dinner—but then I had to go and complicate matters by suggesting you look smitten with me and you did such a good job of it that you've convinced yourself you're attracted to me and you aren't. You couldn't be."

"Because you're divorced and have two children," he repeated incredulously.

"You're forgetting my manipulative mother."

Steve clenched his fists at his sides. "I haven't forgotten her. In fact, I'm grateful to her."

Dianne narrowed her eyes. "Now I *know* you can't be serious."

"Your mother's a real kick, and your kids are great, and in case you're completely blind, I think you're pretty wonderful yourself."

Dianne fumbled with the pearls at her neck, twisting the strand between her fingers. The man who stood before her was every woman's dream, but she didn't know what was right anymore. She knew only one thing. After the way he'd humiliated her this evening, after the way he'd let her actually pay him to take her to the Valentine's dinner, make a total fool of herself, there was no chance she could see him again.

"I don't think so," she said stiffly. "Goodbye, Steve."

"You really mean it, don't you?"

She was already halfway to the front door. "Yes."

"All right. Fine," he said, slicing the air with his hands. "If this is the way you want it, then fine, just fine." With that he stormed off to his car.

Dianne knew her family would give her all kinds of flack. The minute she walked in the door, Jason and Jill barraged her with questions about the dinner. Dianne was as vague as possible and walked upstairs to her room, pleading exhaustion. There must have been something in her eyes that convinced her mother and children to leave her alone, because no one disturbed her again that night.

She awoke early the next morning, feeling more than a little out of sorts. Jason was already up, eating a huge bowl of cornflakes at the kitchen table.

"Well," he said, when Dianne walked into the kitchen, "when are you going to see Steve again?"

"Uh, I don't know." She put on a pot of coffee, doing her best to shove every thought of her dinner companion from her mind. And not succeeding.

"He wants to go out on another date with you, doesn't he?"

"Uh, I'm not sure."

"You're not sure?" Jason asked. "How come? I saw you two get mushy last night. I like Steve. He's fun."

"Yes, I know," she said, standing in front of the machine while the coffee dripped into the glass pot. Her back was to her son. "Let's give it some time. See how things work out," she mumbled.

To Dianne's relief, he seemed to accept that and didn't question her further. That, however, wasn't the case with her mother.

"So talk to me," Martha insisted later that day, working her crochet hook as she sat in the living room with Dianne. "You've been very quiet."

"No, I haven't." Dianne didn't know why she denied it. Her mother was right, she had been introspective.

"The phone isn't ringing. The phone should be ringing."

"Why's that?"

"Steve. He met your mother, he met your children, he took you out to dinner…"

"You make it sound like we should be discussing wedding plans." Dianne had intended to be flippant, but the look her mother gave her said she shouldn't joke about something so sacred.

"When are you seeing him again?" Her mother tugged on her ball of yarn when Dianne didn't immediately answer, as if that might bring forth a response.

"We're both going to be busy for the next few days."

"Busy? You're going to let busy interfere with love?"

Dianne ignored the question. It was easier that way. Her mother plied her with questions on and off for the rest of the day, but after repeated attempts to get something more out of her daughter and not succeeding, Martha reluctantly let the matter drop.

Three days after the Valentine's dinner, Dianne was shopping after work at a grocery store on the other side of town—she avoided going anywhere near the one around which she and Steve had fabricated their story—when she ran into Beth Martin.

"Dianne," Beth called, racing down the aisle after her. Darn, Dianne thought. The last person she wanted to chitchat with was Beth, who would, no doubt, be filled with questions about her and Steve.

She was.

"I've been meaning to phone you all week," Beth said, her smile so sweet Dianne felt as if she'd fallen into a vat of honey.

"Hello, Beth." She made a pretense of scanning the grocery shelf until she realized she was standing in front of the disposable-diaper section. She jerked away as though she'd been burned.

Beth's gaze followed Dianne's. "You know, you're not too old to have more children," she said. "What are you? Thirty-three, thirty-four?"

"Around that."

"If Steve wanted children, you could—"

"I have no intention of marrying Steve Creighton," Dianne answered testily. "We're nothing more than friends."

Beth arched her eyebrows. "My dear girl, that's not what I've heard. All of Port Blossom is buzzing with talk about the two of you. Steve's been such an elusive bachelor. He dates a lot of women, or so I've heard, but from what everyone's saying, and I do mean *everyone*, you've got him hooked. Why, the way he was looking at you on Saturday night was enough to bring tears to my eyes. I don't know what you did to that man, but he's yours for the asking."

"I'm sure you're mistaken." Dianne couldn't very well announce that she'd paid Steve to look besotted. He'd done such a good job of it, he'd convinced himself and everyone else that he was head over heels in love with her.

Beth grinned. "I don't think so."

As quickly as she could, Dianne made her excuses, paid for her groceries and hurried home. Home, she soon discovered, wasn't exactly a haven. Jason and Jill were waiting for her, and it wasn't because they were eager to carry in the grocery sacks.

"It's been three days," Jill said. "Shouldn't you have heard from Steve by now?"

"If he doesn't phone you, then you should call him," Jason insisted. "Girls do that sort of thing all the time now, no matter what Grandma says."

"I…" Dianne looked for an escape. Of course there wasn't one.

"Here's his card," Jason said, taking it from the corner of the bulletin board. "Call him."

Dianne stared at the raised red lettering. Port Blossom Towing, it said, with the phone number in large numbers below. In the corner, in smaller, less-pronounced lettering, was Steve's name, followed by one simple word: *owner*.

Dianne's heart plummeted and she closed her eyes. He'd really meant it when he said he had never intentionally misled her. He assumed she knew, and with good reason. The business card he'd given her spelled it out. Only she hadn't noticed…

"Mom." Jason's voice fragmented her introspection.

She opened her eyes to see her son and daughter staring up at her, their eyes, so like her own, intent and worried.

"What are you going to do?" Jill wanted to know.

"W.A.R."

"Aerobics?" Jason said. "What for?"

"I need it," Dianne answered. And she did. She'd learned long ago that when something was weighing on her, heavy-duty exercise helped considerably. It cleared her mind. She didn't enjoy it, exactly; pain rarely thrilled her. But the aerobics classes at the community center had seen her through more than one emotional trauma. If she hurried, she could be there for the last session of the afternoon.

"Kids, put those groceries away for me, will you?" she said, heading for the stairs, yanking the sweater over her head as she raced. The buttons on her blouse were too time-consuming, so she peeled that over her head the moment she entered the bedroom, closing the door with her foot.

In five minutes flat, she'd changed into her leotard, kissed the kids and was out the door. She had a small attack of guilt when she pulled out of the driveway and glanced back to see both her children standing on the porch looking dejected.

The warm-up exercises had already begun when Dianne joined the class. For the next hour she leapt, kicked, bent and stretched, doing her best to keep up with everyone else. By the end of the session, she was exhausted—and no closer to deciding whether or not to phone Steve.

With a towel draped around her neck, she walked out to her car. Her cardiovascular system might've been fine, but nothing else about her was. She searched through her purse for her keys and then checked her coat pocket.

Nothing.

Dread filled her. Framing the sides of her face with her hands, she peered inside the car. There, innocently poking out of the ignition, were her keys.

Ten

"Jason," Dianne said, closing her eyes in thanks that it was her son who'd answered the phone and not Jill. Her daughter would have plied her with questions and more advice than "Dear Abby."

"Hi, Mom. I thought you were at aerobics."

"I am, and I may be here a whole lot longer if you can't help me out." Without a pause, she continued, "I need you to go upstairs, look in my underwear drawer and bring me the extra set of car keys."

"They're in your underwear drawer?"

"Yes." It was the desperate plan of a desperate woman. She didn't dare contact the auto club this time for fear they'd send Port Blossom Towing to the rescue in the form of one Steve Creighton.

"You don't expect me to paw through your, uh, stuff, do you?"

"Jason, listen to me, I've locked my keys in the car, and I don't have any other choice."

"You locked your keys in the car? *Again?* What's with you lately, Mom?"

"Do we need to go through this now?" she demanded. Jason wasn't saying anything she hadn't already said to herself a hundred times over the past few minutes. She was so agitated it was a struggle not to break down and weep.

"I'll have Jill get the keys for me," Jason agreed, with a sigh that told her it demanded a good deal of effort, not to mention fortitude, for him to comply with this request.

"Great. Thanks." Dianne breathed out in relief. "Okay. Now, the next thing you need to do is get your bicycle out of the garage and ride it down to the community center."

"You mean you want me to *bring* you the keys?"

"Yes."

"But it's raining!"

"It's only drizzling." True, but as a general rule Dianne didn't like her son riding his bike in the winter.

"But it's getting dark," Jason protested next.

That did concern Dianne. "Okay, you're right. Call Grandma and ask her to come over and get the keys from you and then have her bring them to me."

"You want me to call Grandma?"

"Jason, are you hard of hearing? Yes, I want you to call Grandma, and if you can't reach her, call me back here at the community center." Needless to say, her cell phone was locked in the car. *Again.* "I'll be waiting." She read off the number for him. "And listen, if my car keys aren't in my underwear drawer, have Grandma bring me a wire clothes hanger, okay?"

He hesitated. "All right," he said after another burdened sigh. "Are you sure you're all right, Mom?"

"Of course I'm sure." But she was going to remember his attitude the next time he needed her to go on a Boy Scout campout with him.

Jason seemed to take hours to do as she'd asked. Since the front desk was now busy with the after-work crowd, Dianne didn't want to trouble the staff for the phone a second time to find out what was keeping her son.

Forty minutes after Dianne's aerobic class was over, she was still pacing the foyer of the community center, stopping every now and then to glance outside. Suddenly she saw a big red tow truck turn into the parking lot.

She didn't need to be psychic to know that the man driving the truck was Steve.

Mumbling a curse under her breath, Dianne walked out into the parking lot to confront him.

Steve was standing alongside her car when she approached. She noticed that he wasn't wearing the gray-striped coveralls he'd worn the first time they'd met. Now he was dressed in slacks and a sweater, as though he'd come from the office.

"What are you doing here?" The best defense was a good offense, or so her high-school basketball coach had advised her about a hundred years ago.

"Jason called me," he said, without looking at her.

"The traitor," Dianne muttered.

"He said something about refusing to search through your underwear and his grandmother couldn't be reached. And that all this has to do with you going off to war."

Although Steve was speaking in an even voice, it was clear he found the situation comical.

"W.A.R. is my aerobics class," Dianne explained stiffly. "It means Women After Results."

"I'm glad to hear it." He walked around to the passenger side of the tow truck and brought out the instrument he'd used to open her door the first time. "So," he said, leaning against the side of her compact, "how have you been?"

"Fine."

"You don't look so good, but then I suppose that's because you're a divorced woman with two children and a manipulative mother."

Naturally he'd taunt her with that. "How kind of you to say so," she returned with an equal dose of sarcasm.

"How's Jerome?"

"Jerome?"

"The butcher your mother wanted to set you up with," he answered gruffly. "I figured by now the two of you would've gone out." His words had a biting edge.

"I'm not seeing Jerome." The thought of having to eat blood sausage was enough to turn her stomach.

"I'm surprised," he said. "I would've figured

you'd leap at the opportunity to date someone other than me."

"If I wasn't interested in him before, what makes you think I'd go out with him now? And why aren't you opening my door? That's what you're here for, isn't it?"

He ignored her question. "Frankly, Dianne, we can't go on meeting like this."

"Funny, very funny." She crossed her arms defiantly.

"Actually I came here to talk some sense into you," he said after a moment.

"According to my mother, you won't have any chance of succeeding. I'm hopeless."

"I don't believe that. Otherwise I wouldn't be here." He walked over to her and gently placed his hands on her shoulders. "Maybe, Dianne, you've been fine these past few days, but frankly I've been a wreck."

"You have?" As Dianne looked at him she thought she'd drown in his eyes. And when he smiled, it was all she could do not to cry.

"I've never met a more stubborn woman in my life."

She blushed. "I'm awful, I know."

His gaze became more intent as he asked, "How about if we go someplace and talk?"

"I…think that would be all right." At the moment there was little she could refuse him. Until he'd arrived, she'd had no idea what to do about the situation between them. Now the answer was becoming clear...

"You might want to call Jason and Jill and tell them."

"Oh, right, I should." How could she have forgotten her own children?

Steve was grinning from ear to ear. "Don't worry, I already took care of that. While I was at it, I phoned your mother, too. She's on her way to your house now. She'll make the kids' dinner." He paused, then said, "I figured if I was fortunate enough, I might be able to talk you into having dinner with me. I understand Walker's has an excellent seafood salad."

If he was fortunate enough, he might be able to talk her into having dinner with him? Dianne felt like weeping. Steve Creighton was the sweetest, kindest, handsomest man she'd ever met, and *he* was looking at *her* as if he was the one who should be counting his blessings.

Steve promptly opened her car door. "I'm going to buy you a magnetic key attachment for keeping a spare key under your bumper so this doesn't happen again."

"You are?"

"Yes, otherwise I'll worry about you."

No one had ever worried about her, except her immediate family. Whatever situation arose, she handled. Broken water pipes, lost checks, a leaky roof—nothing had ever defeated her. Not even Jack had been able to break her spirit, but one kind smile from Steve Creighton and she was a jumble of emotions. She blinked back tears and made a mess of thanking him, rushing her words so that they tumbled over each other.

"Dianne?"

She stopped and bit her lower lip. "Yes?"

"Either we go to the restaurant now and talk, or I'm going to kiss you right here in this parking lot."

Despite everything, she managed to smile. "It wouldn't be the first time."

"No, but I doubt I'd be content with one kiss."

She lowered her lashes, thinking she probably wouldn't be, either. "I'll meet you at Walker's."

He followed her across town, which took less than five minutes, and pulled into the empty parking space next to hers. Once inside the restaurant, they were seated immediately by a window overlooking Sinclair Inlet.

Dianne had just picked up her menu when Steve said, "I'd like to tell you a story."

"Okay," she said, puzzled. She put the menu aside. Deciding what to eat took second place to listening to Steve.

"It's about a woman who first attracted the attention of a particular man at the community center about two months ago."

Dianne took a sip of water, her eyes meeting his above the glass, her heart thumping loudly in her ears. "Yes…"

"This lady was oblivious to certain facts."

"Such as?" Dianne prompted.

"First of all, she didn't seem to have a clue how attractive she was or how much this guy admired her. He did everything but stand on his head to get her attention, but nothing worked."

"What exactly did he try?"

"Working out at the same hours she did, pumping iron—and looking exceptionally good in his T-shirt and shorts."

"Why didn't this man say something to...this woman?"

Steve chuckled. "Well, you see, he was accustomed to women giving him plenty of attention. So this particular woman dented his pride by ignoring him, then she made him downright angry. Finally it occurred to him that she wasn't *purposely* ignoring him—she simply wasn't aware of him."

"It seems to me this man is rather arrogant."

"I couldn't agree with you more."

"You couldn't?" Dianne was surprised.

"That was when he decided there were plenty of fish in the sea and he didn't need a pretty divorcée with two children—he'd asked around about her, so he knew a few details like that."

Dianne smoothed the pink linen napkin across her lap. "What happened next?"

"He was sitting in his office one evening. The day had been busy and one of his men had phoned in sick, so he'd been out on the road all afternoon. He was ready to go home and take a hot shower, but just about then the phone rang. One of the night crew answered it and it was the auto club. Apparently some lady had locked her keys in her car at the community center and needed someone to come rescue her."

"So you, I mean this man, volunteered?"

"That he did, never dreaming she'd practically throw herself in his arms. And not because he'd unlocked her car, either, but because she was desperate for someone to take her to the Valentine's dinner."

"That part about her falling in your arms is a slight exaggeration," Dianne felt obliged to tell him.

"Maybe so, but it was the first time a woman had ever offered to pay him to take her out. Which was the most ironic part of this entire tale. For weeks he'd been trying to gain this woman's attention, practically killing himself to impress her with the amount of weight he was lifting. It seemed every woman in town was impressed except the one who mattered."

"Did you ever stop to think that was the very reason he found her so attractive? If she ignored him, then he must have considered her a challenge."

"Yes, he thought about that a lot. But after he met her and kissed her, he realized that his instincts had been right from the first. He was going to fall in love with this woman."

"He was?" Dianne's voice was little more than a hoarse whisper.

"That's the second part of the story."

"The second part?" Dianne was growing confused.

"The happily-ever-after part."

Dianne used her napkin to wipe away the tears, which had suddenly welled up in her eyes again. "He can't possibly know that."

Steve smiled then, that wonderful carefree, vagabond smile of his, the smile that never failed to lift her heart. "Wrong. He's known it for a long time. All he needs to do now is convince her."

Sniffing, Dianne said, "I have the strangest sensation that this woman has trouble recognizing a prince when she sees one. For a good part of her life, she was satisfied with keeping a frog happy."

"And now?"

"And now she's…now *I'm* ready to discover what happily-ever-after is all about."

* * * * *

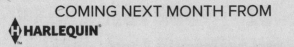

REQUEST YOUR FREE BOOKS!
2 FREE NOVELS PLUS 2 FREE GIFTS!

♦ HARLEQUIN®

American Romance®

LOVE, HOME & HAPPINESS

YES! Please send me 2 FREE Harlequin® American Romance® novels and my 2 FREE gifts (gifts are worth about $10). After receiving them, if I don't wish to receive any more books, I can return the shipping statement marked "cancel." If I don't cancel, I will receive 4 brand-new novels every month and be billed just $4.74 per book in the U.S. or $5.49 per book in Canada. That's a savings of at least 12% off the cover price! It's quite a bargain! Shipping and handling is just 50¢ per book in the U.S. and 75¢ per book in Canada.* I understand that accepting the 2 free books and gifts places me under no obligation to buy anything. I can always return a shipment and cancel at any time. Even if I never buy another book, the two free books and gifts are mine to keep forever.

154/354 HDN GHZZ

Name _____ (PLEASE PRINT)

Address _____ Apt. #

City _____ State/Prov. _____ Zip/Postal Code

Signature (if under 18, a parent or guardian must sign)

Mail to the **Reader Service:**
IN U.S.A.: P.O. Box 1867, Buffalo, NY 14240-1867
IN CANADA: P.O. Box 609, Fort Erie, Ontario L2A 5X3

Want to try two free books from another line?
Call 1-800-873-8635 or visit www.ReaderService.com.

* Terms and prices subject to change without notice. Prices do not include applicable taxes. Sales tax applicable in N.Y. Canadian residents will be charged applicable taxes. Offer not valid in Quebec. This offer is limited to one order per household. Not valid for current subscribers to Harlequin American Romance books. All orders subject to credit approval. Credit or debit balances in a customer's account(s) may be offset by any other outstanding balance owed by or to the customer. Please allow 4 to 6 weeks for delivery. Offer available while quantities last.

Your Privacy—The Reader Service is committed to protecting your privacy. Our Privacy Policy is available online at www.ReaderService.com or upon request from the Reader Service.

We make a portion of our mailing list available to reputable third parties that offer products we believe may interest you. If you prefer that we not exchange your name with third parties, or if you wish to clarify or modify your communication preferences, please visit us at www.ReaderService.com/consumerschoice or write to us at Reader Service Preference Service, P.O. Box 9062, Buffalo, NY 14240-9062. Include your complete name and address.

HARI5

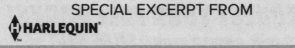
She wasn't sure about that. "Yeah, but look at all the time I'm taking from you. You're stuck babysitting me until the Quinns get home."

He leaned back in the chair, and she couldn't help but stare at his muscular chest and those massive shoulders. Did the military do that for him, or the ranch work?

He caught her stare and she quickly glanced away.

"Hey, I'll take your kind of trouble any day. You rescued me yesterday by helping me pack up all that wedding stuff. You took charge yesterday like a drill sergeant."

She felt a blush cover her cheeks. "What can I say? I have a knack for getting things done."

Those dark eyes captured her attention for far too long. She couldn't let this man get to her. Once he learned the truth about her, he might not like that she'd kept it from him.

He rested his elbows on the table. "Have you ever ridden?"

She swallowed hard. "You mean on a horse?"

He gave her an odd look, but she could tell he was trying not to laugh. "Yes, as far as I'm concerned, it's the best way to see the countryside."

"You want to take me riding?"

"You seem surprised. I'm sure your sister will want to show you around, too."

"To be honest, I've never been on or around a horse until today."

Brooke's first instinct was to say no, but then she realized she'd never taken time just for herself. And why wouldn't she want to go riding with this rugged cowboy? "I'll go, but only if you put me on a gentle horse. You've got one named Poky or Snail?"

"Don't worry, I'll make sure you're safe."

She wanted to believe him, but something deep inside told her if she wasn't careful she could get hurt, and in more ways than one.

Don't miss
COUNT ON A COWBOY by Patricia Thayer,
available March 2016 wherever
Harlequin® American Romance®
books and ebooks are sold.

www.Harlequin.com

Turn your love of reading into rewards you'll love with
Harlequin My Rewards

**Join for FREE today at
www.HarlequinMyRewards.com**

Earn **FREE BOOKS** of your choice.

Experience **EXCLUSIVE OFFERS** and contests.

Enjoy **BOOK RECOMMENDATIONS**
selected just for you.

PLUS! Sign up now
and get **500** points
right away!

Earn
FREE
REWARDS
Join
Today!
HarlequinMyRewards.com